The Blackwater
Lightship

COLM TÓIBÍN

The Blackwater Lightship

PICADOR

ACKNOWLEDGEMENTS

Yaddo, where some of this book was written.

First published 1999 by Picador
an imprint of Macmillan Publishers Ltd
25 Eccleston Place, London SW1W 9NF
Basingstoke and Oxford
Associated companies throughout the world
www.macmillan.co.uk

ISBN 0 330 38985 8

1 3 5 7 9 8 6 4 2

A CIP catalogue record for this book is available from
the British Library.

Typeset by SetSystems Ltd, Saffron Walden, Essex
Printed and bound in Great Britain by
Mackays of Chatham plc, Chatham, Kent

FOR AIDAN DUNNE

The Blackwater
Lightship

ONE

Helen woke in the night to the sound of Manus whimpering. She lay still and listened, hoping that he would quieten and turn on his side and sleep, but when his voice became louder and more insistent and she could vaguely make out words, she got out of bed and moved towards the boys' room; she was unsure whether he was dreaming or awake.

She had left the landing light switched on and she was able to see, as soon as she came into the room, that Cathal had his eyes wide open. He looked at her from the bed, an uninvolved spectator in the scene about to be enacted; he then looked over at his brother, who was crying out hoarsely and fending off some unknown terror with his arms. She woke Manus gently and pulled back the blanket which covered him. He was too hot. Only half awake and rubbing his eyes, he began to whimper again. It took him a while to realise that she was there and the dream was over.

'I was frightened,' he said.

'You're all right now. Maybe you'll go back asleep.'

'I don't want to go back asleep,' he said, and began to cry.

'Will I carry you into our bed?' she asked.

He nodded. He was motionless now, sobbing, waiting to be comforted. She knew that it would be better if she stayed with him and soothed him until he fell asleep again, but she lifted him and let him cling to her. Always, when she held him like this, he became quiet.

Cathal was still watching them.

Helen spoke to him across the room as though he were an adult. 'I'm going to take Manus into our bed so that it will be easier for you to sleep,' she said.

He pulled the blanket over himself and closed his eyes. At six, Cathal was clever enough to know that she was not carrying Manus into their bed for his sake, but because she was prepared to treat Manus like a baby. She wondered what Cathal thought about this, if he were hurt or disturbed – but he would be too proud to let her know, too ready to play the part of the grown-up big brother.

The half-light of dawn had broken through the landing window. She moved slowly into the bedroom. Hugh lay curled up sleeping, his arm across her side of the bed. She stood watching him, wondering at how easy it was for him to fall in and out of sleep. Manus stirred in her arms and turned to see why she had remained motionless in the room. He, too, watched his father sleeping and then turned away and huddled against her. Somewhere in the distance she could hear a car moving. She brought Manus over to the bed.

'Will you sleep on my side?' she whispered to him.

'No, I want to be in the middle.'

'You know what you want, don't you?' She smiled at him.

'I want to be in the middle,' he whispered.

She put him down with his back to Hugh and pulled

4

the sheet over him. Some time in the night Hugh had pushed the duvet off the bed; she left it on the floor, it would be too hot now with the three of them in the bed. She rested her head on the pillow, relieved that Manus was lying quietly between them and trying to reassure herself that Cathal had fallen back asleep in the other room.

They had gone to bed early when there was still vague light in the sky and made love and she was filled now with a tenderness for Hugh and a wish, something which had become a joke between them, that she could be more like him, even-tempered, easy to please – easy to please? he had laughed when she said that – with nothing secret, nothing held inside.

As Manus edged towards sleep he began to pull at her, he wanted her full attention. He did not want her to turn her back on him. 'Come around this way,' he whispered.

She looked at the clock. It was only a quarter to five. Suddenly, she was cold. She reached to the floor, found the duvet, pulled it on to the bed and arranged it over them. They would need to be warm for a while.

★

When Helen woke again, Hugh and Manus were sound asleep. It was just after eight o'clock; the room was hot. She slipped out of the bed and, carrying her dressing-gown and slippers, she went downstairs, where she found Cathal, still in his pyjamas, watching television, the zapper in his hand.

'I've finished in the bathroom if you want to have a shower,' she said to him. He nodded and stood up.

'Are they still asleep?' he asked.

'They are,' she said and smiled.

'I'd better go before they wake up,' he said.

This was their secret language; they mimicked adults, they spoke to one another like a married couple. Cathal hated instructions or orders or being spoken to like a child. If she had told him to go to the bathroom, he would have dawdled and delayed. When Manus is his age, she thought, I will have to carry him to the bathroom.

They were the first to live in this house, and the first in their estate to build an extension – a large, square, bright room which served as kitchen and dining-room and playroom. Hugh had wanted the house for the beech tree which, through some miracle, had been left in their back garden, and the park behind the house. She had liked only the newness, the idea that no one had ever lived here before.

She washed up from the night before and noticed from the kitchen window a breeze flit through the leaves of the beech tree and the fir trees at the edge of the park, and then a sudden darkening in the air, a sense of rain. She turned on the radio – Hugh, as usual, had it tuned to Raidio na Gaeltachta – and found Radio One just as the pips sounded for the nine o'clock news. She would be able to listen to the weather forecast.

As she and Cathal were having breakfast, Cathal engrossed in a comic, the shouting and laughing began upstairs. Manus was squealing at the top of his voice.

'Listen to them,' she said. 'It's hard to know which of them is the bigger baby.'

Cathal smiled at her and took a slice of toast and went back to his comic. They ate in silence as the noise upstairs continued, Hugh shouting something in Irish at Manus, and then both of them shouting at the same time until one of them – she presumed it was Manus – landed on the floor with a thud.

Soon, they both appeared, Hugh in his dressing-gown carrying Manus, still wearing his pyjamas.

'I fell out of bed,' he said.

'We know, we heard you,' Helen said.

His cheeks were flushed. He began to squeeze Hugh's nose.

'Stop that. Sit down and have your breakfast.'

As soon as Manus was seated, he saw Cathal's comic and reached across the table and grabbed it. Cathal tried to hold on to it, but Manus was too quick for him.

'Give it back.' Helen said to him.

'He's finished with it,' Manus said.

'Give it back and say you're sorry.'

He looked at her, calculating what the chances were of her losing her temper. He laughed. 'Don't be silly,' he said.

'We're all waiting here. No one is moving until you hand it back and say you're sorry,' she said.

Cathal sat with his hands by his sides, content to be the injured party. Manus looked at Helen and then at Hugh, who spoke gruffly to him in Irish. Manus sighed and handed the comic back to Cathal.

'And say I'm sorry,' Helen said.

'I'm sorry.'

'And I won't do it again.'

'And I won't do it again.'

'You're becoming a bit of a monster,' she said to him and turned to the sink.

'You're becoming a bit of a monster,' he repeated.

She looked out at the garden and wondered how she should respond; she was grateful when she heard Hugh saying something to him. It was, she thought, her own fault for calling him a bit of a monster. She would leave it, forget about it, feed him his breakfast. He hated being smaller and younger than Cathal. What age would they be, he had asked her, when they would both be the same size? Would it be long? Cathal never hit him or bullied him, but he was always aware that he was at an advantage. Even though Cathal was only two when Manus was born, he had immediately seized on his new role – the one who didn't cry, who didn't have a dirty nappy, who didn't want to be brought into his parents' bed, who didn't grab comics from his brother, who didn't give back-answers to his mother.

When she had given Manus his cornflakes and cold milk and left Hugh to fend for himself – Hugh was more at home in the kitchen than she was – she went out to the line to hang a few dishcloths she had washed. She made a note in her head to find out if there was a good book about bringing up boys, which might make things easier to handle. Once again, as she stood there, the sky darkened. She walked down to the bottom of the garden to take in a deckchair which Hugh must have left out overnight.

She remembered once, perhaps a year earlier, when her brother was in the house and witnessed the boys going to bed. Hugh was in charge and both Cathal and Manus, but especially Manus, did everything to be allowed to stay up, such as clinging to their mother and refusing to do anything their father said. When the house was all quiet and the boys fast asleep, Declan said it was proof, if they needed proof, that boys wanted to sleep with their mother and kill their father.

'They just wanted to stay up late,' Hugh said. 'It just happened that I was in charge.'

'Did you want to sleep with your mother and kill your father?' Helen asked Declan.

'No, no,' he laughed, 'gay boys want the opposite, or at least eventually they do.'

'Sleep with your father?' Hugh asked. His tone was earnest, dead serious.

'Yeah, and have a baby, Hugh,' Declan said drily.

'I still want to kill my mother,' Helen said. 'Not every day, but most days. I cannot imagine anyone wanting to sleep with her.'

She had not forgotten the exchange: Hugh's uneasiness, his innocence, his attempts to suggest to her when Declan had left that talking about killing your parents, or sleeping with them, even in jest, was a sort of blasphemy. She was careful not to seem too impatient with him, aware that she and Declan could without any effort join forces and make Hugh feel that they were laughing at him. Maybe that is what brothers are for, she thought as she walked back into the kitchen, perhaps even now Cathal and Manus are involved in unspoken conspiracies.

'The forecast is for showers,' she said to Hugh, 'and I've worked it out. If it rains, all the tables will fit in here and in the front room and we can put all the drinks in the hall. But we don't have to decide until later.'

It was the end of June, Hugh's end of term; the next morning he would take the boys to Donegal. Tonight, he had invited the teachers from his all-Irish school to celebrate the school's first year in existence, and other friends — musicians, Irish-speakers. Helen had made him invite all the neighbours, including the Indian doctor and his wife and their children who lived at the top of the road.

'No one can complain about the noise if they've just been fed in the house,' she said.

'Half of them looked at me like I was collecting taxes. I bet that guard in the corner house is from Offaly. He has a big, thick accent.'

'Who is that friend of yours who sings "The Rocks of Bawn"? The guard'll have a big, thick accent when he hears him.'

'Mick Joyce. He's loud, all right. Is your brother coming?'

'I haven't asked him,' she said. 'He wouldn't mix. I don't think he likes "The Rocks of Bawn".'

'Has he fallen out with us?'

'He's busy. He's doing research full-time.'

'He has plenty of time so.' Hugh laughed.

'My mother says he's in the laboratory day and night.'

'Is your mother coming?' he laughed.

'Imagine what she'd say about wasting all this money!'

'She'd be great on the door, though,' Hugh said.

★

Hugh spoke Irish to the boys, to his mother and his brothers and sisters, and to at least half of his friends. He insisted that Helen understood more than she pretended to understand, but it was not true. She found his Donegal accent in Irish too difficult, and she made out very little of what he said. Tonight, she knew, she would be irritated by the two or three who would continue to speak to her in Irish, indifferent to the fact that she could not follow, but it was an irritation which would fade easily.

There would be no friends of hers at the party, nobody from the comprehensive school of which she was principal – she was still the youngest principal in the country – nobody from home, nobody from her schooldays or college days. She had one or two women she knew and liked and saw sometimes, but no close friends.

She had given up a long-cherished belief that she was self-contained, or happiest when alone. She could still shut her eyes and bite her lip at how unexpected it was, this life she had made. Nonetheless, she wanted three or four, maybe more, days alone here now after the party, to sit in the garden or an old armchair in the kitchen and read the novels she had saved in the winter, and do nothing else except go to a meeting in the Department of Education, interview prospective teachers and move around the house knowing that, unless there was an emergency, no one would call her or want her immediate attention. But it was important for her to know too that Hugh and the boys were just away for a short while, she would see them soon.

Tomorrow morning, then, Hugh would take the boys to Donegal in the car and she would follow in a while, catch the train to Sligo or the bus to Donegal town, and even now she could imagine Hugh there to meet her, recognising when he saw her how much she feared her own passionate attachment to him, how much she would hold back for a while. After a lot of difficulty, he had learned, as much as he could, to trust her, even though she knew it was hard sometimes.

★

When the janitor from Hugh's school, Frank Mulvey, and his son came in a van with the tables and chairs, she had to restrain herself from telling them where to put everything; she wondered, as she watched them, at how blindly they moved, planning nothing, moving forward without direction. She smiled at herself minding so much about this.

She decided to go to the supermarket to buy the food and the beer. Hugh had already collected the wine and the glasses. She watched from the kitchen window as the boys played aeroplanes in the back garden, circling each other, dipping and diving, their arms outstretched as wings. She called Manus and when he ignored her she called again. He moved reluctantly towards her.

'I want you to come with me to the supermarket,' she said.

'Is Cathal going?'

'No, just you.'

'Why just me? Why can't Cathal go?'

'Come on quickly,' she said.

'I don't want to go,' he said.

'Come on, wash your hands, we're in a hurry.'

'I don't want to go.'

By this time, Cathal had approached and was observing them both.

'Cathal is going to help your daddy with the tables and chairs,' she said.

'I want to do that,' Manus said.

'Manus, you're coming with me,' she said.

He placed himself in the back of the car so that he could see her face in the rear-view mirror.

'But why am I going with you?' he asked.

'Do you think you need to get your hair cut before you go to Donegal?' She would have said anything to distract him as she set off for the supermarket.

'I'm not getting my hair cut,' he said.

'No, you decide. I just asked you.'

'Cathal isn't getting his hair cut.'

'It's up to you. You're old enough to decide yourself.'

This was the plan, this was why she had made him come with her; she had thought about it as she lay awake in the night: she would have to stop treating him like a baby, she would have to begin to talk to him as though he were an adult. But it was having the opposite effect.

'Cathal can get his hair cut, but I'm not doing it and that's that.'

She drove in silence through Rathfarnham and parked in the shopping-centre car park.

'We'll have to get a trolley,' she said.

'Can I have a Ninety-nine?'

'After.'

'After what?'

'After you behave. How are you going to behave?'

'Impeccably,' he said. It was a new big word he had learned. When he looked at her, seeking her approval, she laughed and that forced him to smile.

'What are we getting?' he asked as they pushed the trolley through the supermarket.

'I have it all on a list. Minced meat, onions, beer, salad.'

'Why do you need me?'

'To mind the trolley when I'm paying at the checkout.'

'It's boring,' he said.

'Do you think we should get large cans or small cans of beer?' Again, she was using an adult tone.

'It's boring,' he repeated.

When she got back, she saw that the tables and chairs were set up in the garden. She checked one of the kitchen drawers for plastic tablecloths. The boys were once more playing aeroplanes.

'If it rains, we'll move everything in,' Hugh said as they both surveyed the garden.

*

At nine o'clock the first guests, two men and a woman, arrived carrying six-packs of Guinness and a bottle of red wine. The woman was carrying a fiddle case.

'Are we the first?' one of the men, tall with spectacles and curly hair, said. They seemed uneasy, as though they were half tempted to turn and go. Helen didn't know them and didn't think she had seen them before. Hugh introduced them to her.

'Sit down, sit down, we'll get you a drink,' Hugh said.

They sat in the kitchen and looked out at the tables and the long garden. They said nothing. The two boys came in and examined them and went out again.

'An bhfuil Donncha ag teacht?' Hugh began to speak in Irish and one of the men spoke back from the side of his mouth, something funny, almost bitter. The others laughed. Helen noticed how unfashionably long the speaker's sideburns were.

Hugh handed them drinks, and two of them went into the garden, leaving the one with the long sideburns. It struck Helen for a moment that she had interviewed the woman for a job, or she had worked hours in the school, but she was not sure. Hugh and his friend talked in Irish. Helen wondered if she was wearing the right clothes for the party; she watched the woman from the window, noted her jeans and white top and hennaed hair, how relaxed and natural she looked. Helen moved towards the fridge and checked again that everything was in order: the chilli con carne would simply need to be reheated, the rice boiled; the salads were all ready, the knives and forks and paper napkins set out. She opened some bottles of red wine.

Just then, another group arrived, one of them was carrying a guitar case and another a flute case. She recognised them and they greeted her. There was one woman among them; Helen watched her looking around the kitchen, as though seeking something, a clue, or something she had left behind on a previous visit. When she went to take the six-pack from the man with the guitar, so that she could put it in the fridge, he said he would hold on to it, and smiled at her as if to say that he had been to more parties than she had. He was too warm and direct for her to be offended.

'If you want more, it's in the fridge,' she said to him.

'If I want more, I'll ask you,' he said.

He smiled again. His eyes were a mixture of brown and dark green. His skin was clear; he was very tall. She realised that he was flirting with her.

'I'm tempted to say something,' she said.

'What?'

'No, nothing.'

'What? Say it.'

'I was going to say that you look like someone who might want more.'

He smiled and held her gaze and then reached into his pocket and took out a small bottle opener. He opened a bottle of Guinness and offered it to her. He seemed somewhat taken aback when she refused it, intimidated.

'It's too early for me,' she said.

'Well, cheers so,' he said and lifted the bottle.

For the next hour she was busy filling glasses and opening bottles and trying to remember names and faces. As it grew dark, Hugh lit the flares which he had stuck into the grass and these gave off a fitful, glaring light. When she brought the food out and Hugh put on the striped apron to serve it, people were already sitting at the tables. Cathal and Manus and several neighbours' children had made a small table for themselves and were eating pizzas and drinking Coke.

'We'd better hold on to a bit of the food,' Hugh said. 'There are a few won't come until after the pubs shut.'

The Indian doctor and his wife had arrived earlier, greeted everyone, accepted a drink of orange juice and left, but their eldest son, who must have been seven or eight, had remained behind and was at the boys' table. Helen had promised that she would walk him to his door and that he would not be too late. The O'Mearas next door – she was unsure what they did for a living – were sitting alone at a table watching all the laughter and good humour around them. Helen knew she would have to go and sit with them; it was clear that no one else was going to pay them any attention. She was glad that the guard and his wife had not come.

'God, we don't have to talk Irish to you, do we?' Mary O'Meara said to her when she sat down beside them. 'I was just saying to Martin that we should have listened more in school. God, I haven't got a word of it. "An bhfuil cead agam dul amach" is all I can remember.'

Helen realised that she did not want them to know that she spoke no Irish either. She was prepared to eat with them, but she was not prepared to join them in being at a loss. She noticed several more people arriving. One of the new arrivals was a friend of Hugh's called Ciaran Duffy who had a case for uilleann pipes with him. Of all of Hugh's friends, he was the one she liked best and found easiest to be with. She didn't think he spoke much Irish either, but he was a well-known piper and she watched a number of others turning to look at him as he arrived. She liked his boyish self-confidence, his clear, open face. He reminded her of Hugh, except he was bigger, stockier. Hugh guided Ciaran Duffy and his friends over to her table. Everybody shook hands and suddenly, she noticed, in just a few seconds, the O'Mearas had lost their forlorn, isolated aura and were busy taking in their new companions. Hugh brought over chilli con carne and rice and salads and went back to get drinks.

As Helen went out to close the front door, which had been left open so that people could walk through, she noticed the six-packs carefully placed everywhere, like parcels of territory. It was something Hugh would never do, she thought; he would never be bad-mannered like that and in time, she reckoned, as his friends became older and more prosperous, they would change too.

When she came back into the kitchen, his friend with

the brown and green eyes appeared. He stood in front of her.

'It's you again,' she said.

'I was wondering where the toilet was, your honour,' he said in a mock country accent.

'Anywhere between here and Terenure,' she said. 'No, seriously, it's upstairs, at the top of the stairs, you'll find it.'

'Right so. It's a pleasure being in your house,' he said and moved away.

She went back and sat with the O'Mearas. Opposite her, Ciaran Duffy caught her eye and winked, as if to say that he had the measure of the O'Mearas, but he would be saying nothing. She smiled at him, as if to say that she knew what he was thinking. He shouted something to her, but she could not hear it for all the noise around.

Before she served the fruit salad and cream she counted the guests at the tables: there were thirty-seven; they had expected four or five more; maybe some of them were, as Hugh had said, in the pub. Closing time was half-past eleven. It was eleven o'clock now and maybe time, she thought, to take the Indian boy home – she must find out his name. He was laughing with Cathal and Manus and the other boys. She decided to leave them for another while.

★

The music started in the kitchen while most of the guests were still at tables outside. The man with the six-packs was playing guitar, his friend the flute, and the woman in the jeans and white top a fiddle. Their playing was casual, unselfconscious, almost loose; Helen knew that any move towards intensity would be frowned upon, or indeed mocked. The flute player was leading them, setting the pace; the music had a strange, repetitive gaiety, and the players continued to give the impression that they were playing to please themselves, or each other, but they were not looking for an audience, nor seeking to impress anybody.

Slowly, people began to carry chairs in from the garden; someone turned off the main light in the kitchen, leaving only the light of two lamps to illuminate the room, and others joined in the playing, another fiddle, a mandolin, a squeezebox. Hugh was still busy opening bottles and filling glasses. She knew that he loved the music, the semi-darkness of the room, the company, the drinking. It reminded him of home, of something which was hardly ever possible in Dublin, something that most of his friends here would not be able to manage, being too modest or lazy, too willing to drift and let things happen.

Suddenly, there was silence all around; a woman had begun to sing. Helen knew her, knew that she had made records in the past with her brother and sister and more recently a solo CD which Hugh had listened to over and over and Helen had slowly grown to like. Helen had met the singer on the stairs earlier in the evening and remembered her shy, friendly smile. Now as she stood against the back wall of the room, she sang with ease and authority, and among the guests there was a hush which was almost reverent. The woman did not often sing in public, and if she had been asked to sing – Helen knew the rules – she would have refused, suggesting somebody else, remaining resolute in not singing. Her voice had come from nowhere during a break in the music. Her family, Helen knew, was from Donegal, but Hugh had only met her in Dublin. Her accent in Irish was pure Donegal, but the strength in the rise and fall of the voice was entirely hers, and even the O'Mearas, Helen could see, watched her with awe. When the song was over and the singer sat down, she smiled and sipped her drink as though it were nothing.

The music started again, this time faster than before; someone produced a bodhrán and began to beat it with his eyes closed. Helen went with the O'Mearas to the front door and then remembered the Indian boy and went back in to find him. He was playing around the tables, being chased by Cathal and Manus and another boy who had permission to stay up until the end of the party. As she broke up the game she wished she had secured permission for the Indian boy to stay on as well.

She walked with him up the street to his house.

'Will your parents not be asleep?' she asked.

'My mother will be waiting,' he said and smiled. She wondered if Cathal and Manus could ever be polite like this.

'I hope she won't blame me for keeping you out so late.'

'No, she will not blame you,' the boy said gravely.

⋆

As Helen walked back to the house, she looked at the road bathed in the eerie yellow light which oozed from the streetlamps, and the cars parked in the drives or the roadway – Nissans, Toyotas, Ford Fiestas; every semi-detached house was exactly the same, built for people who wanted quiet lives. She smiled to herself at the idea and stood outside the house as a taxi, flashing its lights, approached. She watched as the driver got out, an electric torch in his hand.

'We're looking for Brookfield Park Avenue,' he said. 'We've found Brookfield everything else. It's the wild west out here.' He flashed his torch at a neighbour's doorway.

'It's here. You're here,' she said.

The doors of the taxi opened and four passengers got out, each with a bag of cans under his arm. 'This is the place,' one of them said. She could not make out any of the faces.

'It's Helen,' one of them said. 'We've been driving around like eejits.'

'I know you,' she said. 'You're Mick Joyce. Is it not too late for you to be out?'

'Hold on until I pay this man,' he said and laughed.

When the taxi drove away, she accompanied the four new guests into the party. Mick Joyce had come to the house several times before; he was a solicitor, he had done all the legal work for Hugh's school. He was the best solicitor in the country, Hugh said, he knew every trick, he was a great man for detail, but once darkness fell – and she had heard Hugh telling the story several times, using the same words – he'd do anything, go anywhere, he'd go to Kerry and back the same night if he thought there was anything going on there. He had a strong Galway accent.

'This is the woman of the house,' he said to the others. They shook her hand. There were no introductions.

'We kept food for you,' she said.

'You're a great woman,' he said.

He walked down the hallway to the kitchen and stood in the doorway as though he owned the place, or was the guest of honour. When the music stopped, several people shouted greetings. Hugh got drinks for him and his companions and then the music started up again.

Helen noticed that Ciaran Duffy was assembling his uilleann pipes, being watched carefully by several people. It was slow, meticulous work, and she realised that those still playing were overshadowed by these preparations. She watched Mick Joyce going into the garden, finding Manus and lifting him on his shoulders, making him laugh and shout; Cathal and his friend followed them as they moved around the garden. She remembered that each time Mick had come to the house he had sought Manus out and acted as though he had come to see him specially. Manus loved him; he was the only friend of Hugh's he ever mentioned.

Mick Joyce and the boys came into the house when the piping began. Some people had already left, but the kitchen was still half-crowded, and there was a silence now which had been there before only for the singer. Those who had been playing left their instruments down: this was, Helen knew, more than anything a world of hierarchies, and no one came near this player's reputation. They listened, full of respect and deep interest in the technique, the movement of chanter and drone, the sense of control and release. Cathal and Manus had been learning the tin whistle; they sat on the floor listening, Manus making sure that Mick Joyce was sitting on the chair right behind him, and paid attention, even though it was after midnight now, and they should have been asleep three hours earlier.

Helen sat on the floor and relaxed for the first time that evening; she noticed the tunes and rhythms changing, becoming faster, a display of pure virtuosity, full of hints and insinuations, good-humoured twists and turns. The room was half full of cigarette smoke; cans and bottles were being used for ashtrays. All around, people sat or stood and listened to the music. Hugh stood with his shoulder against the wall; he caught her eye and grinned at her.

When the piping stopped, the crowd began to thin out. It was then that someone shouted at Mick Joyce that he hadn't sung yet, and that the night would not be complete until he did.

'I'm too drunk to sing,' he shouted. He stood up and pointed to the man with the guitar and his companion with the mandolin. 'Don't try and join in,' he instructed them. 'You'll put me all wrong.'

'I thought you were too drunk to sing,' one of them said.

'I'll give you singing now, if you want singing,' he said.

He began 'The Rocks of Bawn'; this time his voice was even louder than when Helen had heard him before. Cathal and Manus still sat on the floor, fascinated by the sheer passion in his delivery, his face all lit up by the rage of the song, as though at any moment he would start a fight or burst a blood vessel. A few people who were at the front door, about to go, came back to witness the end of the song:

I wish the Queen of England would write to me in time
And place me in some regiment all in my youth and
    prime.
I'd fight for Ireland's glory from the clear daylight 'til
    dawn
And I never would return again to plough the Rocks of
    Bawn.

When he had finished he lifted Manus up and laughed
when the child pulled his ears. He looked at Helen as if
to say that he had fooled them all again. Helen brought
him a cold can of lager; he opened it and offered some to
Manus first, but he refused. Manus didn't like the taste of
beer. Cathal put his hand up and asked for some and
when Mick Joyce handed him the can he put his head
back and drank the beer. He saw Helen watching him.
He knew he was allowed to take sips of beer, but he was
still uncertain about her reaction.

'He gave it to me,' he said as he handed back the can.

'You'll be drunk,' she said and laughed. 'You'll have a
hangover in the morning.'

★

Helen closed the doors to the garden. The party was
nearly over. She remembered Hugh telling her that Mick
Joyce knew only one song, and she was relieved about
this. His singing could have been heard by the neighbours
on both sides, and possibly further down the street. She
wondered about Mick Joyce: since he liked children so
much, why he didn't have children of his own, and how
he managed to pretend, in his manners and speech, that
he was in the west of Ireland. She wondered what it

would be like to be married to someone like that – the mixture of control and anarchy, the unevenness. She turned around and watched as Hugh began to sing in Irish, his voice nasal and thin, but sweet as well and clear. His eyes were closed. There were only about ten people left, and two of these joined the song, softly at first and then more loudly. She stood there and thought about Hugh: how easygoing he was and consistent, how modest and decent. And she wondered – as she often did in moments like this – why he had wanted her, why he needed someone who had none of his virtues, and she felt suddenly distant from him. She could never let him know the constant daily urge to resist him, keep him at bay, and the struggle to overcome these urges, in which she often failed.

He tried to understand this, but he was also frightened by it, and often succeeded in pretending that it was nothing, it was her period, or a bad mood. It would pass, and he would wait and find the right moment and pull her back in again, and she would lie beside him, half grateful to him, but knowing that he had wilfully misunderstood what was between them. As she watched him now, his voice soaring in the last verse of the song, clearly in love with the sounds of the words he was singing, she knew that anybody else would have laid bare, in the way that he had covered, the raw areas in her which were unsettled and untrusting.

TWO

She woke early, with a strange feeling of disappointment, as though she had missed something important. Her mouth was dry. She realised that she would not get back to sleep, and she lay there going over the events of the party. It struck her that she felt the way a child feels when a buzz of excitement is replaced by bedtime or dull duty.

It was eight o'clock; she had been asleep for only four hours. She got up and, when she was washed and dressed, began to clean up from the party, emptying and refilling the dishwasher, tying up black plastic bags full of rubbish and leaving them outside the back door. By the time Hugh appeared, it was almost done. He was wearing boxer shorts and a T-shirt.

'You should have left it for me,' he said.

'It's all finished,' she said, 'so you can concentrate on packing.'

He came over to the sink, where she was standing, and held her.

'I'm going to miss you,' he said. 'I'm going to think all the time of things I want to say to you but you'll not be there.'

'If I didn't have this meeting in the Department and

the school interviews I could change my mind, but it's only a week or so,' she said.

She closed her eyes and put her mouth against his bare neck. The lack of sleep served only to intensify a sudden desire for him, and now she began to fondle him and he slowly began to kiss her. When she opened her eyes she saw that Cathal was studying them carefully from the kitchen door. She smiled and pushed Hugh away gently with her hands.

'Cathal,' she said, 'your breakfast things are on the table. We're going to lie down for a while. We won't be long.' She wondered if Hugh's erection was apparent through his shorts.

Cathal remained silent, watching them as he moved towards the kitchen table. They went up to the bedroom and closed the door.

'Poor Cathal,' she said. 'I hope he's all right. It would be worse I suppose if we were having a big fight.'

'Much worse.' Hugh laughed. 'Much worse.'

⋆

By eleven o'clock the boys' suitcases were in the boot of the car and Hugh's rucksack was on the back seat. Helen had written out a list of instructions.

'You're to go up through Ballyshannon,' she said. 'You're not to drive into the North.'

'Yes, ma'am,' Hugh said.

'I'm sure you've forgotten something,' she said.

'We've forgotten to kiss you farewell,' he said.

'And you're to mind all those Donegal people,' she said lightly. 'They're sly.'

She made sure that the boys had their seatbelts on in

the back seat. Manus was impatient to be gone. He refused to kiss her goodbye. 'I'm bored waiting,' he said.

She waved at them as the car drove off.

★

She knew as she walked back into the house that this next hour or two would be special, a time when she could savour and appreciate the empty, silent rooms and the sweet energy which Hugh and Cathal and Manus had left behind them.

Before lunch, Frank Mulvey and his son came to collect the tables and chairs. When he learned that Hugh and the boys had gone to Donegal, he nodded his head and looked at her. 'And will you be all right here now?' he asked.

'I'll be fine. It's just a few days.'

'My missus', he said, 'never lets me out of her sight.'

As she stood at the front gate watching the last of the tables being stacked into the van, she noticed a white car edging its way into the street and a man's head peering at houses as he drove by. She watched the car pass as Frank and his son closed the back door of the van.

'It's quiet enough around here.' Frank Mulvey surveyed the road as he got into the front.

'You should have heard us last night,' she said.

'You're not a Dublin woman, are you?' he asked.

'No, I'm from Wexford. Enniscorthy,' she said.

'Wexford,' he said. 'We used to travel to Courtown years ago on motorbikes.'

'Dublin fellows were all the rage in Courtown, I'd say.'

'We were the bee's knees, but that's all years ago,

29

before you were born.' He closed the door. She watched him and his son, who had not spoken, put their seatbelts on. He beeped the horn as he drove away.

The white car had now turned in the road and was slowly coming towards her. She realised that the driver was looking for directions. When he drew up to her he pulled down the window.

'I'm looking for O'Dohertys', number fifty-five,' he said.

'This is it,' she said.

'Are you Helen?' he asked.

There was something both eager and friendly about him, but formal as well, and it occurred to her that he was a teacher looking for a job, coming with references or a CV to her house. She wondered how he had got the address. Her face darkened.

'Yes, I'm Helen,' she said stiffly.

'Hold on, I'll park the car,' he said.

She had spent the previous two weeks interviewing teachers and she thought she recognised the type: cocky, self-confident, lacking all reticence, the potential scourge of the staffroom and useless in the classroom. She waited for him at the gate.

'I'm Paul,' he said. 'I'm a friend of your brother's.'

She said nothing, still half sure that he was a teacher to whom Declan had given her address. She wondered if it was something Declan would do, but she did not know, it was years since she had met any of Declan's friends.

'You can come inside, but there's been a party here, the house is a mess.'

'A party?' he asked. His tone was odd and unconvincing.

'Yes, that's what I said – a party,' she said drily.

She brought him to the kitchen and sat down. She did not offer him anything. She expected him to sit down as well but he remained standing.

'Declan's in hospital. He's in St James's. He asked me to come out here and tell you.'

Helen stood up. 'I'm terribly sorry. I thought you were a teacher looking for a job.'

'No, I have a job, thanks.' It was his turn to be dry.

'Did he have an accident? I mean, is he OK?'

'No, he didn't have an accident, but he'd like to see you.'

'How long has he been in hospital? Sorry, what's your name again?'

'Paul.'

'Paul,' she said.

He hesitated. 'He said he'd like to see you. I don't know how you're fixed now, but I could drive you to St James's.'

'He wants to see me now? Hey, is this serious?'

Again he hesitated.

'I mean, is he all right?' she asked.

'I saw him this morning and he's in good form.'

'You don't sound very reassuring.'

It was when he did not reply to this that she stopped herself asking any more questions. She looked at her watch; it was ten-past one.

'I have a meeting in the Department of Education in Marlborough Street at four.'

'If you come now you can be in Marlborough Street by four,' he said.

She realised that he was waiting for another question.

'Right. I'll come now,' she said. 'But it will take me a few minutes to get ready.'

Upstairs, as she changed into her navy-blue suit and white blouse – her nun's costume, Hugh called it – she went over what Paul had said and not said. It would have been easy for him to have said that it was just something minor. Even if he was an alarmist, someone who thrived on bad news, he could still have said something which would indicate that it was not serious. Maybe when he said that he had seen Declan that morning and he was in good form, maybe by this he meant to say that there was nothing wrong really. She stood in front of the bathroom mirror and put on a discreet amount of make-up. She felt a sudden urge or longing, which at first she could not identify, but then knew that it was an urge to be back in the house before Paul's arrival, to be back half an hour ago without his heavy, ominous presence in the room below.

She brushed her hair and checked herself in the full-length mirror and then, reluctantly, she went downstairs. As she saw him in the kitchen, she felt an intense hostility to him, which she knew she would have to keep under control.

She found her briefcase in the front room and emptied it of books, leaving only a notepad and some biros. She made sure that the downstairs windows were closed, turned on the answering machine, checked she had her keys and then told Paul she was ready.

They drove in silence through Rathfarnham and into Terenure. Helen knew that the next question she asked would elicit information which would leave her in no doubt.

'You'd better tell me what's wrong,' she said.

'Declan has AIDS. He's very sick. He sent me to tell you.'

Her first instinct was to run from the car, to watch for the next traffic lights and try to open the door and run to the pavement, and become the person entering a news-agent's shop or waiting for a bus, become anyone but the person she was now in the car.

'I'll pull in if you like,' Paul said.

'No, go on, I'll be OK,' she said. 'How long has he been sick?'

'He tested positive a good while ago, but he's only been sick the last two or three years, even though he's looked OK. He was very bad last year, but he pulled through. He has a line in his chest which gets infected, and he has problems with one eye and he gets chemo once a month. He's much weaker now than he was. He's very worried about your mother.'

'So he hasn't told her either?'

'No. He decided, or I don't know if "decided" is the word, to leave it all until the last minute.'

Once again, she was left feeling unable to face the answer to the next question she might ask. She wished she knew Paul better so she could judge whether he had used the phrase 'the last minute' casually or deliberately. She thought about it: everything else he said had been measured and deliberate; he would hardly have used a phrase like 'the last minute' without meaning to.

'Is he dying then?' she asked.

'It will be harder this time.'

'Has he been in hospital long?'

'On and off, but mostly he goes to the clinic.'

'My mother told me he was busy.'

'He hasn't been working. Also he's been avoiding seeing you and your mother.'

'What's he been living on?'

'He has money saved, and he's been working on and off.'

'Does Declan have a boyfriend, you know, a partner?'

'No,' Paul said flatly.

'Has he been living alone?'

'No, he's been staying with friends. He's been travelling a bit. He went to Venice at Easter – two of us went with him – but he doesn't have much energy. He went to Paris for a weekend, but he got very sick there.'

'It must have been hard looking after him,' she said.

'No, it's hard now, because he's weaker and he hates being in hospital, but he is the best in the world.'

'And why didn't he tell us?'

They were stopped in traffic on Clanbrassil Street now. Paul glanced at her sharply.

'Because he couldn't face it.'

She realised from the way he spoke that he considered her an outsider, a remote figure who had to be brought into the picture. Declan, she thought, had replaced his family with his friends. She wished he had thought of her as a friend.

They said nothing as they drove along Thomas Street. She still could not figure Paul out – the mixture of the dry, factual tone and the something else, which was softer, more sympathetic. They passed the brewery and then turned left into the hospital grounds. He drove into a car park at the side.

'Does Declan have a doctor he sees all the time, or a

consultant?' she asked as they walked towards one of the hospital buildings.

'Yeah, but I don't think she's here today.'

'She?'

'Yeah, Louise. She's the consultant.'

'Does Declan like her?'

'He likes her, she's a good person, but "like" isn't really the word.'

As they walked into the reception hall she asked him what he did for a living.

'I work for the European Commission,' he said. 'I'm taking time off at the moment.'

This wing of the hospital was old, with high ceilings, shiny walls and echoing corridors. Paul led the way without indicating how far they were from Declan's room. She did not know at what point he would turn and open a door and she would find Declan. It astonished her that less than an hour ago she was in her own house, undisturbed.

'Sorry, Paul.' She stopped him in the corridor. 'I have to ask you – are we talking about days, or weeks, or months? What are we talking about?'

'I don't know. It's hard to say.'

As they spoke, a young doctor in a white coat with a stethoscope around his neck came up to them.

'This is his sister,' Paul said. The doctor nodded into the distance.

'Don't go in for a while,' he said. He seemed distracted.

Helen looked at her watch; it was two o'clock.

'She has to go at half-three,' Paul said.

'I can always cancel the meeting,' she said.

'Hold on here,' the doctor said. 'I'll go in and look.' He walked down the corridor and quietly opened a door on the right.

'I have a name, you know,' she said to Paul.

'I'm sorry, I should have introduced you properly.'

'What does Declan want to do about my mother?' she asked.

'He wants you to tell her.'

Helen smiled sourly.

'I speak to her on the telephone sometimes, but I don't know exactly where she lives. I mean, I have her address, but I haven't been there. We don't get on.'

'I know all that,' Paul said impatiently. He sounded like someone chairing a meeting.

'And?' she asked.

'He wants you to go and tell her. You can have his car. It's in the car park. I have the keys.'

The doctor came back and beckoned them to come with him. 'He wants you both to go in at the same time,' he said.

The room was darkened but Helen could make out Declan in the bed. His eyes followed her; he smiled. He was thinner than when she had last seen him three or four months before, but he did not look sick.

'Paul,' he said in a hoarse whisper, 'could you open the window and pull the curtains a bit.' He tried to sit up.

A nurse came in and took his temperature and wrote it on a chart and then left. Helen noticed a dark, ugly bruise on the side of Declan's nose. He began to speak to Paul as though she was not there.

'So what do you think of her?'

'Your sister? She would have made a great reverend mother,' Paul laughed.

Helen remained motionless and silent. She tried to smile and forced herself to remember how hard this must be for Declan. She wanted to strangle Paul.

'She's nice, though,' Paul added.

'Hellie,' Declan said. 'Will you deal with the old lady?'

'Do you want to see her?'

'Yes.'

'When?'

'As soon as she can. And will you tell Granny as well?' He closed his eyes.

'You should meet my granny, Paul,' he said. 'She's the one would put manners on you. She's a real paint remover.'

'It won't be a problem, I'll drive out to Granny's as well,' Helen said. 'I'll make sure it's not a problem. Hugh and the boys are in Donegal.'

'I know,' Declan said.

'How do you know?'

'A friend of mine was at your party last night.'

'Who?'

'Seamus Fleming. He knows Hugh.'

'What does he look like?'

'Tall and skinny. Gorgeous eyes. He flirts,' Paul interjected.

'Does he play the guitar?'

'Yeah,' Declan said.

'Is he gay?' she asked.

'As the driven snow,' Declan said. Paul laughed. Declan closed his eyes and lay back and said nothing.

Helen knitted her brow in exasperation. No one spoke

for a while. Declan seemed to be asleep but then he opened his eyes. 'Do you want anything?' she asked him.

'Do you mean Lucozade or grapes? No, I don't want anything.'

'This is a real shock, Declan,' she said.

He closed his eyes again and did not reply. Paul put his finger to his lips, signalling to her to say nothing more. They stared at each other across the bed.

'Hellie, I'm sorry about everything,' Declan said, his eyes still closed.

★

Before they left the hospital, they spoke to the doctor again. Helen noticed how friendly Paul was with him and how familiar. The doctor told them that the consultant – he too called her Louise – would be there all the next day, and she would see Helen and her mother at any time.

'I have to keep convincing myself', Helen said when they got outside, 'that this is really happening. You're all so matter-of-fact about it, but the truth is that he is dying in there and I have to go and tell my mother.'

'No one is being matter-of-fact,' Paul said coldly.

He walked with her to the car park in front of the new hospital. He opened Declan's car – a battered white Mazda – and handed her the keys. 'Have you driven one of these before?' he asked.

'I'll be OK, I'm sure,' she said.

'I'll be here most of the day tomorrow,' he said, 'but here's my home number anyway, I have it written down for you. Also, it seems to me that they don't really need to have him in hospital. He has to have a line put back in and that will be done early tomorrow morning, I imagine. But after that they probably won't do anything else with him, just monitor him. It's really easy to get into hospital, but really hard to convince them to let you out. If you and your mother told Louise that you wanted to take him out, even for a day, then she would listen to you.'

'The main thing tomorrow is my mother,' Helen said.

'No, hold on,' Paul said. 'The main thing is Declan, not your mother. He gets depressed in that hospital room, so it's not just a small detail. It's a priority.'

'Thanks for the correction,' she said.

She got into the car and closed the door, pulling down the window so she could still talk to him. 'I'm really grateful to you for everything,' she said. She tried to sound as though she meant it, regretting the hostility in her earlier tone.

'Yeah,' he said and looked away. He was about to say something and then stopped himself. He looked at her, his expression almost hostile. 'I'll see you,' he said.

She started the car and drove out of the hospital grounds and into the city centre. She found a parking space in Marlborough Street, took her briefcase from the car, put money in the meter and made her way to the reception desk of the Department of Education.

★

She was early and she sat there waiting. If Hugh were here now, she knew, he would make her go home. She wished he were waiting out in the car for her and were coming to Wexford with her. He would probably be in Donegal by now, settling the boys into his mother's house. She would phone him before she left. Her mind kept skipping as she thought about him and the boys and the meeting she was about to attend, and she found that each time she could not focus on what the trouble was, it was like a dark shadow in a dream, and then it became real and sharp – Declan, the hospital, her mother. Mostly, when she worried or was concerned, it was about things which could be solved or would pass, but this was something new for her – and that was why, she believed, her mind kept avoiding it – something that would not go away, that could only get worse. She would do anything, she realised, to wish it away.

When some other school principals arrived, a porter came to take them upstairs.

'The Minister is here,' the porter said, 'and he wants to be introduced to you all before the meeting.'

A year earlier, the Minister had come to open the new science laboratories in Helen's school, and he had stayed afterwards for more than an hour in her office, asking questions, listening carefully.

When Helen walked into the room, she saw a few civil servants whom she recognised, including one with whom she had constant problems. Now, because of the Minister's imminent arrival, they were all polite and cowed. They shook hands and made small talk until the Minister came in.

'The Minister says he's met all of you at some time or another, but I'm going to introduce you all nonetheless.' John Oakley, the most senior civil servant, spoke.

The Minister greeted each person introduced and then politely asked them to take a seat. He remained standing.

'You're all welcome here,' he began. 'I know you're busy and I know you're going on holidays and we're all grateful to you for coming in today. These meetings are informal. However, there will be a report at the end and John Oakley here is going to write it and it will be done by Christmas. We've asked you to come here specifically because each of your schools has excelled in a certain area, areas which are particularly weak in other schools. The ones which come most to mind are absenteeism, in both teachers and pupils – Helen O'Doherty here has the lowest absentee rate or sick-leave rate for pupils or teachers anywhere; European languages – Sister here has been getting extraordinary results, especially in the spoken languages, and girls doing well in physics and higher maths, and George Fitzmaurice's school in Clonmel has excelled in that. These are just a few of the areas, and we want to know how it's done and apply it elsewhere. If you want to submit written reports, by all means do so, but please come to a few of these informal meetings between now and Christmas. And, as I think you know, if you have any particular concerns or problems, come to me with them, either directly or through John Oakley, our door is always open. That's all I'm going to say now. Thank you all, and I'll leave you to it.'

The Minister smiled at them and spoke briefly to one of the civil servants. On the way out of the room, he caught Helen's eye.

'I've been meaning to talk to you,' he said. 'I think you told me the day I was out at the school that you were from Enniscorthy and your father was a teacher too. But I heard more about you when I was down there at the Mercy Convent and the nuns said that one of their past pupils was a school principal in Dublin and that your maiden name was Breen and that your father was Michael

Breen. I knew your father well. We were both on the committee, the very first one, of the Irish Branch of the Association of European Teachers.'

'My father is dead twenty years,' Helen said. 'I didn't think you'd remember him.'

'It was a great loss, Helen,' the Minister said. 'You know, you might be too young to remember this about him, but he was brilliant and dedicated, one of the very best. He'd be very proud of you now, Helen.'

The Minister's tone was so personal and confidential, so unreserved, that Helen wanted to say something else to him, talk to him more, but he squeezed her hand and moved away and was soon talking to one of the other principals.

Helen waited until the Minister had left and then approached John Oakley.

'I have to go,' she said. 'I can't stay. I'll send you in a report and I'll be in touch.'

'Even if you could stay for half an hour,' he said.

'I can't.'

'Was it something the Minister said?' he asked suspiciously.

'I have to go to Wexford,' she said. 'I'll be in touch.'

As she walked down the corridor, she began to cry. A civil servant coming out of a doorway with a bunch of files looked at her, astonished. She walked down the stairs to the lobby and went out to the car. She sat there until she felt composed and then drove home to Ballinteer through the evening traffic.

★

By seven o'clock she was on the road to Wexford. Hugh, when she phoned him, had wanted to drive back down to Dublin; the boys, he said, had already forgotten he existed, they were so taken up with their cousins and the strand and their granny's house. He offered to get into the car immediately and come down, but Helen said no, she would go to Wexford on her own and phone him the next day.

She told him about Seamus Fleming, and Hugh said that he remembered Seamus asking when he was going to Donegal, but he never knew he was a friend of Declan's, he didn't even know he was gay.

'I hate the idea', she said, 'of him coming to the party, knowing that we didn't know.'

'Declan must have told him not to tell us,' Hugh said.

★

As she drove south, the sky began to brighten. Declan's car was old, and she had to be careful not to overtake on these narrow roads beyond the dual carriageway. At times she felt she was driving in a dream, one of those dreams that you wake from still unsure that it is over, but she was certain now as she drove on past Rathnew towards Arklow that she was wide awake. The evening light was clear, the sky blue with white clouds banked in the distance. She had not put a single thought into what she would say to her mother. When she began to picture the time they would spend together, whether in Wexford or in Dublin, she realised she would do anything to avoid it. She began to work out options.

She thought of booking into a hotel in Wexford and going to find her mother in the morning, but it was only when she stopped at Toss Byrne's in Inch, on the road into Gorey, that she knew for certain what she would do. She would not drive to Wexford that night. Instead, she would drive to Cush on the coast, where her grandmother lived, and tell her first. She would stay the night there; her grandmother would know how her mother should be handled.

★

She realised as she went into the lounge that she was starving. She had never stopped here before and, even though she had spotted the sign which said *Food All Day*, she was surprised to find a full-dinner menu on each table. She waited at the counter for a while, expecting to be told that the kitchen was closed, but a barman came and took her order and told her that he would bring the food down to her table. There was something typically Wexford about his accent and tone, a slightly awkward friendliness and openness which she had forgotten and which she now recognised, and it made her feel lighter as she went to the table and sat down. She had believed that nothing could lift her spirits, and now the barman's angled smile had made her almost cheerful. She knew, however, that what had really changed her mood had been the decision to postpone meeting her mother.

Her grandmother Dora Devereux lived alone in her former guest-house near the cliff in Cush. She was almost eighty and, except for her failing sight and fits of intense bad humour, was in good health. Helen pictured her now: her long neck and long thin face, grey hair pulled back in a bun, thick glasses, thin bony wrists, her expression alert, curious, watchful, tuned into every change in the wind or news in the neighbourhood. Helen smiled to herself as she thought about how her grandmother, in a rambling phone call a few weeks earlier, had told her about selling three sites for £15,000 each. She had done the deal without consulting Helen's mother, she had said defiantly. Her tone was that of a conspirator, seeking Helen as an ally and friend.

Helen had asked her grandmother if she was not getting on with her mother. Instead of replying, the old woman had gone on to remind Helen of how good she had been to Helen's mother in the time after her father died, how she had comforted her and consoled her, had sat up with her at night, slept in the room with her. How little she had got in return, her grandmother had said. She had seemed surprised, almost affronted, when Helen did not reply.

As Helen drove through Gorey and then turned left down the coast road, she thought to herself that with her grandmother it would somehow be easy to come like this, with bad news, looking for help. It would not be so easy to approach her mother. As she drove through Blackwater, Helen found herself unable to imagine what telling her mother would be like. She realised that the bitter resentment against her mother which had clouded her life had not faded; for a long time she had hoped that she would never have to think about it again.

When she turned at the ball-alley, she felt she was entering a new realm. For the first mile or so there were no houses, and then a new bungalow appeared on a corner just after the turn into the forest. She was overwhelmed now by sadness, a feeling which replaced the sense of foreboding and shock which had filled her. It was a feeling which she could deal with; there was no fear in it. The sudden rise in the road and then the first view of the sea glinting in the slanted summer light made it easier. The sadness brought tears to her eyes: she felt it sharply – that this would all go, that Declan would never see it again, never walk these lanes again, just as her father never would; soon they would only be a memory, and that too would fade with time.

She passed a mud ruin where old Julia Dempsey had lived out her days, and she would have given anything then to go back to the years before their father died, when they were children here and did not know what was in store for them.

★

At her grandmother's gate she stopped the car, pulled up the handbrake and turned off the engine. Her grandmother appeared at the door, her hand shading her eyes even though she stood in shadow.

'Here you are now, Helen,' she said as Helen approached from the car.

She had never in her life kissed her grandmother, or shaken her hand; now as she came close to her she did not know what to do.

'Granny, I'm sorry for barging in on you like this.'

'Oh, it's a great surprise, Helen, it's a lovely surprise.'

Her grandmother searched her face and then looked back towards the gate to check that no one else was coming. She turned and walked into the house. The big old Aga cooker in the kitchen was on full, and the room was warm. As Helen came in, the two cats jumped up to the top of the dresser — their constant presence there looking down on the room had amazed Cathal and Manus the previous year — and sat there watching her suspiciously.

'Now, Helen, there's tea on and I could make you up a fry.'

'No, Granny, I'll just have tea. I had a meal on the way down.'

She realised that her grandmother was biding her time, asking nothing, waiting to be told.

'Granny, I have very bad news.'

Her grandmother turned and put her two hands into the pockets of her apron as though searching for something. 'I know, Helen. I knew that as soon as I saw you.'

She remained standing as Helen told her the story. She concentrated fiercely on what was being said so that Helen felt, when she was finished, that the old woman could have repeated every single word she had said. There was something which she had forgotten: in the corner of the kitchen sat a huge television; her grandmother had access to all the English channels as well as the Irish ones. She watched documentaries and late-night films and prided herself on being well informed on modern subjects. She knew about AIDS and the search for a cure and the long illnesses. 'There's nothing can be done, Helen, so,' she said. 'Nothing can be done. It was the same years ago with your father's cancer. There was nothing the doctors could do. And poor Declan's only just starting his life.'

'What will I do about my mother?' Helen asked.

'You'll go into Wexford in the morning and you'll

47

break the news to her softly, Helen. Let her sleep tonight now. It's the last night's sleep she'll have for a long time.'

Her grandmother made tea and put biscuits on a plate. She sat down opposite Helen. It was still bright outside, and Helen felt a desperate need to go down to the strand, to get away from the intensity of her grandmother's attention.

'I'll make you up a bed now,' her grandmother said. 'The room hasn't been used since you were here last summer. Your mother never stays, and she hasn't been here much recently.'

'Have you fallen out with her?' Helen asked.

'Ah, not really. She still thinks she's going to get me to move into Wexford. What if I broke my leg out here, she asked me. And I told her I've plenty of money now that I sold the sites; that old field that was full of ragwort. I never consulted her or asked for her opinion. And that's all is wrong with her, but she's well over it now. She's good at forgetting things, putting them behind her. And I had the central heating installed without as much as a by-your-leave from her. Come on until I show you.'

She stood up and Helen accompanied her into the old dining-room. She pointed at the new white radiator, and then opened the doors of the two bedrooms off the dining-room with iron beds and bare mattresses. These two rooms also had radiators.

'I had it put in all over the house, and a big oil tank out the back. I bought a deep-freeze as well, so I have no worries. Your mother came down when the work was half done and said that the house would rot. She said that she had everything set up for me in Wexford. "It's a wonder, Lily," I said to her, "that you don't look high-up or low-down at me and I only ten miles out the road and you with your big car. Isn't it funny now that you've started to call when you know I have money?" Oh, she was raging. That was Easter and I didn't see her again until the end of May. She brought me down this.' She took a mobile phone from her apron pocket. She held it in her left hand as though it were a small animal. 'Oh, I told her I couldn't have a phone in the house. I'd worry about it, so I keep this here, it's turned off, I never use it.'

'But, Granny, you didn't mean it about the money.'

'No, Helen, but it was the only thing I could say that would make her stop trying to move me into the town. Oh, she was raging. And she'd be even more raging if she thought I told you. God help her, she'll have other things to think about now.'

Her grandmother went over to the window and peered out through the curtains.

'Is it easy to get down to the strand this year, Granny?' Helen asked.

'Oh yes, Helen, they dug steps and the steps have stayed, except for the last bit which is all marly and mucky.'

'I'd like to go down, just for a minute, just so I can think, it's been the longest day I've ever spent.'

'You go down, Helen, and I'll make up your bed, and I'd be glad if you'd drive the car into the yard or I'll have dreams about it rolling over the cliff.'

'I won't be long.'

★

The last strong rays of the sun could be seen over the hill behind the house. The air was still, with hardly a hint of the night about to fall. She felt almost healed and enclosed by her grandmother, but she knew, too, that her grandmother's attempt to suggest that nothing could hurt her was half pretence; the other half was a hardness built up over a lifetime of expecting the worst and then watching it unfold.

As Helen walked down the lane, she could see only the soft blue horizon and she could not imagine what the sea would look like in this light. And when she came to the edge she saw it down below: blue with eddies of dark blue and green in the distance. The sea was calm and the waves rolled over with an easy, whispering crash. There was no barrier at the end of the lane; a car could easily be driven over and would tumble down the clay and marl on to the sand below. But no strangers were expected here; even in the summer it was not a place for casual visitors.

She found the steps and began to make her way down to the strand. The first stretch was easy, but soon she had to move carefully, holding on to weeds and tufts of grass, trying and failing to avoid the muck and the wet marl. She had to run down the last bit; it had always been like that, there was always too much loose sand at the bottom.

She stood on the narrow strand and shivered. Down here in the shadow of the cliff it seemed darker, colder, more like late August than late June. A line of sea birds flew a hand's distance above the calm water. And as each wave came in, it looked as though it might not break, but merely casually spill in and then get sucked back, but every time there came the inevitable lift and curl and a sound that was almost remote, a sound that, she believed, had nothing to do with her and had no connection to anything she knew, the quiet crashing of a wave.

From here as far as Keatings' the erosion had stopped or slowed down. No one knew why. Years earlier, it had seemed just a matter of time before her grandmother's house would fall into the sea, just as Mike Redmond's and Keatings' outhouse had done. And now Keatings' old white house itself was falling, but there was still one house between her grandmother's and the sea.

The erosion had stopped, but when she watched now she noticed fine grains of sand pouring down each layer of cliff, as though an invisible wind were blowing or there was a slow, measured loosening of the earth. It was bright enough still while she looked south to see Raven's Point and Rosslare Harbour. The strand, as she walked along, became narrower and stonier; she listened to the waves hitting the loose stones, unsettling them, knocking them against each other and then withdrawing. She saw, as she walked towards Keatings', that some of the red galvanised iron from a shed at the side had fallen now, and raw walls with strips of the old wallpaper were open to the wind, and soon they would fall too, until only a few people would remember that there had once been a hill and a white house below it way back from the cliff.

Here, the county council had put huge boulders to protect the cliff, but they had no impact. When she turned back, she saw that the line of coast from Cush to Parle's Gap and Knocknasillogue was as it had been ten or fifteen years before, as though time had stood still. The colours were darkening now, night was coming down. She would walk up the gap where Mike Redmond's house had been and then along the lanes to her grandmother's house or along the clifftop if it seemed easier.

She noticed something out of the side of her eye, and when she turned she saw it again: the lighthouse flashing in the distance, Tuskar Rock. She stood again and watched it, waited for the next flash, but it took a while to come, and then she waited again as the rhythm of the night set in.

She walked on, knowing what she was facing into now. She imagined Declan in Dublin, afraid, wondering what had happened, alone in the small hospital room with the long night ahead. It was something which she could barely imagine, and as soon as she started thinking about it she stopped herself, and began to dream about him now arriving in his car, hearing the sound of it approaching and seeing him turn in the lane, and knowing that he was, most of the time, able to get around his grandmother in a way that Helen never could. He could talk to her as no one else was able to; he pretended to share her prejudices, he managed to laugh at her in a way she never minded. Declan would have loved her showing him the central heating and the mobile phone. He would have known what to say.

The climb was easy at Mike Redmond's, easier than the steps to her grandmother's lane. Helen walked through the ruin of the house, the front wall having long since fallen into the sea. She looked at the old chimney and the back wall still in place, and then stood at the edge waiting for the next flash from Tuskar. It seemed brighter now, stronger, from this height. She could feel the dew falling and could hear the sound of cattle somewhere in the distance as she made her way back to her grandmother's house.

THREE

The bed was uncomfortable and the nylon sheets, she felt, had not been used for years. They must have been from the time of the guest-house; they had a thin, almost slippery feel. The mattress sagged. She was so tired that she had gone to sleep as soon as she lay down, but she woke an hour or two later, unsure where she was, reaching out for a light, unable to think what house she was in, and feeling a strange, hard thirst. Then she remembered where she was and how she had got here. She put her head on the pillow and wondered how she had let this happen. Earlier on, it had seemed a good idea to come and spend the night here, but she had not bargained for being wide awake like this, the light from Tuskar through the curtains flitting across the wall over her bed, and a smell of must and damp in the room.

She got out of bed and made her way to the kitchen. She filled a mug of water and brought it back to the bedroom. The lino in the room was torn, some of the wallpaper had peeled, the paint on the ceiling was flaking, and the presence of the shiny modern radiator made the room seem even more dingy and depressing. When she pulled the old candlewick bedspread back, she found that the blankets were stained. She didn't feel tired or sleepy. She shivered. The smell seemed sharper now, and sour, and it was the smell more than anything which brought her back to the time she and Declan had lived in this house.

★

This had been her room, Declan's the one behind. But after a while his bed had been moved in here. She remembered the hammering apart of the iron bed and the feeling as they stood and watched that they were causing all this trouble.

Declan was afraid. He was afraid of the black clocks which darted awkwardly across the floor, afraid that if you stepped on one of them all the bloody insides would be on your feet. He was afraid of the dark and the cold and of his grandparents' movements upstairs which seemed to echo in the rooms below. And Helen knew that there was another fear, which was never mentioned in all that time: the fear that their parents would never come back, that they would both be left here, and that these days and nights – Helen was eleven then, Declan eight – would become their lives, rather than an interlude which would soon come to an end.

Helen remembered how it began. It must have been just after Christmas, maybe early January, and it was her last year at primary school. She remembered the day when she arrived home, dropped her schoolbag inside the door and found her parents in the back room, standing in a pose she had never seen them in before. They were both looking into the mirror which was over the fireplace, and when they saw her coming into the room they did not turn. Her mother spoke. It was a new voice, soft, with a tone of entreaty.

'Helen,' she said, 'your father is going to have to go to Dublin for tests.'

She looked at the two of them as they stared at her and at each other, as though any second now the mirror would flash and take a photograph of them. In her memory, these moments – her father's slow smile, her mother's gentle tone – were mixed up with their wedding photograph, taken in Lafayette's in Dublin. She was sure that the scene in front of the mirror could have lasted only a few minutes, maybe less even, enough for a glance from each of them and a sentence – 'Helen, your father is going to have to go to Dublin for tests' – and maybe nothing more. In any case, it was the last memory she ever had of seeing her father. She knew she must have seen him later that evening and perhaps the next day, but she had no memory, absolutely none, of seeing him again.

Her only other memory of that day was of Sister Columb from St John's arriving and standing in the hallway, refusing to come in. Helen remembered whispering and half-talk in the hallway and then the nun departing.

'The nuns in St John's are going to knock on the tabernacle tonight,' her mother said.

Who did she say this to? And then, Helen remembered, someone had asked what this meant and her mother had explained that it was something which the nuns hardly ever did, but one of them would approach the altar and knock on the tabernacle, and that would be a special way of asking God for a favour.

Her next memory of that evening was the clearest of

all. She was upstairs in her bedroom when Declan came in. He told her that their mother was going to Dublin as well.

'What's going to happen to us?' she asked.

'We're going to Granny's. We have to pack. She says you're to pack warm things.'

She went downstairs. Her mother was in the kitchen.

'How long are we going for? What are we going to do about school?'

'Your father's sick,' her mother said.

'I thought you said that he was going to Dublin for tests.'

'There's a suitcase under my bed. You can use that,' her mother said. 'Bring all your schoolbooks.'

She wondered had this really happened, the non-answers to questions, the sense of her mother as being utterly remote, lost to her. In the morning Aidan Larkin, who was in Fianna Fáil with her father, drove them to Cush. Dr Flood, later, was going to drive her parents to Dublin. Her mother and father must have been in the house that morning, and must have spoken to her and to Declan, but she had no memory of it, just the car journey and the arrival. Her grandparents in Cush had no telephone, so she had no idea how they had been alerted to the imminent arrival of the two children. Nonetheless, Helen and Declan were expected in this house they had come to previously only on summer Sundays, or in the early summer when the guest-house was not full. Helen had no memory of ever visiting the house before in the winter. This, then, was the first time she noticed the patches of damp on the walls and the smell of damp which was everywhere except the kitchen, and the draughts which came under doors and the fierce wind which came in from the sea.

The sea was just twenty or thirty yards away, but in all those months – from January to June – she caught sight of it maybe once or twice from the clifftop: this turbulence below them, the waves crashing hard against the cliff-face. Her grandparents, she remembered, behaved as though it were not there. In all the years her grandmother had been in Cush, she had hardly ever been on the strand. They paid no attention to the sea, and Helen and Declan learned to pay no attention to it either.

The first dispute arose over food. Declan would eat only sliced bread, it had become a sort of joke in the family. But there was no sliced bread in Cush, only brown bread and soda bread that her grandmother made, and loaves of white bread with a hard crust which they bought in Blackwater. There were other things which Declan wouldn't eat – cabbage or turnips, carrots or onions, eggs or cheese. He was obsessive about this, carefully finding out about each meal, or possible visits to other houses, and making sure that the food would be to his taste, and making himself pleasant in every other matter, and always getting his way.

On Sunday visits to Cush their mother packed sandwiches for Declan, and during longer visits she brought and cooked their own food. But Declan knew that their grandmother disapproved of this.

'You don't eat because you like the food, you eat to live, that's why you eat,' was one of her sayings.

As they drove from Enniscorthy to Cush, Helen knew that Declan thought only about food, and what was going to happen. The first dinner in the middle of the day was a stew; her grandmother served out four plates of stew with a big ladle and then put a plate of potatoes in the middle of the table. Her grandfather took off his cap and sat down and blessed himself. Helen made a sign to Declan to say nothing, do nothing. She peeled two potatoes for him and he mashed them up and slowly began to eat them. But he didn't touch the stew. Her grandfather read the *Irish Independent* and said very little. Her grandmother bustled about – she seldom sat at the table – and when, that first day, she went out into the yard, Helen took Declan's plate and scraped the stew into the bucket of waste her grandmother kept for the hens. She put the plate back in front of Declan; he sat there amazed, trying not to smile. Neither of their grandparents noticed anything.

When teatime came, Helen helped her grandmother set the table. For tea there was brown bread, thick slices of white bread and boiled eggs. Declan came into the kitchen as the eggs were being taken from the boiling water.

'These eggs now are fresh,' his grandmother said, 'not like the ones you get in the town.'

'Yuck,' Declan said.

'Declan doesn't eat eggs,' Helen said.

'I never heard worse,' her grandmother said. 'The things your mother has to put up with. She's too soft.'

And so the battle began, the battle that raged daily, Declan filling his pockets with crusts, Helen reaching for the waste bucket, and days when there was no way out, when Declan put the onions and the carrots or the cabbage and the turnips to one side of the plate and refused to eat them, and their grandmother insisted that he stay at the table until he had them eaten, only to relent as soon as he started to cry.

'He can't eat them, Granny, he'll get sick,' Helen would say.

'Stop giving back-answers, Helen.'

'I'm not giving back-answers.'

As soon as her grandmother began to talk about sending them to the two-teacher school in Blackwater, Helen set up a classroom at the kitchen table and for much of the day, in between meals, she and Declan worked at their schoolbooks, Helen playing the role of teacher. They discovered school as a way of excluding their grandmother, until she put a paraffin heater into the dining-room for them so that she could listen to the radio in peace. They did algebra or Irish or decimal points at the times of the day when she was most likely to hover around them; often they did the same exercises over and over, pretending this required total concentration and not looking up if their grandmother came into the room. They opened Declan's books at random and went through lessons he had done long before, or began entirely new ones without fully understanding them or finishing them. When they were bored, they laughed and whispered and played cards.

Their mother wrote short letters to their grandmother saying there was no news and mentioning tests and prayers and hoping that Helen and Declan were not too much of a burden on her. Their mother was staying in Rathmines with her cousin, one of the Bolgers of Bree, and his wife, and they too sent their regards. There was no mention of their father.

Helen and Declan found a box of games under one of

the beds and amused themselves in the long, dark evenings playing Ludo and Snakes and Ladders. Helen found boots she could wear and went often with her grandfather to fetch the cows for milking or to open and close gates for him. Declan had no boots; he hated the muck of the yard and the lane, he seldom went out and often in the afternoon, in the clammy heat of the parlour, he became tired and irritable. Alone together in these first months, they never mentioned home or their mother or their father, or how long they would be here. They worked out strategies to get them through the day without confrontation.

Slowly, their grandmother began to treat Helen as an adult and Declan as a child, although Helen and Declan continued to treat each other as equals, even if Helen remained in the role of protector. In the first week or so, Helen had an argument with her grandfather; it was the only time he said much during their entire stay in the house. He was reading something in the newspaper about Fianna Fáil – he himself was a member of Fine Gael, which was strong in Blackwater – and he turned to Helen and her grandmother and said, 'They're only a shower of gangsters, bloody gun-runners. Liam Cosgrave will put manners on the whole lot of them.'

'Jack Lynch is not a gangster or a gun-runner,' Helen said.

'The rest of them, then,' her grandfather said. 'And I'd string Charlie Haughey up. He's a feckin' gangster.'

'Oh, language now,' her grandmother said.

'But Jack Lynch is the leader,' Helen said.

'Oh, I know who you've been listening to,' her

grandfather said. 'Did we ever think that Lily would have a little Fianna Fáiler for a daughter?'

'And the *Irish Independent* is only Fine Gael propaganda,' Helen said.

'Propaganda? Where did you learn that word?'

'Oh, Helen knows all the words,' her grandmother said.

'It's saying your prayers you should be,' her grandfather said and went back to reading the paper.

'Good girl, you stand up to him now,' her grandmother said later when he had left the room.

From then on, her grandfather let her watch the news on television and, after a few weeks, one Saturday night Helen realised that she was going to be allowed to watch *The Late Late Show*, which her mother and father had never permitted her to watch at home, except for the night when Lieutenant Gerard from *The Fugitive* was a guest on the show and she was called downstairs. Now in Cush she sat on one of the armchairs in the kitchen and wondered if they had forgotten about her as the news ended and then the break for advertisements ended and the music for the show began and Gay Byrne appeared.

'If something comes on that's not fit for her now,' her grandmother said, 'she'll go to bed.'

Helen remembered the slow preparations for the programme, her grandmother making sure that all the housework was done. Tea things and biscuits were set out on a tray, the kettle filled to be put on a hotplate during the second break. Her grandmother loved the programme, and, Helen realised, loved having Helen to discuss the guests and the controversies in the days that followed.

Her grandfather, on the other hand, disliked it and muttered to himself when something was said of which he disapproved.

During that season, Helen remembered, hardly a Saturday night passed without a group of women wanting rights, or a priest in dispute with the hierarchy, appearing on the programme.

'Oh, look who it is now, look at her, look at her hair!' her grandmother would shout at a woman who appeared on the panel.

Her grandmother commented throughout, but her comments mostly took the form of exclamations of shock or wonder at what was being said, and on the personal appearance of guests. But sometimes, with extraordinary vehemence, when women's rights or politics were being discussed she would bang her fist against the armchair and shout her total agreement with an opinion being expressed. 'She's right, she's absolutely right!' she would roar.

She hated breaks for music and the appearance of writers or film stars or English people. They told too many funny stories; she wanted argument, not amusement. But she remained silent and tense when religion was discussed, watching some nun or priest or concerned layperson out of the side of her eyes. Once or twice, during these discussions, her grandfather threatened to turn the television off, but he never did so. All three stayed up until the end of the show, and it often went on until close to midnight, as an ex-nun cast doubt on the power of the Pope, or a student leader denounced the Irish bishops or the education system. Contraception and divorce were discussed regularly; her grandparents watched in embarrassed silence, but the only time when they threatened to send Helen to bed was when a woman on the show pointed out that most Irish couples had never seen one another naked, even people who'd been married for years.

'Oh, Lord bless us and save us!' her grandmother said.

The item on *The Late Late Show* which unsettled them most, however, was not about sex or religion. It was when an American woman, middle-aged, with permed hair, and glasses, wearing a red dress, appeared on the show. She could, she claimed, make contact with the dead. She did not use the word 'dead', but talked about people who had passed away, people on the 'other side'. Gay Byrne asked her questions as though he believed her.

'Did you ever hear such nonsense?' her grandmother asked. 'Did you ever hear worse?'

The woman stood in front of the live audience with Gay Byrne beside her. She held a microphone and pointed at individuals in the audience.

'Yes, that woman there,' she said. 'I'm getting very strong messages for you. You have only one sister, is that right?'

The woman in the audience nodded.

'And she's been ill, hasn't she?'

The woman nodded again.

'The message is confused now, but are you twins or very close in age?'

'We're very close in age.'

'But when you were children, you are the one who was ill, right?'

'Yes, that's right.'

'Could this be your mother, dear, could this be your mother? I know that she wants to protect you and she's worried about your sister, but things are better now, and she's watching over you both.'

There was silence in the kitchen as Helen and her grandparents watched the television. The woman on *The Late Late Show* moved on to someone else.

'I'm getting strong signals again,' she said to a woman. 'Did you have a little boy who was killed or died as a baby?'

'No,' the woman said.

'I'm getting strong signals. Did you have a brother who died young?'

'Yes, I did,' the woman said.

'And he's still watching over you and he knows that you're a very strong person and you've just moved house, have you?'

'Yes,' the woman said.

'And is your mother living with you?'

'No, she was, but she's not now.'

'Well, he's worried about her, he thinks the change is for the best, but he's worried about her. I think you might know what he means by that.'

The woman nodded.

'Now I have to talk to somebody else. There's something important. Is there somebody called Grace here?'

There was no response.

'Is there somebody called Grace? Maybe even a surname?'

A hand went up. 'Grace is my surname,' a man said.

'And your first name?'

'Jack.'

'Jack,' the woman said, 'I think you're about to make a big decision. Now it's somebody very close to you. Jack, the ties are very close between this person and you. It's someone you think about every day, a few times a day. You know who it is, I think?'

Jack nodded.

'She says you mustn't go. That's the message, it's very clear. But there's something else as well, there's a relationship that's very important for you. You're unsure about it, but she wants to give it her blessing, and she says she still loves you and is protecting you and guarding you.'

When the break for advertisements came, Helen's grandmother did not move from the chair. She motioned Helen to turn down the sound.

'I wonder if you can write to that woman.'

'Enclose a postal order, I'd say,' her grandfather said.

'Who would you like to get in touch with, Granny?'

'Oh, Helen, I'd love to get in touch with my sister Statia, and I'd a brother Daniel who died of TB. I'd love to hear from them, no matter what it was, even if it was just a message. And it must be terrible hard for that American woman, having that power.'

'She's making all that up,' Helen's grandfather said.

'No,' her grandmother said, 'she has the power, I'd know by her. And did you see that man's face? It must have been his wife that was getting in touch with him. I'd give anything now to talk to Statia.'

★

Around that time, maybe a week or two later, Declan began to have nightmares. The first night Helen could not think what the sound was. She woke and tried to go back to sleep, but the noise persisted, and then she heard her grandmother moving in the room above and coming down the stairs. As though alert to her movements, Declan began to scream, and Helen jumped out of bed and ran into his room. He had sounded as though someone were attacking him.

They woke him, but he could not come out of the dream. He continued to scream and cry, even when they brought him into the kitchen and gave him a drink of milk and offered him a biscuit. He was frightened by something, and did not fully recognise either of them, and then slowly he began to calm down, but he said nothing, stared ahead of him, or at the light, and for a while they were unsure whether he was still living in his dream. And then he was fine again, but he would not go back to his room until the light was left on.

The nightmares changed him; during the day he became withdrawn, and often, as they went through a lesson or played cards, he became forgetful and distant and she would remind him where he was and that became a joke between them. But the dream did not stop, although some nights he would sleep soundly. On the other nights, as soon as his shouting began, both Helen and her grandmother would run to him and always – it was the same each time – it would take five or ten minutes to calm him down and bring him back to the world they lived in.

His grandmother wondered if he had worms or if he might be sickening for something, and she brought him to the doctor in Blackwater. He refused to go into the surgery unless Helen came as well. She watched the doctor examine him, check his tongue and tonsils and the whites of his eyes, listen to his breathing through a stethoscope. The doctor asked him if he was afraid of anything and he said no.

'And so what are your dreams about?'

Declan looked at the doctor and thought for a while.

'If I think about it too much, it'll come back,' he said.

'But just tell me what it is.'

'I'm small, I'm tiny, like the smallest things, and everything is huge and I'm floating.'

'You mean everything else is huge.'

'Yes.'

'And is that frightening?'

'Yes.'

'And he won't eat,' his grandmother interrupted. 'I can't get him to eat.'

'Oh, he's well nourished,' the doctor said. 'I wouldn't worry about that.'

Declan was still staring ahead, thinking. 'I kind of forget the dream after I've had it,' he said.

The doctor said that Declan should move his bed into the room with Helen and maybe he'd feel safer then. 'A lot of boys have nightmares for a while like that and they just go away.' He pinched Declan's cheek.

★

Helen watched the post. The postman came at eleven. He delivered the newspaper as well, and if there was no post he dropped the newspaper in the door, but if there was post he knocked on the door and handed the letters to her grandmother. Her mother's letters were short and vague; she used the same words each time. Helen wondered if her father were really having tests, why the tests could not be over, why they did not produce results.

One day – she could not remember what month it was – a letter came from her mother which her grandmother did not show her and which later, when Helen asked about it, her grandmother told her did not arrive. Helen was sure it had been delivered and searched with her eyes over the mantelpiece where the letters were kept, but it was not there. Her grandmother knew how to hide things. And the next day she heard her grandmother whispering to Mrs Furlong, and she felt she understood the reason for the whispering: there was something in the letter which she could not be told.

In all the months in Cush – by this time, she was sure, they had been there for three or four months – Helen and Declan had never discussed how long they would be there or what was happening to them, but as soon as Declan brought up the subject they could not stop discussing it.

'Hellie,' he began one day over lessons in the parlour. 'I want to go home.'

'Ssh,' she said. 'She'll hear you.'

'I don't think they're in Dublin at all. I think they're in England or America.'

'Don't be silly.'

'Why has she never come down here?'

'Because she's visiting him in hospital.'

'Why has she not come even once?'

'Because we're all right here.'

'We're not all right.'

Helen told him nothing about the letter. She tried to talk him out of his new idea, but it became an obsession.

'I saw a programme about it on the television,' he said. 'The father and mother left their children behind.'

'Behind where?'

'In an orphanage.'

'This is not an orphanage.'

'What will happen when she needs the rooms for summer visitors?'

'They'll be back by then.'

'They're in England.'

'Declan, they're not.'

'How do you know?'

It was around the same period she heard the word 'cancer' for the first time. Her grandmother was talking to Mrs Furlong in the hallway and did not know that Helen was listening on the other side of the door.

'When they opened him up, they found that he was riddled with cancer,' she said.

Helen knew that if she asked a question she would get no answer. One day, when her grandmother had gone into Blackwater, she searched for missing letters, but she could not find any.

By now, Declan was consumed by the possibility of escaping.

'You could get a job in Dublin,' he said. 'We'd be much better off.'

'Where?'

'In Dunnes Stores, that's where you can work if you leave school.'

'I'm not even twelve.'

'How would they know?'

In the days that followed she looked at herself carefully when she was in the bathroom. She remembered the opening of the novel *Desirée*, where the heroine had placed handkerchiefs inside her blouse to look like breasts. Helen was tall for her age, and she wondered, if she claimed to be fourteen, would she be believed?

Something changed in the house as the days grew longer. Their grandmother's softening attitude towards them, the length of Mrs Furlong's visits, a long visit from Father Griffin, the curate in Blackwater, all convinced Helen that it was her father who was riddled with cancer, and this must mean that he was dying, or maybe needed another operation which would take longer. Although she and Declan talked about escaping and going to Dublin and Helen finding a job and a flat and Declan going to school, Helen always treated it like a game, a fantasy. Declan, however, took it seriously. He worked out plans.

'Declan, you've hardly even been in Dublin,' she said.

'I was loads of times. I know Henry Street and Moore Street.'

'But only for a day,' she said.

One evening, he came to her in her bedroom with an old brown leather wallet which was full of twenty-pound notes.

'Where did you get it?' she asked.

'He keeps it in the kitchen press in a hole,' Declan said.

'Leave it back.'

'We can use it when we escape. Now you know where it is.'

'Leave it back.'

★

Their father died in Dublin on 11 June. This seemed strange to her and even now, twenty years later, as she lay in bed in this house, wide awake, her grandmother upstairs asleep and Declan in hospital in Dublin, she had no memory of that early summer in Cush, of May passing into June. Some things, however, were still sharp in her memory: the changed atmosphere in the house, at least two other letters arriving and not being mentioned, the smell of damp and paraffin. Years afterwards, she realised that her childhood ended in those few weeks, even though she did not have her first period until six months later.

She knew something had happened on that morning: early, it must have been around eight o'clock, a man arrived, she saw him passing by the window; he spoke to her grandparents and then he left. And then, not long afterwards, Father Griffin from Blackwater arrived. She decided to stay in bed until he had gone, and told herself it was still possible that something else, or nothing much, had happened. She lay there and waited. Declan was fast asleep in the other bed.

After a while she heard her grandmother tiptoeing across the parlour. She opened the door to the bedroom quietly and told Helen in a whisper to dress as quickly as she could.

When Helen came out of the bedroom her grand-mother was standing by the window.

'Helen, we've bad news now; your father died last night at eleven o'clock. He died very peacefully. We'll all have to look after your mother now. You and Declan are going to go into Enniscorthy with Father Griffin.'

'Where are we going?'

'I've got clean clothes out for you. Mrs Byrne of the Square is going to look after you and Declan.'

Helen felt a sudden surge of happiness that they were leaving here and would never have to come back, but she quickly felt guilty for thinking about herself like this when her father had just died. She tried not to think at all. She went into the kitchen, where Father Griffin was drinking tea.

'We'll all kneel down and say a prayer for his soul,' her grandmother said.

Father Griffin led a decade of the Rosary. He said the words of the prayers slowly and deliberately and when he came to the Hail Holy Queen he recited the prayer as though the words were new to him: 'To Thee do we send up our sighs, mourning and weeping in this valley of tears.' Softly, quietly, Helen began to cry, and her grandmother came over and knelt beside her until the prayers ended.

They sat and drank more tea in silence; her grandmother made toast and aired clothes.

'Why isn't Declan up?' Helen asked.

'Oh, I let him sleep, Helen. It'll be time enough for him when we're packed to go.'

'Have you not told him?'

'We'll let him sleep.'

'He'll be awake.'

As Helen was packing their schoolbooks in the parlour, Declan called her. 'What are you doing?' he asked.

'I'm packing. We're going to Enniscorthy.'

When he looked at her from the bed, she thought that he knew, but she was not sure.

'How are we getting there?'

'Father Griffin.'

He looked at her again and nodded. He got out of the bed and stood on the floor in his pyjamas.

'I want to pack my own schoolbag,' he said.

★

Somewhere on the road between The Ballagh and Enniscorthy, with Father Griffin driving and Helen in the front seat, she realised that Declan didn't know their father was dead.

'Are Daddy and Mammy already back from Dublin?' he asked.

Even now, twenty years later, as she lay between the sticky nylon sheets with her hands behind her head, staring at the ceiling as the lighthouse flashed on and off, Helen could still feel the terror in the car as neither she nor Father Griffin answered the question. She expected Declan to ask again, but he sat back and said nothing and they drove on towards the town.

Helen desperately did not want to go to Mrs Byrne's house in the Square. Declan was friendly with the two boys, it would be easy for him, but she had no friends there and knew that Mrs Byrne would treat her like a child. Mrs Byrne was like all the shopkeepers' wives in the town: they were always watching everything, always on the lookout, even their smiles were sharp, and she did not want to be under the control of Mrs Byrne or any other Mrs in the town.

They drove past Donoghue's Garage in silence and crossed the bridge and drove up Castle Hill. Helen was determined not to go into Mrs Byrne's house.

When Father Griffin double-parked in the Square and left them alone in the car, Declan asked her nothing and she told him nothing. Mrs Byrne came out, all smiles. She opened the driver's door and put her head into the back of the car.

'Now, Declan,' she said, 'when Thomas and Francis come home for their dinner, maybe they'll both take the afternoon off so you can play upstairs.'

Helen got out of the car and stood beside Mrs Byrne. 'My granny says I'm to go up home and have the place tidy for Mammy.'

'Helen, I'm sure some of the neighbours will do that.'

'Granny said I was to go and Father Griffin was to drive me up and Declan was to stay with you.'

Father Griffin stood there listening carefully. Helen knew that she had sounded too sure of herself for him to disagree. He was a mild man, uncomfortable now and anxious to get away since his car was blocking the traffic.

'So,' Helen said, 'if you could take Declan's things and then we'll see you later.' She was trying to sound brisk, like somebody from the television.

'Hold on a minute,' Father Griffin said, 'and I'll park.'

Declan took his bag from the boot and they stood outside Byrne's shop waiting for Father Griffin.

'Isn't your grandmother very good?' Mrs Byrne said to Helen.

'She's marvellous,' Helen said.

Mrs Byrne looked up and down the street. 'Your poor mammy now will be glad to see you,' she said.

'I'll go and wait in the car,' Helen said, and she walked across the Square to where Father Griffin had parked. As he left the driver's seat, she opened the passenger's door.

'Will you be all right here?' he asked.

'Yes, perfect,' she said confidently.

She watched him walk across the Square and go into Byrnes' with Declan and Mrs Byrne. She knew what he was doing: he was telling Declan that his father was dead. She wondered why he was taking so long. Two passers-by saw her in the car and came over. She rolled down the window.

'Are you waiting for your mammy?' they asked.

'No,' she said. 'No, I'm not.'

'Is she still in Dublin, the poor thing?'

'Yes,' Helen said. She was trying to sound grand, as though used to being accosted by people like this.

'Well, we're very sorry for your trouble.'

'Thank you.' She knitted her brow and rolled up the window.

When Father Griffin came out of Byrnes', he walked with his head down, hunched.

'I'm not sure that we can leave you up there on your own,' he said. 'Mrs Byrne wants you to come back in.'

'Oh, Mummy is very particular. Everything will have to be spick and span for her.'

'But you can't be on your own in the house.'

'No; I'll call on Mrs Russell, she's the one who's closest to Mummy, and she'll come in with me.'

She pretended that she was a Protestant girl being driven to Lymington House by this slow country priest. She knitted her brow again. Father Griffin started the car. She wondered what had happened with Declan, what he was doing now.

'Are you sure you'll be all right?' Father Griffin asked her.

'Perfectly sure, father, perfectly sure. I'll go in and then I'll call on Mrs Russell.'

He drove along John Street and then up Davitt Avenue.

'You can leave me here, father, and we're very grateful to you.'

He drove her to the house. She did not want him to know that she would have to climb in the kitchen window. She would have tried anything to make him drive away.

'I'll take my case from the boot,' she said nonchalantly. 'I left it open. It's better to reverse back down, father, easier than trying to turn here.'

She closed the door of the car and fetched her case and waved at him casually as she opened the garden gate. She walked around the side of the house without looking behind. She stood the case up, using it to reach the ledge of the kitchen window, and then levered herself up until she was able to kneel on the ledge. The clasp on the lock had been broken for years. She pulled the bottom part of the window up with all her strength. It opened just enough for her to lean in on to the draining board beside the sink, and edge her way into the kitchen. As soon as she stood up, she did not wait to close the window but went and opened the front door and found Father Griffin, as she expected, still sitting in his car looking at the house. With her right hand, she motioned him imperiously to go. She shut the door again and put her back to it, and closed her eyes. When she went into the front room and looked out of the window, she saw that he was already reversing the car; he was on his way. Now she had the house to herself.

★

She listened: there was no sound at all. She had never noticed silence before. It was five months since she had been in this house. She looked around the room, touched the cold tiles of the fireplace, sat on one of the armchairs. She walked into the back room and opened the curtains. It was the stillness which surprised her, the emptiness. She had thought about these rooms so much in Cush, she now expected them to come to life for her, but they did nothing. She opened the back door and collected the suitcase from under the kitchen window; she came back in and closed it. She sat in the back room and thought about Mrs Byrne's big living-room over the shop, and everybody being nice to her because her father had died, and she shivered.

She was glad she had come back here. When she put her hand on the kitchen door handle, she had realised that her father's hand would have touched it too, his fingerprints or the print of the palm of his hand had probably – no, definitely – been left there. His hand was dead now, lying cold in his coffin. And this house, every inch of it, had his traces imprinted on it: the chair where

79

he sat, the cups and glasses he used must still have some trace of him, the knives and forks he touched, in all the years he would have touched every one of them. She went to the front door and touched the handle and lock that he must have touched.

Upstairs, in her parents' bedroom, his suits and jackets and trousers and shirts and ties lay in the wardrobe. She opened the wardrobe and touched one of the suits and it swayed on its hanger. When she pushed the hangers along, she found a pair of braces that he must not have worn for years. She ran her fingers along them and then recoiled, putting all the hangers back evenly in place.

She went to the window and looked across the valley at the Turret Rocks and Vinegar Hill, and then down into the street, at the carefully tended front lawns bordered with flower-beds. There was no one on the street. The neighbours must have not seen her arriving or they would have come to knock on the door immediately.

Her father's shoes under the bed surprised her more than anything. They needed polish on the toes, and the laces on one of them were somewhat frayed. More than anything else in the room, they suggested her father's presence rather than his absence, as though he could arrive at any moment to sit on the bed and slip them on, and lean over to tie up the laces.

On the back of the door was her mother's dressing-gown and behind it hung two ironed white shirts. She took one of them down and held it up against her and looked in the mirror. She put her feet into his shoes, which were much too big for her. She opened the wardrobe again and found a dark grey suit. She put it on the bed and went through the ties, searching for one which was dark but not too dark, with dots or stripes. She put a few ties against the suit, as she had observed her mother do, to see if they matched, and eventually chose one with grey and white stripes on black. She opened a drawer and found a white vest and white underpants and in another drawer she found a pair of socks.

She laid the suit full-length on the bed. She put the shirt inside the jacket and stuffed the sleeves of the shirt into its arms, and opened the buttons of the shirt and put the vest inside, and then closed up the buttons. She put the tie around her own neck, as if it were her school tie, and tied a knot in it and placed it inside the collar of her father's shirt and tightened it. Then she put the underpants inside the trousers and laid the trousers out, tying up the buttons of the fly, and tucking the shirt into the trousers. She found the socks and put one inside each shoe and placed the shoes at the bottom of the trouser legs, but they didn't look right.

She went downstairs and picked a pile of books from the bookcase in the front room and brought them upstairs. She placed books on either side of the shoes, and, on realising that she needed more, she went downstairs and carried up another armful. She propped the shoes, the toes facing upwards, between the books.

She looked at the figure on the bed and decided he needed something else. She went downstairs to the press under the stairs where the coats were kept and she found a cap hanging on a hook. She found a small pillow in her bedroom and brought it into her parents' room. She put the pillow resting against her parents' pillows, close to the neck of the shirt; she placed the cap over the pillow, as though her father had fallen asleep with his cap on his face. And then she stood back and watched.

She closed the wardrobe door and the drawers, and then left the room and stood out on the landing with her eyes shut. Slowly, she walked back into the bedroom. It was the shoes that made the difference, made it seem that he was lying there asleep and she could come and lie beside him. She placed herself on her mother's side of the bed, carefully and gingerly so as not to disturb him. She reached out and held the hand that should be there at the end of the right-hand sleeve of the jacket. She reached over and lifted the cap and kissed where his mouth should be. She snuggled up against him.

★

By the time she heard them, Mrs Morrissey and Mrs Maher were already in the hall. She realised she would have to move very fast and very quietly, but she knew that if they came upstairs now she would be caught and it would be impossible to explain. She reached for the shoes and put them on the floor, leaning over the figure she had made of her father. Without making a sound, she bundled up the suit and shirt and tie and underwear and socks. She placed the books on the floor and took the clothes and the pillow and the cap and moved slowly towards her own room, knowing that the creaking floor-boards would soon alert the two women downstairs to her presence. She did not have time to smooth the bedspread or check the room.

'Oh Jesus, Mary and Joseph, is there someone upstairs?' Mrs Morrissey shouted.

Helen shoved the clothes under her own bed and sprang to attention, calling over the bannisters.

'It's me! It's Helen!'

'Helen!' Mrs Maher shouted. 'You're after giving us a terrible fright. What are you doing here in the name of God? What are you doing here? You're meant to be down in Mrs Byrne's.'

'My granny said I was to come up here,' Helen said, and then rushed into her parents' bedroom to check that she had left nothing important on the bed. She smoothed out the bedspread and went back to the landing and walked downstairs.

'Well,' Mrs Maher said, 'you gave us a fright.' She had put white plastic bags full of large sliced pans on the kitchen table, and other bags on the draining board and the kitchen floor.

'You shouldn't be here on your own,' Mrs Morrissey said. 'If your mammy heard you were here on your own!'

'That's what my granny said, I was to come here,' Helen said.

'Well, I'll get Jim to drive you down to Mai Byrne's. Isn't Declan down there?'

'But they're all boys down there,' Helen said. 'They'll just tease me. I can't go down there.'

'Isn't she very precocious! Isn't she a little lady!' Mrs Maher said.

For the next two hours, Helen worked with them, buttering the bread, making ham sandwiches, chicken sandwiches, salad sandwiches for people who would come back to the house after the removal of her father's remains.

'There'll be a big crowd tonight,' Mrs Maher said.

'And an even bigger crowd tomorrow. The whole of Fianna Fáil in the county Wexford will be there.'

Mrs Maher and Mrs Morrissey talked while they worked, but Helen only half listened to them. She wondered was her father in his coffin yet, and did they open the coffin again, or was it closed now for ever? She wondered if they covered his feet, or left them bare.

As each pile of sandwiches was made, it was placed back into the greaseproof wrapping paper to keep the bread fresh. Mrs Maher held a cigarette between her lips while she worked. Each time the ash grew long, Helen watched to see if it would fall into one of the sandwiches, but she always tipped it into the sink before it fell.

Mrs Morrissey hoovered the downstairs rooms. After a while, when she knew that they were both busy, Helen slipped upstairs to her room and found the underpants, the vest and the socks and put them back into the drawers where they had been. She checked downstairs again by looking over the bannisters and, when she was sure that she would remain undisturbed, she disentangled the rest of the clothes, untying the tie and putting the shirt back on its hanger. Her mother would believe, she thought, that it had wrinkled because it had been unused there so long. As she left it on the back of the door, she tried to crease the other shirt which hung there too. She put the suit back in the wardrobe and closed the wardrobe door. She flushed the toilet before she went back downstairs. She had forgotten the tie, but she knew she would be able to deal with that later.

She carried on helping their two neighbours make the sandwiches. When they were finished, Mrs Morrissey said, she could come over to their house and have her dinner and wait for her mammy to come. It would be quiet, Mrs Morrissey said, and it was a sad day and she'd have to look after her mother.

'She must be broken-hearted,' Mrs Maher said.

the same confidences that had been given to Nietzsche were given to other intimate friends. We have Glasenapp discussing quite calmly, in his fourth edition, the possibility of Geyer having been Wagner's father—a discussion which we may be sure he would not have permitted himself had there been any possibility of its being repugnant to Cosima and the Wagner family. We have the record of his being gratified to discover that the eight-year-old Siegfried resembled Geyer. We have the letter of January 1870 to Cäcilie, upon which only one construction can be put—that the letters of Geyer which Cäcilie had sent him have confirmed his previous surmises. At some time or other Wagner must have obtained, from sources that he felt to be reliable, the information as to the flightiness of Friedrich Wagner and the consequent strain upon the domestic relations of the latter and his wife; and in the light of all our other knowledge it is not a farfetched conclusion that this reference to Geyer in *Mein Leben* was a veiled hint that he had already surmised that the relations of the latter with Frau Wagner had been unusually intimate.

Mr. Sonneck quotes the four letters from Geyer to the widow Wagner which have been published, and asks, not unjustly: "Are these letters in address, signature, form, contents and tone the utterances of a man who has possessed a woman, soul and body, for several years?" [9] That indeed is a difficulty. I fully agree with Mr. Sonneck when he says: "I do not believe that the parties to a clandestine love-affair would go to that unnecessary trouble in confidential letters after the death of the husband." But I cannot agree with Mr. Sonneck in his further deductions. "Supposing this, for a moment, to be true," he says, "what would follow? That Richard Wagner must have seen less harmless and more incriminating letters which compelled

---

[9] The "several years," however, is an exaggeration. The letters all belong to the period from December 22, 1813, to February 11, 1814, and "possession" need not be assumed before the late summer of 1812.

P

FOUR

Her grandmother was waiting for her in the kitchen.

'I don't think you slept, Helen,' she said.

'I lay awake for a long time, but then I slept for a while,' Helen said.

'I knew you were awake.'

Her grandmother put slices of bread into an electric toaster and then made tea.

'I lay awake,' Helen said, 'thinking about all the things that happened years ago. Maybe it was the room and the lighthouse brought it all back, and Declan being in hospital I suppose. Anyway, I went over everything, Daddy dying and us being down here.'

'That was a very hard time, Helen,' her grandmother said. She poured tea and took a boiled egg from a saucepan on the Aga. When the toast was done, she put it on a plate.

'Do you remember us coming down here in the year after he died? You mentioned it on the phone the day you rang me,' Helen asked.

'I do, Helen,' her grandmother said.

'You know, I would come out of school and Mammy would be sitting there in the car, the old red Mini, with Declan in the back, and as soon as I'd get in, she'd start up the engine without saying a word. I used to dread it. God, I used to dread it.'

'She couldn't manage, Helen, that's what it was. She couldn't get over losing him.'

'She'd drive us up to school in the morning from here, and I'd close my eyes when I came out at the end of the day and hope when I opened them that she wouldn't be there. But often she'd be waiting there again, and we'd know that she hadn't been home, she'd spent the day driving around the country or sitting in the hotel or in Murphy Flood's. I used to dread coming out of school.'

'You and Declan were all she had,' her grandmother said.

'I don't want to criticise her, Granny,' Helen said, 'we've been through all that, and I know it was hard for her, but the whole journey down and back she wouldn't speak to us. I have my own children now and I couldn't imagine doing that.'

'Helen, she was doing her best. She couldn't manage. She was very good to me when your grandfather died. I remember that you were doing your Leaving Cert. She looked after me then, even though she was back working herself.'

'When you rang me, Granny, you said she had never done anything for you.'

'Well, that was wrong, Helen,' her grandmother said.

★

Helen drove towards Wexford. The drizzle became blustery rain as she approached Curracloe. It was past ten o'clock now and her mother would, she supposed, be at work. She was glad she did not have to tell her the news at the door of her house; it would be easier to arrive at the office.

As she was having breakfast with her grandmother that morning, a memory came to her which she put out of her mind. It was something she could not mention. Now, as she reached the main road into Wexford, the wipers criss-crossing the windscreen of the car, she pictured the scene which had earlier come back to her.

It was a Sunday in the summer the year after her father died. For the previous few months, they had not travelled much to her grandmother's at Cush during the week, but had always gone on Sunday, setting out from Enniscorthy after twelve o'clock Mass. This Sunday – it might have been June or early July – she noticed that they were driving along the Osborne Road towards Drumgoole. She said nothing, but Declan, from the back of the car, asked why they were not driving the usual way.

'I think we'll go to Curracloe instead,' her mother said.

'Are we not going to Granny's?' Declan asked.

'I made sandwiches so we can have them on the strand if it stays fine.'

Curracloe had a car park, a shop, sand dunes and a long strand. It possessed, for Helen and Declan, a tinge of glamour and newness; Ballyconnigar and Cush were, on the other hand, stale and dull. There were, Declan maintained, too many country people in Cush and Ballyconnigar, whereas people from Wexford town came to Curracloe.

'And we're not going to Granny's?' Declan asked.

There was no reply. They drove to Curracloe and made their way to the strand, carrying the picnic which their mother had prepared without their knowing, a rug and their swimming gear. Helen wanted to ask her mother if their grandmother knew they were not coming to Cush, or if she was there waiting for them now, keeping the dinner hot, listening out for the sound of the car.

In Cush, in all the years, her mother had never gone into the sea for a swim. She would come down to the strand with them, and watch them bathe, and on a hot day she might change into a bathing suit, but she would never even get her feet wet. On this Sunday in Curracloe, Helen and Declan presumed that she changed into her bathing suit because it was hot. When she put on a bathing cap, Declan began to laugh. 'Your face looks all funny,' he said.

The sea was rough and few bathers went beyond the point where the waves broke. Declan always stood at the edge of the water for a while and then made his way in as though walking on glass. Helen had learned that it was easier if you didn't think about it, it was easier just to wade in and swim out, but it was still hard. Now, suddenly, as they both stood at the edge of the water, their mother walked past them, blessed herself, waded in confidently and, as soon as she was up to her waist, dived under the water. She looked up at them and waved and dived again and then emerged just as a huge wave broke. Declan ran into the water as the wave pulled back and tried to reach her, but he was knocked over by a second wave. Helen saw that he was laughing as the wave pushed him in towards the shore. She moved in his direction and caught him and held his hand.

'I want to get out to where Mammy is,' he said.

Close by was a group of children and adults standing waiting for the next wave to roll in, shouting at each other in delight and letting themselves be lifted by the high waves and pulled in towards the shore. As Helen and Declan picked themselves up, having been knocked over, their mouths full of salt water, they could see that their mother was still swimming out beyond where the waves broke. When they got her attention, she began to swim in to where they were.

'You said you couldn't swim,' Declan said.

'I haven't been in the sea for years,' she said.

For most of the afternoon, then, Helen and her mother, with Declan in between them catching their hands, stood waiting for the waves to crash. A few times, when they went back and sat on the rug, Declan was not content until they returned to the water. As soon as a wave appeared, he would shout that this was the biggest one, and when some of them turned out to be small and mild, this did not put him off. He would point to the next one, and the next one, and the next one, laughing all the time, until, finally, a huge wave came and knocked the three of them over.

As the afternoon faded, they sat on the rug and ate their sandwiches and drank tea.

'This is the best place,' Declan said. 'Can we come here every Sunday?'

'If you like,' his mother said.

Helen wanted to ask if her mother had told her grandmother that they would not be coming to Cush, but she knew, as they dressed and got ready to go back to the car, that she had not.

She wondered, as they drove into Curracloe village,

would she turn towards Blackwater and call into Cush, but her mother turned left and took the road to Enniscorthy. Declan sat in the back of the car and talked all the way back home, addressing questions and remarks to his mother. It was the first memory Helen had of what became a constant scene: Declan and his mother in deep conversation, him laughing and his mother smiling and Helen unable to keep up with them, but smiling too, enjoying Declan's jokes and comments, his good humour and his inexhaustible need for his mother's attention and approval.

She drove towards Wexford. She knew that her mother's offices were on the quays overlooking the old harbour, and she wondered if she would get parking near there. She thought she should phone Hugh – he would surely wait at home this morning until she rang – and then she would face her mother.

Two years after her father died, her mother went back to teaching, getting a job, with the help of Fianna Fáil, in the local vocational school. Soon – Helen was not sure when – she began to give commercial courses in the school in the evening, until the designing of these courses to suit the needs of the students and the finding of jobs for those who took part became an obsession with her.

Then, with the arrival of computers, her mother began to talk to business groups and others about the need to computerise. She was the first in the county to include computer skills in her commercial course. And this led, eventually, to the setting up of her own computer business, where she taught basic skills and later began to sell machines to businesses and individuals. The previous summer, her grandmother had shown Helen a full-page advertisement in the *Wexford People* for Wexford Computers, with quotes from clients in Waterford and Kilkenny who said that they came all the way to Wexford because the courses made using computers easy and the sales force made installation and maintenance problem-free. There was a large photograph of Helen's mother at the top of the page.

'Will you look at Lily!' her grandmother said.

★

When she had parked the car, Helen phoned Hugh and told him where she was and what she was about to do. She realised as she spoke to him that she had put no thought into what she would say to her mother, and that she would make any excuse – phone the school, move the car, have tea in White's – to postpone her visit to Wexford Computers Limited.

The boys had been up since early light, Hugh said, and had gone down to the strand with their cousins, wearing their raincoats. Everything was fine, he said, and he would come down whenever she wanted him. She told him that she would call him later in the day.

'Things are never as bad as you think they're going to be,' he said.

She was surprised when she saw the lift in the hallway of the Wexford Computers building, and surprised, too, by the lighting and tiling and paintwork, which were all modern and cool, as though from a magazine, and not like anything she expected to find on the quayfront in Wexford. A sign in the lobby told her that the showrooms were on the first floor and the reception on the second floor. She pressed the button for the second floor.

She was checking herself in the mirror, expecting to arrive into a hallway or lobby. She wondered if she would be able to find a bathroom up there and put on make-up before she saw her mother. But when the lift doors opened, she stepped into a vast room with windows looking on to both the harbour in front and the street behind, and skylights in the high-beamed ceiling, the attic having been removed. There were twenty or more people seated on chairs in the room; some of them turned to look at her, but most of them continued to face her mother, who was standing.

Her mother was in mid-sentence when she appeared. Helen found herself helpless, exposed; she could not retreat or try to find a bathroom. She moved forward until she found a chair. She noticed how beautiful and bright the room was, and how expensive-looking. Her mother kept talking, and acknowledged Helen's presence merely by moving her spectacles from her hair to her nose and peering short-sightedly in Helen's direction. A few others looked behind as her mother continued to lecture, slowly, almost absent-mindedly putting her glasses back where they had been.

'Now you must all remember', she was saying, 'that we are here for you. If your company installs a new system, or if you find that you need to expand your skills, then simply call us, just as you would call a plumber if you had a leak in the house, and we'll sort you out as quickly as possible, even if it means coming here in the evening or at the weekend. Just call us and we'll be here for you.'

Her mother stopped for a moment and put her glasses on again, peering once more at Helen as though to make sure that she had not been mistaken the first time.

'Now,' she went on, 'we began only as a provider of courses in computers and word processors, but, as we worked, we found that almost everyone coming here had a horror story about buying or installing a system, or about maintenance. So it is by default that we have the best range and the best sales and technical force in the south-east. And I can tell you that it wasn't hard to be the best. You can laugh all you like, but you'll find that our prices are lower, and we have a twenty-four-hour service. Our showrooms are on the floor below, but you're not here to buy computers, you're here to use them, and for each of you we have a special programme; we've studied your needs, and we're ready to start now. There's a machine here for each of you as well with your name on it, and if you could move your chairs to the computers, we'll start. The staff are the ones with name-tags on.'

Helen watched her mother moving towards the table beside a window which looked on to the harbour. Her mother spoke to one of the staff, then picked up a sheet of paper and looked at it. Helen resisted an urge to go back down to the street in the lift, drive to Dublin and inform Declan that he could send his friend from the European Commission to tell his mother. She waited as her mother moved about the room, checking names and details, clearly in command. Eventually, her mother moved towards her, but suddenly thought better of it and went back to the table beside the window. Once she had satisfied herself about something there, she crossed the room and approached Helen.

'I thought it was you when you came in, and I wondered had you come all the way down here to learn computers,' her mother said.

'No, thanks. Your offices are lovely.'

'It's all new,' her mother said.

'I need to talk to you. Is there a private office?'

'I don't have much time,' her mother said, but as soon as she had said it, she stopped and searched Helen's face. 'Has something happened?' she asked.

They went into a small private office opposite the lift. Her mother closed the door.

'What is it?' she asked.

Helen sighed. 'It's Declan.'

'Helen, tell me!'

'He's in hospital, in Dublin, and he wants to see you.'

'Has he had an accident? Has he hurt himself?'

'No, not that. He's sick, and he'd like to see you. He's been there for a while, but he didn't want to trouble us.'

'Trouble us? What is it you're talking about?'

'Mammy, Declan is really sick. Maybe it would be better if you talked to the doctors about it.'

'Helen, do you know what's wrong with him?'

'No, not exactly. But he wants to see you today. I have his car outside and I can drive you to the hospital. He's in St James's.'

Her mother went to a desk and flicked through her diary until she found the right week.

'What day's today?' she asked.

'Wednesday.'

'Right. You wait outside and I'll make two phone calls and then I'll be with you.'

'Why don't I see you in White's?'

'If you wait outside, I won't be a second.'

★

They drove to Dublin as the day brightened. Her mother did not speak until they were beyond Gorey.

'I hate this road,' she said. 'I hate every inch of it. I never thought I would have to travel on it again on my way to a hospital.'

'I stayed with Granny last night,' Helen said.

'You went down to her first? Why didn't you come to me first?'

Helen did not reply; she stared straight ahead, concentrated on the road.

'Oh that's right, don't answer me now,' her mother said.

'Hugh and the boys are in Donegal,' Helen said.

'I don't know how he puts up with you,' her mother said.

They drove in silence until they reached the dual carriageway. Her mother pulled down the sunshade and began to put on lipstick using the small mirror.

'I have to tell you what's wrong,' Helen said.

'You've left me waiting for an hour and a half,' her mother said, looking at her watch.

'He has AIDS, he's had it for a long time, and he has kept it from us.'

She could feel her mother holding her breath as a dark shadow seemed to pass in front of the car.

'How long have you known?' her mother asked.

'Since yesterday.'

'Does your granny know?'

'Yes, I told her.'

Her mother pushed back the sunshade and put the lipstick back into the make-up bag. 'Is he very sick? How sick is he?'

'He's very sick, but it's not clear how sick.'

'And there's no cure, is there?'

'No, there's no cure.'

'And how long has he had it?'

'For years.'

'And how long has he been in the hospital?'

'I don't know.'

'Why did he keep it from us?'

Once more, Helen did not reply. Suddenly, it started to rain, and when she switched the wipers on, they began to tear against the windscreen. She turned them off, but the rain was coming too hard and she could not see, so she turned them on again. Her mother remained silent until they reached Bray. Battling with the windscreen wipers distracted Helen from her mother's sighing and clenching her fists and facing towards her as though about to say something and then facing away again.

Eventually, she spoke. 'Just when I have managed to pick myself up, this happens now.'

The rain stopped and Helen turned the wipers off.

'Why couldn't Declan have told me himself?' her mother asked.

'He was very worried about how you would react,' Helen said.

'And is that why he sent you to tell me?'

Helen stared at the road ahead. When she saw a double-decker bus, she thought of asking her mother to make her own way to the hospital, but it was a thought which she did not entertain for long. She softened and tried to imagine what it must be like for her.

'I think he felt that at a time like this we would all forget our differences,' Helen said.

'Well, I don't notice any difference in you,' her mother said.

'Bear with me, I'm making an effort,' Helen said. She could not keep the dry tone out of her voice.

★

By the time they reached the hospital Helen believed that the car would explode if either of them tried to speak. She parked it in the car park Paul had used, and they walked to the wing where Declan was.

'The doctor said that the consultant will see us at any time.'

'Is Declan in a private room?'

'Yes.'

'What does he look like?'

For one moment Helen felt a great tenderness towards her mother and wanted to say something which would make things easier. She was close to tears.

'No, he looks all right. I think he's afraid.'

'And the consultant? What's he like?'

'It's a she. I didn't meet her, but they say she's nice.'

At reception, they asked for the consultant, and when she could not be located Helen asked for the doctor whom she had met the previous day. They waited in silence. After a while, the consultant and the young doctor arrived together. The consultant was much smaller and younger than Helen had imagined. She was almost girlish. It took her mother a while to realise that this was the consultant. She brought them down a corridor to an office.

'Now, doctor,' Helen's mother said as soon as they sat down, 'could you give us your considered opinion on the case?'

99

'I'm afraid I'll have to be very blunt,' the consultant said.

'There's no point in mincing words with me,' Helen's mother said.

'Declan's very sick. His T-cell count, which is how we measure the progress of the disease, is almost down to nil. Most people have more than a thousand. He's open to any number of opportunistic infections. He had a small operation this morning to put a line back into his chest, and that went all right. He could go on for a while, but he could also go very quickly. It depends on each individual. I should say about him that he's very brave and very resilient but he won't survive too many more onslaughts.'

'Are there any drugs you can use?'

'There's one drug, called AZT, but I'm afraid it isn't a cure, and we are developing better medicine for each infection as it arises.'

'And what are the chances of a cure?'

'There's nothing in the pipeline, although you never know; but I think that most doctors would agree that Declan's immune system has been destroyed and it would be hard to envisage a way for that to be restored.'

'Could anything be done for him in America?'

'Our systems here are just as advanced.'

'Is he in pain?'

'No, he was actually sitting up in bed half an hour ago when I saw him. He has a group of friends who make sure that he is well looked after. I'll take you down to him and we can talk afterwards, if you want.'

As Helen opened the door, her mother turned to the

consultant. 'Could I speak to you alone for a minute, please?'

Helen waited outside and then walked down the corridor and stood looking out of the window. She knew what her mother was asking: the question she had refrained from asking Helen in the car. She had always wondered if her mother knew about Declan being gay, and was not sure now whether the consultant would tell her or not. But as she watched her mother walking out of the consultant's office and coming with her down the corridor, she knew that she had received a reply. Her mother's shoulders were hunched and she kept her eyes on the ground. It was years since Helen had seen her look defeated like this.

When they walked into Declan's room, he was sitting up in bed listening to music on a Walkman. Paul, who was sitting on a chair beside the bed, stood up immediately, nodded at Helen and left the room.

'I've brought you a visitor,' Helen said.

'I knew the last time I saw you that you weren't looking well,' their mother said, approaching the bed and smiling at Declan. 'But you look much better now.' She held his hand.

'I didn't think you'd be up so soon,' he said.

'This room is a bit dark, isn't it? Are they treating you properly at all?' her mother asked.

'Oh, it's fine, it's fine,' he said.

'We're only here to make everything nice for you, isn't that right, Helen?'

'Yes, Mammy,' Helen said.

'Could you find out when I was getting out?' Declan asked.

'We met the consultant, but she didn't say anything about it,' his mother said. 'But I'll go down now and ask her if you like.'

'No, wait for a while,' he said.

'Have you any pain?' his mother asked.

'I don't feel great today. I had a local anaesthetic in my chest this morning, and it always leaves you feeling drowsy.'

A nurse came in with a small plastic cup with pills which Declan took with a glass of water.

'You know,' his mother said, 'if you wanted to come down to my house, everything would be set up for you. There's a great view, as you know, and we could have a nurse call around if there were any problems.'

'I don't know what I'll do,' Declan said.

'Whatever you want now,' his mother said. She put her hand on his forehead. 'Well, you don't have a temperature, anyway.'

★

Helen found Paul waiting in the corridor outside the room. Her mother stayed with Declan while they had lunch in a pub close to the hospital. Afterwards she drove across the city to her school. The previous week, letters had gone out to certain applicants for teaching jobs calling them for a second interview. She wanted to check dates and times for the interviews.

Anne, her secretary, read her a list of phone messages which she had, as instructed, taken verbatim in shorthand. Most of them were routine; one was from John Oakley in the Department of Education. Helen looked through the post. Anne told her that one of the teachers had phoned up to ask why they were doing a second interview since no other school had adopted this practice.

'What does she teach?' Helen asked.

'Irish and English.'

'Could you read me her message exactly?'

The secretary read her out the phone message. Helen thought for a minute and then said: 'We'd better write to her. Could you type out a note saying that the position has been filled, and thank her for her interest, and I'll sign it before I go. She sounds like a real nuisance.'

'Also,' Anne said, 'there's a problem with Ambrose. He was drunk, or at least he had a lot of drink on him on Monday. He implored me not to tell you.'

'When was the last time he was drunk?'

'The sixth of April,' Anne said.

'He's the most obliging handyman in Ireland,' Helen said.

'He's afraid of his life of you,' Anne said.

'But he was sober yesterday, and is he sober today?'

'Yes, and really sorry.'

'I'm going to do nothing about it,' Helen said. 'But tell him you told me, and I've gone off to think about it. Frighten him a bit.' She laughed, and Anne shook her head and smiled.

She walked around the empty, echoing corridors of the school, then went upstairs and sat on a bench opposite the staffroom. Suddenly, the whole weight of what had happened and what was going to happen hit her as though for the first time: her brother was going to die, and they were going to watch him sicken further, suffer and slowly fade. A vision came to her of his lifeless, inert body ready to be put in a coffin and consigned to darkness, closed away for all time. It was an unbearable idea.

She tried to put it out of her mind. She felt tired now, worried that if she stayed too long in one place she would fall asleep and be found by Anne. She walked slowly down to the office and signed the letter and then drove home, desperately wishing that she could lie down on the bed and sleep until the morning. She had a shower and changed her clothes. When she phoned Hugh in Donegal, there was no answer. At four o'clock, she drove back across the city to the hospital.

She met her mother and Paul in the corridor outside Declan's room.

'They're just doing a general check-up on him now,' her mother said. 'They're going to let him out for a few days.'

'Does he want to come to my house?' Helen asked.

'No, he wants to go to Cush, to his granny's house,' her mother said. 'I don't know why he wants to go there.'

'To Granny's house?'

'Of course, when I tried to phone her, she had the phone turned off,' her mother said.

'He's been talking a lot', Paul said, 'about Cush and the house by the sea.'

'If he wants to go there, then we'll take him there. I told him that.'

'When?' Helen asked.

'If he's going he'll have to go now, because he might have to be back here in a couple of days,' her mother said.

The consultant and the doctor came out of the room. 'He has the all-clear for a few days anyway,' Louise said. 'I'll make out a list of drugs and as soon as pharmacy has them ready he can go.'

'One day we waited here two hours for pharmacy,' Paul said.

'I'll take the prescription up there myself and if you come with me, Paul, and stand there looking at them, then they might do it now,' the consultant said.

★

Helen and her mother went into the room, where Declan was sitting on the side of the bed.

'I feel all dizzy when I sit up like this,' he said. 'But I'll be all right in a minute.'

'Declan, I stayed in Granny's house last night,' Helen said. 'The beds are really uncomfortable and the sheets are ancient.'

'I'll get sheets from home,' her mother said.

'How was Granny when you told her?' Declan asked.

'She was worried about you,' Helen said.

They went outside while Declan dressed.

'Do you know who this Paul is?' her mother asked.

'He's an old friend of Declan's. I think he's been very good.'

'This whole thing is a nightmare,' her mother said.

'Yes, I know. He seems so well. It's hard to believe.'

'You can drive us down,' her mother said. 'You're on holidays, aren't you?'

'Not exactly, but I can drive you down.'

★

When the drugs came, Paul and Declan began to clear out the room, putting rubbish into a black plastic bag and clothes and CDs into a holdall. Declan began to give Paul detailed instructions on how to get to his grandmother's house in Cush. Helen and her mother looked on, puzzled, as Declan told Paul to give these directions to Larry as well – Helen did not know who Larry was – and ask him to come down to Cush too as soon as he could.

They set out for Wexford. Her mother fussed over Declan's comfort in the car and wondered whether he would be better in the front or the back. As they drove through the city, Declan in the back seat, her mother turned to him and said: 'Helen said on the way up that you were worried about how I'd react. Well, you needn't worry about that at all. You and Helen are the two people I care about most, and nothing would ever change that.'

'I should have told you before,' Declan said, 'but I couldn't bring myself to.'

They stopped at Dunnes Stores in Cornelscourt, where Helen left them in the car park and filled up a trolley in the supermarket with things they would need over the next few days. She did not know how her grandmother would respond to their arrival. She realised that for the first time in years – ten years, maybe – she was back as a member of this family she had so determinedly tried to leave. For the first time in years they would all be under the same roof, as though nothing had happened. She realised, too, that the unspoken emotions between them in the car, and the sense that they were once more a unit, seemed utterly natural now that there was a crisis, a catalyst. She was back home, where she had hoped she would never be again, and she felt, despite herself, almost relieved.

On the journey to Cush, her mother talked about her staff and her clients; she was trying hard, Helen believed, to be witty and bright. A few times they thought that Declan was asleep, but he turned out only to have his eyes closed. Her mother said that at some stage that evening Helen could drive her into Wexford and she could get her own car and bedclothes from home.

'We'll make you very comfortable, Declan,' her mother said.

'Do you think Granny will mind us barging in on top of her like this?' Declan asked.

'She's always loved you, Declan.'

'Yes, but will she not mind?' he asked.

'If she'd turn her telephone on, we could find out.'

'I think she'll want to help in every way she can, Declan,' Helen said.

★

It was still early evening when they arrived in Cush. Their grandmother came out and looked into the car, unable to make out who its occupants were.

'Is it Declan you have in the back?' she asked Helen when she opened the front door.

'He wanted to come down here for a while, Granny,' Helen said. 'We couldn't refuse him.'

'Oh come in, all of you. Lily, come in and bring Declan in with you.'

They left the car in the lane and came into the house. Their grandmother turned off the television and moved over to the sink, where she began to fuss with the teapot and kettle. She kept her back to them while they remained uneasily in the kitchen. When Helen looked at Declan in this light, she saw for the first time how sick he was, how tight and drawn the skin on his face was, how tired his eyes seemed, and how shrunken his whole body had become.

Her mother had Declan sit down while her grandmother stood, washing up cups in the sink, although there was a row of clean cups on the dresser. The two cats watched them from their perch.

'Mammy,' their mother said, 'maybe we shouldn't be barging in on you like this.'

'No, Lily, I was worried about you all day.' Her face, Helen could see when she turned, was as unreadable as stone. 'I'll make tea,' she said, 'and I'll make sandwiches if you like, or will you be having a meal when you go home?'

Helen could not tell whether she was pretending not to understand that they wanted to stay here in the house, or whether she genuinely believed that they were on their way to Wexford. She tried to think back to what she had said to her when she got out of the car, but she was too tired to remember.

No one answered her grandmother, who now went outside, leaving the three of them to look at each other.

'Declan,' their mother said, 'we can drive into Wexford and you and Helen can stay in my house.'

He did not reply, but stared straight ahead of him. Helen wondered if he had built up a picture over days in bed of this house and the cliff and the sea and now the sight of it had disappointed and depressed him. He looked miserable.

Her grandmother came in with a bucket and left it down beside the sink. She filled the teapot from the kettle, once more turning her back to them. Declan closed his eyes and sighed. Her mother glanced sharply at Helen.

'Granny,' Declan said, 'they've let me out of hospital for a few days and I thought of coming down here and looking out at the view, and staying for a few days, but maybe it's too much for you.'

His grandmother turned and looked towards the window. 'Declan,' she said, 'you can always come down here. There's always a bed for you. Let us have a cup of tea first, and then we'll make sure you're all fixed up.'

By half-past nine they had been assigned beds. It was arranged that Declan would have the room he and Helen had shared all the years before, which gave on to the front of the house. Helen would have the room behind and her mother would have one of the upstairs rooms.

Some of Declan's medicine had to be put in the fridge; his grandmother made space for it, and they watched, half fascinated, half repelled, as Declan attached a small plastic container to a tube which ran directly into his chest. He went through his pills and took four of them with a glass of water.

'Granny, the doctor says I'm allergic to cats. It's not a problem as long as they don't come near me.'

'Oh, they stay up there if I have visitors, so I don't think they'll be troubling you.'

'I'm sure it's not a problem,' Declan said.

'Look at them, they know we are talking about them,' his grandmother said.

★

As darkness fell, Helen drove her mother into Wexford.

'She doesn't want us here,' Helen said as they came near Blackwater.

'Oh that's just pretence and nonsense,' her mother said. 'She likes company, you know.'

'She doesn't want us here,' Helen said again.

They remained silent until they reached the other side of Curracloe.

'How long have you known about Declan?' her mother asked.

'Since yesterday. I told you.'

'I mean, how long have you known that he had friends like Paul?'

'Like what?' Helen asked.

'You know like what.' Her mother sounded irritated.

'I've always known.'

'Don't be so stupid, Helen.'

'I've known for ten years, maybe more.'

'And you never told me?'

'I've never told you anything,' Helen said firmly.

'I hope nothing like this ever happens to you.'

'You sound as though you hope it does.'

'If I meant that, I would say it.'

'Oh you would, all right.'

They drove along the quays in Wexford until they came to Helen's mother's car. She did not speak before she got out; she banged the door as she left as though in temper and walked to her car. She drove towards

110

Rosslare, Helen following close behind, and then turned into a maze of side roads for several miles. Even the indicator of her car was in a rage, Helen felt.

Until she turned into her mother's driveway, Helen did not know that the house had a view of the sea, a view even clearer than her grandmother's because the house stood on higher ground. They were closer here to Tuskar; its beam skimmed across the front of the house as Helen stopped the car. Her mother went into the house without paying her any attention, so Helen waited in the car for her to come out again. Declan had told her that the house was grand and had cost a fortune, but it looked to her like an ordinary, detached bungalow with a tiled roof. It was the site, she thought, that must have cost a fortune.

In the dark she could only vaguely make out the line of horizon in the dwindling light. She realised that the house would catch the sun first thing in the morning. She wondered why her mother had not put more glass in the front of the house. The beam of the lighthouse came again and washed over her.

Her mother emerged now with her two arms full of sheets and pillows and put them in the back of her car, still ignoring Helen. Helen wondered if she should drive back to Cush and let her mother follow whenever she wanted, but she realised that a certain curiosity was now tempting her to go into the house. She opened the door of the car and was surprised by the stillness, the pure silence here, not a breath of wind, and the sea too distant for its roar to be heard. Her mother came out again with duvets; she almost bumped into her at the door.

'I'll need your help with the mattress,' she said brusquely.

The hallway and the bedroom to the right seemed ordinary, like rooms in any new house, but it was the room on the left which caught Helen's attention: it was, she thought, more than thirty feet long, like an art gallery rather than a living-room, with white walls and pale parquet floors and high ceilings with roof windows. In the middle was an enormous fireplace, and the end wall – the gable wall of the house – was all glass. It seemed barely credible that her mother could live alone here.

When her mother came upon Helen looking at the room, she brushed past her.

'What an amazing house!'

'Helen, we have to get the mattress out of the small bedroom.'

Helen ignored her and walked into the room, noting an armchair and a sofa and a television in one corner, but aware more than anything of the emptiness in the room. And then it struck her what the room looked like; it resembled her mother's offices on the top floor of the building in Wexford. It also had a high-beamed ceiling and the same roof-lights, the same cool austerity. It must have been done, she thought, by the same designer. She wondered if there was another smaller, cosier room where her mother could sit in the evenings and at weekends, but she realised as she went back into the hall that there were only two bedrooms, a kitchen and a bathroom. There were no other rooms.

Her mother came into the hallway pulling a mattress. 'Are you going to stay there gawking?' she asked.

'I can't get over your house,' Helen said.

'We can put the mattress on the roof-rack. I have a thing that will tie it down.'

'It would be nice to bring a lamp that we could put beside the bed for him,' Helen said.

'God, that house in Cush is depressing,' her mother said. She went into her own bedroom and unplugged a bedside lamp. 'Will he need anything else?' she asked. 'He seemed very sick just there when we were going. I can hardly bear to look at him.'

'I think he's happier now that you know the whole story,' Helen said.

'I hope it doesn't rain on the mattress,' her mother interrupted.

They carried the mattress out to the car. In the darkness, they could see the row of lights at Rosslare, and when the lighthouse flashed, it was like a moment from a film as they were caught in its glare. They tied the mattress to the roof-rack and put the lamp in the boot.

'I'll see you back there, so,' Helen said.

'Do you know your way into Wexford?' her mother asked.

'I'll find it,' she said.

★

She phoned Hugh from the coinbox in Blackwater. His mother answered the phone and was full of worry about Declan and Helen's mother and grandmother.

'It's a hard time for all of you,' she said, 'and you can be sure our prayers are with you.'

Hugh told her that the boys were fast asleep. Manus

had to be carried sleeping all the way home from the pub, he said.

'The pub?' she asked.

'They remembered the pub from last year, and they forgot I existed until they needed money.'

'Are they all right?'

'They're fine, they're asleep. I'm going back down to the pub myself.'

'Don't fall into bad company,' she said.

'I won't,' he said. 'I am keeping myself pure and holy.'

★

She drove back to Cush to find her mother and grand-mother dragging the mattress into the house. She felt that she could have lain down here on the cold cement in front of the house and fallen into a deep sleep. She was worried about the night to come, that she would once more sleep deeply for a short time and then wake and spend the night brooding over things.

When they had placed the mattress on the bed-frame they began to make the bed. Helen thought that all the linen her mother had brought was brand new, had never been used before. Her mother must be making a lot of money. They plugged in the lamp and put it on a chair beside the bed.

The cats stared down suspiciously as Helen came into the kitchen to find Declan watching television. The bruise on his nose seemed much darker and uglier under electric light.

'Are you really allergic to cats?' she asked.

'Yeah, they would do something to my stomach.'

She told him that she had been in their mother's house.

'It's amazing during the day,' he said. 'It's really beautiful.'

'Why didn't you want to go there?'

'It gives me the creeps,' he said.

'Does this place not give you the creeps too?'

'I need these creeps,' he said. 'I don't know why.' He laughed.

★

Helen noticed that her mother and grandmother seemed happier and more satisfied now that they had made the bed and lit the lamp. Declan, too, seemed brighter.

'It's great being out of hospital,' he said.

Helen wondered if he knew how close to the end he was, or if he could live for much longer than anyone predicted. She wondered how much they had told him; it was something, she thought, she must remember to ask Paul. She imagined for an instant them turning on the news and hearing that a cure for AIDS had been invented and would have instant success even for people who'd had the disease for years.

When Declan went to bed, the three women sat in the kitchen eating sandwiches. There was an uneasy peace between them; they chose topics with care and then moved cautiously, alert to the friction which even a stray word could cause. Eventually Helen went out to Declan's car and brought in the groceries she had bought in Dublin and also the rest of the bedclothes from her mother's car.

As she passed Declan's room, she saw that the lamp was still on. He was lying on his back staring at her.

'It's strange being here, isn't it?' he said.

'Yes, I couldn't sleep last night thinking about it.'

'You can close the door,' he said. 'I'm going to turn off the lamp and try and sleep.'

'Declan,' she said, 'if you wake in the night and need someone, you can come into my room and wake me.'

'I'll be all right,' he said. 'I hope I'll be all right.'

FIVE

Helen woke and looked at her watch; it was ten o'clock. She heard sounds: voices and something being pulled or pushed. She lay back and dozed, and then woke fully and lay with her hands behind her head. Her mind kept wandering back to her mother's house, and the glimpses she had had the previous day of her new life. She could not understand how her mother faced going back to that house after a day's work, or why she had chosen to live alone so far from the town.

She remembered hearing from Declan how the old house had been sold. Declan had mentioned this casually, as though he were telling her that their mother had changed her car. He was surprised at how upset Helen had become, and admitted that although he had known it for some time he did not think it was important enough to tell her. When had the sale happened, she had asked him, and he told her that their mother had moved to Wexford four or five months before. And who had bought the house? Declan told her that he had not the slightest idea. And what had happened to the furniture, the ornaments, the pictures, the photographs? Declan laughed at her concern about these and said he didn't know.

'There were things belonging to me in that house,' Helen said to him.

'What things? Don't be so stupid!'

'Things in my room. Books, photographs, things that mattered to me.'

'She cleared out your room years ago.'

'She had no right to do that.'

The house was gone now. In her mind, she went through the rooms again, how each door closed – the door to her parents' room almost noiseless, the door to Declan's room more stubborn, impossible to open or close without alerting the whole house – or the light switches – the one outside the bathroom which Declan when he was tall enough loved turning off while someone was inside, the light switch inside her bedroom door, firm and hard, to be turned on and off decisively, unlike the light switch in her parents' room, which could be switched on and off with a little flick.

She pictured the house empty and ghostly, like a ship under water, as though it had been left as it was on the last day she saw it. The box of Mass cards and sympathy cards for her father under her parents' bed, and another box full of old photographs. The opening to the attic covered by a square of wood which could be shifted sideways on a windy night.

Someone else lived there now. This was what happened to houses, Declan told her. Get over it, he said in a mock American accent.

In the days after she heard about it, however, nothing about the sale of the house seemed to her normal or inevitable. In the first year of their relationship, she had made an agreement with Hugh that she would tell him when she was upset or worried, that she would not keep things bottled up, as was her habit, withholding something important from him so that he would find out only months later the cause of a period of silence and blackness. But she could not tell him about the house and her feeling on hearing the news of the sale because she could not think why she should mind so much.

She was angry with her mother, having tried to feel nothing about her for years, and having believed that her mother would never be able to provoke her again. She remained for days in a silent rage. Hugh watched her pretending it was nothing until she realised that she would have to tell him what it was. He was puzzled by the source of the anger, and he wondered if it was not about something else.

He told her that she would have to resolve it by talking about it; he loved the language of emollience and reconciliation. They went to bed early and she talked for hours while he held her and listened. He tried to understand, but the conflicts were too sharp and too deeply embedded for him to fathom. She felt she needed to revisit the rooms of the old house, even in her imagination, knowing that something had ended. She needed, she thought, to let it end, to ease it out of herself. These rooms no longer were hers; instead, now, the rooms of the house she shared with Hugh and the boys belonged to her.

It was a few days later as she was driving home from school that a thought struck her which caused her to pull in and sit in the car and go back over everything again. It was this: she could not put the house and its sale out of her mind because she believed that she would some day go back there, that it would be her refuge, and that her mother, despite everything, would be there for her and would take her in and shelter her and protect her. She had never entertained this thought before; now, she knew that it was irrational and groundless, but nonetheless, as she sat in the car, she knew that it was real and it explained everything.

Somewhere in the part of her where fears lay unexplored and conflicts unresolved, there was a belief that the life she had made with Hugh would fail her; not precisely that he would leave her, but more exactly that she would some day or night appear at her mother's door asking to be taken in and forgiven and her mother would tell her that her room was always there for her, and that she could stay as long as she liked. The boys did not exist in this scenario, nor the possibility that she could ever take refuge in her mother's new house, and she realised that it was a fantasy, and something that she must not think about. However, it overcame her like a sudden nausea, and she knew that she could not tell Hugh about it, it would seem too dark and disloyal to him, it would frighten him even more than it frightened her.

She had it in the open now – she was sure she was right about it – and she would have to combat it quietly herself, tell herself over and over that she would never need to appear at her mother's door like this, or sleep, comforted by her mother, in her old room. The house was gone, she thought. I have a new house. But the dark thoughts about the old house continued to trouble her.

And it was only now that it struck her that Declan had just the previous evening enacted the fantasy that she had feared so much. He had come back asking for comfort and forgiveness, as she had felt she would, and they had been ready for him, as though they too had always been alert to their side of the bargain. She was frightened by the symmetry in this, but she did not know what it meant.

Her grandmother came in with a cup of tea and put it on the locker beside her bed.

'Declan's just up,' she said. 'He's in the bathroom. Lily went into Wexford at the crack of dawn, she said she'd be back sometime this morning.'

As soon as Declan had finished in the bathroom, Helen got up and had a shower and dressed herself. The day was overcast and windy. When she went into the kitchen, Declan and her grandmother were there, Declan sitting beside the Aga looking frail and uneasy.

'It's a terrible day,' he said. 'Granny says it might clear up, but it's a terrible day.'

She realised that he was trapped here now, that he had dreamed about this house and the cliff and the strand, but the dreams had not included the possibility of an ordinary morning, with a grey sky and a whistling wind, had not included his trying to talk to his grandmother as she washed up. Her first urge was to think of an excuse to go into the village, offering perhaps to take Declan with her, and to stay there for as long as she could. Her grandmother, she presumed, was as uncomfortable as they were, her routine destroyed by these two half-strange interlopers.

'Do you go into Wexford much, Granny?' Helen asked as her grandmother sat down at the kitchen table.

'Oh, I go in once a week,' she said and sipped her tea.

'How do you get in?' Helen asked.

'This only started last year when I sold the sites,' her grandmother said, moving over to sit at the kitchen table. 'I decided that I would go to Wexford every Wednesday. So I asked around and I discovered that Ted Kinsella in Blackwater ran a sort of hackney service. So I arranged with him that he would drive me into Wexford on a Wednesday morning and collect me outside Petit's supermarket at four o'clock. And I paid him very well for this, as you can imagine. And it was lovely.' Her grandmother smiled and continued. She appeared to relish this opportunity to talk. 'I had the day to myself. I would buy a paper and a magazine and sit in White's or the Talbot and have tea and then I'd wander through the town and look at the shops, and I tried out every place for lunch in the whole town. You'd have to go early or late, or else you'd get into a crush with all the office people. And, of course, I'd avoid your mother.' She laughed, almost maliciously. 'And then I'd go to the supermarket and I'd do the whole week's shopping. I didn't know myself. But it couldn't last, of course. Didn't Ted Kinsella let it be known around that he was driving into Wexford twice of a Wednesday, and didn't he start bringing in all sorts of people with him? Oh, they'd want to know all your business, and they'd look up in your face as they'd ask you were you going to sell any more sites. And then one day – this was the week before Christmas – Ted arrived and told me, if you don't mind, that he had to collect another passenger at five and would I like to wait in the car or would I like to wait somewhere else. And he was already ten minutes late! Oh, I cleaned his clock for him now. I was raging. And

122

I was paying him the same as I was paying him when I drove in on my own. So when I got home I sent him a note with Tom Wallace the postman saying that I wouldn't be going into Wexford any more. I gave no reason. Sure he knew the reason.' She paused and pursed her lips as though she was indignant once again.

'So I thought about it and after a week or so – and I had got used to going in there, it brightened up my whole week – I rang Melissa Power, who's Lily's secretary. I used to know her father and she's very private. Lily had sent her out here a few times with messages when she was too grand to come herself. And I told her not to tell Lily I rang – I was in the phone box in Blackwater – and I asked her who the best taxi driver in Wexford was. I knew there were a few because I had seen ads for taxis in the *People*. And she gave me the name Brendan Dempsey and I rang him, and he said that it would be expensive all right, but in actual fact it was less than that old fool Ted Kinsella had charged me, and he sounded very nice, very refined, and I go in with him now – oh, he has a beautiful car, I don't know what it is, and I tell him I feel like the Queen of Sheba sitting in it, and some days he knows I don't want to talk, and he always asks me if he can turn the radio on. And he's interesting, he follows the news and he doesn't put his nose into my business, so I have a lovely day on a Wednesday.'

She sat at the table and looked at them both, as though defying them to contradict her.

'You're a great woman, Granny,' Declan said.

'Did you go to Wexford yesterday?' Helen asked.

'I did, Helen,' she said. 'So, with what you brought, we're well stocked up now with plenty of groceries.'

They sat in silence for a while until they heard a car approaching.

'Whisht now,' their grandmother said; 'that's not Lily's car.' She went to the window and parted the lace curtains, and then she walked out into the hallway, closing the kitchen door. Helen and Declan could hear a man's cheerful voice asking her if she was Declan's granny.

'Oh Jesus!' Declan said.

'Who is it?' Helen asked.

'It's Larry. I didn't think he'd come today.'

Helen remembered that Declan had told Paul to give directions to a Larry as well, and tell him to come as soon as possible, but clearly he was now embarrassed by his friend's arrival. She wondered if he was content now with simply her and her mother and her grandmother, or if he felt awkward at the arrival of another uninvited guest.

Her grandmother came into the kitchen accompanied by Larry, who began to talk as soon as he arrived.

'Will you look at you?' he said to Declan. 'You look as though you haven't left that chair since you arrived. I'd say all the women are spoiling you.'

Helen watched as Declan instantly brightened up.

'God, it's very hard to find this place,' Larry continued without getting his breath. 'I went all over the country. No one knew any Breens, and then I realised that your granny mightn't be called Breen.'

'My granny is standing behind you,' Declan said.

'Will you look at the cats?' Larry said, pointing to the top of the dresser. 'What are they called?'

'The black fat one is Garret and the other one is Charlie,' Mrs Devereux said.

'Are you serious?' Larry asked.

'Yeah, Larry,' Declan said drily, 'she's serious.'

'The skinny one looks just like Charlie,' Larry said. 'The names are gas. And is this your sister?' He spoke without pause, smiling all the time.

Larry was too friendly, Helen thought, too open in his manner, but nonetheless he was, she felt, a relief after Paul, who was too formal and distant.

'Don't mind him,' Declan said. 'He only talks non-stop when he's nervous.'

'What?' Larry asked. 'Who's nervous?'

'Hey, Larry,' Declan said, 'shut up.' He smiled at Larry.

'Would you like a cup of tea, Larry?' Mrs Devereux asked.

'No, no, I'm all right, thank you,' he said. 'God, it's gas the names of the cats.'

'Stop, Larry,' Declan said.

'God, it's a great place this,' Larry said.

'Did you bring your measuring tape?' Declan asked. 'I'm sure Granny wants some renovations done.'

'I did, as a matter of fact,' Larry said. 'I have it in the car. Do you know I had real trouble finding this place?'

'If you don't shut up, we're going to drown one of the cats.'

'Declan!' his grandmother said.

'Granny, I have to say something drastic to shut him up.'

'OK, OK, I'll shut up,' Larry said. 'God, it was a long drive down.'

'Both cats,' Declan said emphatically. 'We'll drown both Garret and Charlie.'

'What's this about a measuring tape?' his grandmother asked.

'Larry', Declan said, 'is an architect.'

★

Helen noticed that Declan ate nothing at lunch, and when she and Larry and her grandmother had finished eating, he lay back in the chair beside the Aga and closed his eyes. Outside, the sky had cleared, but there was still a wind and no certainty that the sky would not cloud up again soon.

'I'd love to go down to the strand,' Declan said. 'Not for long, just for a minute before it starts raining again.' He kept his eyes closed.

'Sure we'll go down with you,' Larry said.

Declan shaded his eyes with his hands all the time as they tried to make their way down the cliff, saying that the light was too much for him. Helen saw how frail he was as they helped him from step to step. When, finally, she and Larry were standing on the strand, having run down the last stretch, Declan stood alone, unable to manage. Larry offered to go back up and help him but then Declan suddenly ran down the bank of loose sand. He seemed pale and exhausted.

'I should have brought my togs,' Larry said and looked at the sea. There was a wind blowing a thin film of sand along the strand.

'I want to stay here on my own for a while,' Declan said. 'I just want to sit here where there's shelter. If the two of you go up, I'll follow you later.'

'Why don't we go for a walk first?' Larry asked.

'No, I'll just sit here,' Declan said.

'We can't leave you here,' Helen said.

'Hellie, I'll be fine. I just want to look at the sea and think, and then I'll come back up.'

Helen told him about the gap to Mike Redmond's house, which was easy to climb; she and Larry walked towards it.

'Is he all right there?' Helen asked Larry.

'I got a big shock when I saw him in the room,' Larry said. 'He looks awful, doesn't he?'

'How long have you known him?'

'Since college.'

'Do you think we should leave him there?'

'If that's what he wants,' Larry said.

'Sometimes you forget he's sick, or you don't realise how sick he is,' Helen said.

'The problem is that he forgets as well,' Larry said, 'or he puts it to the back of his mind and then he remembers. It's very hard.'

They walked up the gap until they came to the ruin of Mike Redmond's house. Larry walked around it, touching the walls and the chimney breast.

'Your granny is lucky that her house is further back from the cliff,' he said.

'There used to be a big garden in front of this house,' Helen said.

'The foundations are very thin and the walls are not very strong,' Larry said.

'Have you brought your measuring tape?' she asked.

He looked at her earnestly. 'Why?'

She laughed until it struck him that she was mocking him.

'You're worse than Declan,' he said.

They walked back along the clifftop in silence, Larry staring out to sea and stopping to look down at the coast. 'I didn't know there were places like this still left in Wexford,' he said.

As they walked up the lane, they saw Lily driving towards them. She stopped at the gate of her mother's house.

'Is Declan inside?' she asked.

'Mammy, this is Larry, he's a friend of Declan's,' Helen said.

'Hello,' she said coldly. 'Is Declan inside?' she asked again.

'No, he's on the strand,' Helen said.

'Who's he with?' her mother asked.

'No one. He's on his own.'

'How did that happen?'

'He asked us to leave him there. He said he wanted to think.'

'Helen, that is irresponsible.' She began to walk towards the cliff.

'Where are you going?'

'I'm going to get him,' her mother said.

'He wants to be left alone.'

Her mother continued walking away from them towards the cliff.

'It's mucky,' Helen shouted at her, but her mother did not turn.

'Look at her shoes,' Helen said to Larry. 'She'll never get down the cliff.'

'A mother's love's a blessing,' Larry said.

'I presume you're being sarcastic?'

'It's not just you and Declan can go on like that,' Larry said.

'I thought you were a nice simple chap,' she said.

'I think I prefer your granny to your mother,' he said.

'I did that for a while too,' Helen said. 'It's a mistake.'

★

They sat in the kitchen and listened as Helen's grandmother moved about upstairs. The cats on top of the dresser had disappeared. When her grandmother came down the stairs and into the kitchen, she had a cat under each arm.

'These two gentlemen', she said, 'are disturbed by all the visitors.'

'You've a great view here,' Larry said.

'View?' she asked. 'You can get fed up looking at the sea. I can tell you that now. If I could turn the house around, I would.'

'It has great character, the house,' Larry said.

The cats jumped out of her arms and made their way to the top of the dresser, where they scowled down at Helen and Larry.

'I'm bad on my feet,' her grandmother said. 'I'd love to make my bedroom downstairs, but then the bathroom's upstairs. There's no justice.' She went to the window and parted the lace curtains. 'Oh, here's Lily now,' she said.

Helen and Larry stood up as they heard Declan and Lily talking. As Helen opened the kitchen door, she noticed her mother's shoes all covered in marl and muck. Declan, she saw, had been crying. They did not come into the kitchen, but turned towards the room where Declan had slept.

'Is he all right?' her grandmother called after them.

'He's fine. He's just going to lie down.'

When Larry went and sat in front of the house, Helen's grandmother guardedly closed the kitchen door and checked the window to make sure no one was coming.

'Helen,' she asked, 'is this man Larry, is he going to stay here as well?'

'I don't know, Granny.'

'Helen, are we going to put them into the same room?'

'I don't know.'

'I suppose we're all modern now,' her grandmother said, going again to the window, 'and I'm as modern as anyone, but I would just like to know. That's all.'

'Granny, do you mean – are they partners?'

'Yes, that's what I mean.'

'No, they're not.'

'So where is Declan's partner?' her grandmother asked.

'He doesn't have a partner,' Helen said.

'Do you mean he has nobody?'

'He has us,' Helen said. 'And he has his friends. That's not nobody.'

'He has nobody of his own,' her grandmother said sadly. 'Nobody of his own, and that's why he came down here. I didn't understand that before. Helen, we'll have to do everything we can for him.'

Her grandmother kept her eyes fixed on a point in the distance and said nothing more. When Larry came in and saw them, he pretended he had been looking for something and he left the room as soon as he could.

★

Helen went to her room and lay down and tried to sleep. She stared at the ceiling, aware of her mother sitting with Declan in the next room, and surprised that the window was just a small slit in the wall, making the room a shadowy, cavernous space, full of damp smells. She had not remembered it like this.

She thought about the previous year when she had come down here with Hugh and Cathal and Manus. The boys had been excited and interested. Manus had a video about hens, and he had spent the journey from Dublin talking about the hens he was going to see in Cush. Cathal, in recent weeks, had become interested in the idea of young and old. His grandmother in Donegal was old; was his grandmother in Cush old? he asked. Helen explained that his grandmother was in Wexford, his great-grandmother was in Cush and, yes, she was old.

The boys had packed their bathing togs and buckets and spades, even though they were only staying one day. Helen explained about the cliff.

'But is there sand?' Cathal asked.

'Yes, plenty of sand,' she said.

'Do they talk English in Cush?' he asked.

'Plenty of English,' Hugh said.

As soon as they got out of the car and stood in front of their great-grandmother's house, the boys looked around them suspiciously. The house seemed decrepit; one of the windows upstairs was broken. When her grandmother came to the door, Helen watched her as though through the eyes of the two boys. There was something frightening about her presence. The boys did not move as Helen and Hugh went towards the old woman. Helen was afraid that Manus might run back to the car, or worse call her grandmother a witch or some other word from his increasingly large vocabulary.

The boys did not want to come into the house. When Helen asked if Hugh could take Manus to see Furlong's hens, Hugh seemed almost too grateful for the excuse to leave.

Helen beckoned Cathal to come inside. He stood in the kitchen, inspecting everything, his gaze critical and utterly unselfconscious.

'Oh, he's the image of your father, Helen,' her grandmother said. 'Isn't he the image of your father!' Cathal looked at her coldly.

When Hugh and Manus returned, it was clear that the trip to see the hens had not been a success.

'They were all dirty,' Manus said.

'Oh now,' Mrs Devereux said, 'Mrs Furlong washes them with soap and water on Mondays, so you came the wrong day.'

'Do you live here?' Manus asked her.

Hugh sat beside the Aga, Helen and Manus and Mrs Devereux at the kitchen table. Cathal would not sit down.

'Your mother now will be here any minute,' her grandmother said to Helen.

'Is she your mother too?' Manus asked.

'No, Manus,' Helen said, 'she's my mother, but she's Granny's daughter. Isn't that a good one?'

Manus wrinkled his face in mock disgust. He hated it when he did not understand things.

'Did you live here?' he asked Helen.

'No, it's my granny's house,' she told him.

'There's an awful stink,' he said.

He began to examine the fly-paper, which hung from the ceiling near the light-fitting. He called Cathal over.

'The flies are dead,' Cathal said, 'and they're stuck to the paper.'

'Lift me up,' Manus said to Hugh.

'You're to be good, Manus,' Helen said. 'It's Granny's house.'

'I want to see the dead flies,' he said.

'The paper is all sticky,' Cathal said.

'It's all manky,' Manus added.

The cats appeared at the window and her grandmother went out and carried them in, one under each arm. As soon as they saw the visitors, they jumped up to their perch on the dresser. Manus wanted someone to help him fetch them down so he could play with them, but Mrs Devereux explained that they didn't like little boys.

'What did you bring them in for?' he asked her sharply.

The day was mild and sunny and Helen thought it might be best for everyone if Hugh took the boys down to the strand. She would go as far as the cliff with them.

She and Hugh were careful to say nothing as they walked down the lane, pretending that this was a normal outing with buckets and spades. Hugh lifted Manus in his arms as they approached the cliff, Helen held Cathal's hand. Just as they came to the edge, the sky darkened and the boys looked down with amazement and alarm.

'Is that the strand?' Manus asked.

'Yes, and you use steps to go down,' Helen said.

'What steps?'

She pointed them out to him.

'And you run down the last bit,' she said.

'I hate it,' Manus said.

'It's lovely when you're down there. And the sea is much warmer than Donegal.'

'It's all dirty,' he said.

'Do we have to go down?' Cathal asked.

'No,' Helen said, 'you can do what you like.'

She realised that they were used to the long sandy beaches in Donegal, and that the marl of the cliff and the short strand seemed strange to them.

'But I think you'd like it down there,' Helen said.

'How long are we staying here?' Cathal asked.

'Just today.'

'We're not sleeping here, sure we're not?'

'No, we're driving back later.'

The boys stood there, downcast and subdued.

'Manus, I'll give you a piggy-back if you come down now,' Hugh said.

'No, I want to sit on your shoulders.'

'All right.'

'And I'm not swimming if it's cold,' Manus said.

Cathal shook his head at Helen, signalling that he did not want to go down the cliff.

'You can come up with me,' she said, 'and sit in the car and read your comic.'

'Can I sit at the steering wheel?' Manus asked.

'When you come back,' she said.

Helen and her grandmother waited for her mother to arrive while Cathal sat in the car reading his comic. When Hugh and Manus came back and her mother still had not arrived, she took the cold lunch she had brought from the car into the kitchen and they all sat around the table. Her grandmother had made soup and wanted to cook pork chops, but Helen insisted that they eat only the food she had brought. As she moved from the table to the dresser, she had a sudden memory of Declan being handed one of those willow-patterned plates with onions and carrots on it which he would not eat. She almost wished now that her grandmother would produce some items that the boys did not eat – cheese, for example, or cabbage – to see their reaction. They would have responded with contempt, they would have refused even to look at the food.

They ate lunch and drank tea afterwards, all the time listening out for Lily's car. They talked about neighbours in Cush, Hugh cut a piece of cardboard for the broken window upstairs, Cathal read his comic and Manus tried to entice the cats from their lair. Helen made sure that there was never silence.

When she brought Cathal to the toilet, he asked if he could look around the house, and she told him he could. Downstairs, when she said to him that she and Declan had once slept in these rooms, he became interested. But when he asked her why they had slept here and not in their own house, she became vague. Cathal, however, persisted, and she told him that her father had died.

'And was your daddy old?' he asked.

'No, Cathal, he was young,' she said.

'And why did he die then?'

'That happens sometimes.'

'Is your mammy old?'

'She's older than me, but she's younger than Granny.'

'And she's not dead?'

'No, we're going to meet her.'

He pondered on what she had said, but he did not seem satisfied.

'Was Declan like Manus when he was small?'

'He was very like Manus,' Helen said.

'What does the image of your father mean?'

'It means you look like him.'

'But he's dead.'

'When he was alive.'

'Did they take photographs of him?'

Her mother did not arrive and the afternoon waned. Finally, they decided to leave. Hugh and Cathal and Manus went to the car.

'I'm nicely hoped up with you all,' Helen's grandmother said to her. 'That Lily is a law on to herself.'

'Tell her we came anyway,' Helen said.

'I'll clean her clock,' her grandmother said and turned towards the dresser, as if to look for something.

Now, for the first time there was silence. Her grandmother did not turn until Helen began to speak.

'We all have a lot to put up with, Helen,' her grandmother said, interrupting her.

Helen said nothing.

'What were you going to say?' her grandmother asked.

'I was going to thank you for the day, and say that you should come up to Dublin and see us.'

Her grandmother looked at her.

'After all those years I suppose it's nice to hear you saying that,' she said. Her tone was bitter, almost angry.

Helen smiled and turned and walked out of the house. In the car, as Hugh started the engine, she rolled down the window and they all waved at her grandmother and Hugh honked the horn as they set off for Dublin.

She waited until later that night, when she had drunk most of a bottle of red wine, to tell Hugh what her grandmother had said.

'We won't go near them for a good while so,' he said.

Now she was back under the same roof with them. She stood up from the bed and studied herself in the old mirror. She could see how tired her eyes looked. She sighed and opened the door and went back out to join her mother and her brother and his friend in their grandmother's house.

★

Later, as she sat in the kitchen, they heard another car in the lane. Mrs Devereux looked out through the curtains. 'Oh, here's another of them now,' she said.

'Who, Granny?' Helen asked.

'Look yourself,' she said.

Helen saw that it was Paul. He was carrying a suitcase. They watched him talking to Larry.

'Someone else deal with him,' her grandmother said.

Helen went to the door and brought Paul, followed by Larry, into the kitchen. She introduced him to her grandmother, who smiled at him warmly.

'It took me a bit longer than I thought,' he said. 'It's very hard to find this place. I had to ask at nearly every house.'

'Oh God Almighty, I'll have them all on top of me now,' her grandmother said. 'I'll have them in droves.'

'What do you mean, Granny?' Helen asked.

'The neighbours', she said, 'will smell the news.'

'How is he?' Paul asked.

'He's lying down,' Helen said.

'And he hasn't eaten since he came,' her grandmother said.

'No, his appetite can come and go,' Paul said. 'I

137

brought him some clean clothes and there are drugs he needs and Complan.'

'Did you bring the Xanax?' Larry asked.

'I brought a packet of it. I used the old prescription.'

'What's Xanax?' Helen asked.

'It cheers him up a bit,' Larry said.

'Cheers him up,' her grandmother repeated. 'Maybe we should all have it.'

Helen's mother came into the room and examined them all disapprovingly.

'He wants a glass of milk and he shouldn't be left alone like that again, and he wants to know if his friends can stay in the spare room upstairs.'

'This new fellow'll have to bring his car in from the lane first, or it'll roll over the cliff,' her grandmother said.

'Paul,' Helen said. 'His name is Paul.'

'We'll have to get sheets and blankets for them,' her grandmother said. 'Are there any more coming?'

'A line of cars from Dublin,' Helen said.

'We should put a sign up saying we're open for business,' her grandmother said.

*

In the late afternoon when Larry and Paul were in the bedroom with Declan, and Helen was in the kitchen with her mother and grandmother, voices could be heard, and then a knock came at the kitchen door.

'Come in,' Helen's grandmother said.

Two middle-aged women, Madge and Essie Kehoe, clearly sisters by their looks and the way they dressed, entered the room and managed to take in everything even before they spoke.

'Dora, we were just passing and we saw all the cars and we were wondering were you all right.'

Helen watched her grandmother moving towards the kitchen door and closing it behind her two visitors. 'I'm as right as rain,' she said.

'You have plenty of visitors, Dora?' Madge asked.

'Just down for the day, Helen and her friends.'

'Her husband isn't down?'

'No, no, he's in Donegal.'

'And the boys?'

'In Donegal too.'

'Donegal,' Madge repeated.

Helen left the room and told her brother and his friends not to make a sound. She went upstairs and flushed the toilet noisily.

'We read all about you on the paper nearly every week, Lily,' Essie was saying as Helen came back into the room.

'Oh, Lily's a big shot now,' Madge said to nobody in particular. 'She's in the IDA.'

'Is the red car your car?' Essie asked Helen.

'That's right,' Helen said.

'But that's the car that stopped and asked us directions,' Madge said.

'No, the white car is Helen's,' Lily said firmly.

'And not the red car?'

'No.'

'Whose is the red car then?'

'They're friends of mine, they teach in my school, and they're staying in Curracloe. They've gone for a walk,' Helen said.

'Well, I hope it doesn't rain,' Madge said. They drank

tea and looked around them. 'And will you be staying here tonight now?'

'I don't know,' Helen said.

'It's a while since you stayed the night here, Lily,' Essie said.

'I might well have passed up and down when you weren't looking, Essie,' Lily said.

'Oh, Madge would see you then,' her grandmother said coldly and stared towards the door.

'You haven't been down here since last year, have you, Helen?' Essie asked, ignoring the last remark.

'No.'

'And what do you think of the improvements she's made, Lily?' Madge asked, pointing to the radiators.

'Lovely, lovely,' Lily said.

★

When they had gone, Mrs Devereux put her finger to her lips and went to the window. 'Say nothing now! They're inspecting the cars!'

Helen and her mother went to the window.

'Stand back both of you!' her grandmother ordered.

When the Kehoe sisters had finally disappeared, the three women began to laugh.

'I was in school with Essie,' Lily said. 'She was a right hunt.'

'If you'd known her mother, you'd know that she never could have been any other way,' Mrs Devereux said.

'How do you put up with them, Granny?' Helen asked.

'I don't put up with them, Helen,' her grandmother said. 'Did you not hear what I said to them? They'll be raging about that.'

'The oul' father, oul' Crutch Kehoe, used to beat them with nettles,' Lily said.

'Well, if that's all he did to them, they're not too bad,' Mrs Devereux said. 'They'll go off now and they'll fill whoever they meet with the news and gossip. The only lucky thing is they have no telephone.'

As Helen went down to Declan's room to tell the others what had happened, she heard them talking animatedly. It was Larry's voice she heard, telling a story, and the other two interrupting, laughing, egging him on. She left them there; she did not go into the room.

★

Her grandmother sat by the window. As the pale light from the sea faded and the shadows grew, Helen focused only on the old woman; she watched her white hair and her long thin face. When her grandmother spoke, the voice was sharp and determined.

'Oh, when I saw you getting out of the car,' she said to Paul, 'when I saw you, I said to myself – here's another of them now.'

'Granny, what do you mean?' Helen asked her.

'I think you know what I mean, Helen,' she said.

'She means homosexuals,' Paul said.

'Granny, you can't talk about people like that.'

'When I saw him getting out of the car' – the old woman spoke as though she were talking to herself, trying to remember something – 'it was the way he walked or turned and I wondered what sort of life he was going to have now, what sort of person he could be.' She raised her head and looked across the room at Helen.

'It's a difficult time for all of us,' Helen said.

'It's difficult for them, Helen, and it always will be.'

'I think she means homosexuals again,' Paul said.

'Well, I'm happy,' Larry said. 'I'm not happy being here now, but my life's happy.'

'It's a stupid word, "happy",' Paul said.

There was silence now. The four of them sat in the gloom as the lighthouse began to flash. Her grandmother looked out of the window as if she had heard a sound or someone approaching. Then she faced back into the room. 'I'm old and I can say what I like, Helen.'

Helen realised that she was still afraid of her grand-mother, that she would not confront her or defy her. She stared at her across the room, knowing that the old woman could not see the resentment, the dislike. Her grandmother turned to Paul and Larry, her two visitors.

'Declan never told us anything about himself. We always thought that he had a great life in Dublin. No one knew he was sick and no one knew he was one of you.'

She said nothing for a while, but it was clear that she had merely stopped so that she could gather strength for what she was going to say next.

'But I knew something. I've known it for a year now and I never told anyone or said anything. Declan came down here last summer. He left his car way back some-where so I heard no car, but for some reason I went out to the lane, and I looked down towards the cliff and I saw him coming towards me. He must have passed the house without calling in, or maybe he went down by Mike

Redmond's and walked along the strand. And now he was coming towards me, but he didn't expect to see me, and I think he didn't want to see me, and I think that he would have passed by my house if I hadn't come out to the lane. I hadn't seen him since Christmas, and I don't think he had been down here for more than a year. And when he came towards me I could see that he had been crying and he was so thin and so strange, like as though he didn't want to see me. He was always so friendly, even when he was a little boy. And he tried to make up for it when he came into the house. He was all smiles and jokes, but I'll never forget seeing him. He had tea here, and both of us knew that there was something awful, something very wrong. I knew he was in trouble, but AIDS was the last thing I thought of, and I thought of everything.'

Helen held her breath in the semi-darkness as the lighthouse started up. She wondered why her grandmother had not told her this before.

'I knew Declan came down here,' Larry said. 'He used to drive out of Dublin on his own, usually to Wicklow, to the mountains; he would drive along those roads for miles. He drove to Wexford a few times, to his mother's house, but it was always late and he never went in. I think he hoped she'd find him there like you did. But he never saw her. And then he'd drive back to Dublin.'

'I knew something would happen and I waited for it,' Mrs Devereux said, as though she had not been listening.

Helen wanted her grandmother to stop talking. She directed a question at Larry and Paul. 'Do your folks know that you're gay?' she asked them.

'Tell her your story,' Paul said to Larry.

143

'I've told it too many times,' Larry said.

'Make him tell it,' Paul said to Helen.

'My grandmother would love to hear it,' Helen said. She knew that this was the nearest she could come to defiance. 'Come on, Larry,' she said. 'We're all full of curiosity.'

'All right,' Larry said. 'But if it gets boring stop me. After I qualified, I was involved in a gay group in Dublin, and we organised fund-raising and we started a news sheet, and we had meetings all the time. I helped out a bit, and I was around a lot, so the time Mary Robinson invited gay men and lesbians to Áras an Uachtaráin, I was on the list and I couldn't say no. It was a big deal. We really enjoyed getting ready for it. I know it sounds stupid, but we thought that because the law still hadn't been changed it might just be a private visit. Anyway, all the newspapers were there, and radio and television. Mary Holland was there and a fellow from RTÉ, it wasn't Charlie Bird, I can't remember his name, but I realised that he was from the six o'clock news and they were going to film us all having tea with the President.'

'Oh she's very nice, Mary Robinson,' Mrs Devereux said, 'she's very refined. There aren't many like her.'

'Yes, we all loved her,' Larry continued, 'but this didn't help me. I still wondered if I could sneak out. I mean it. I actually wondered what would happen if I disappeared. I realised that I would never be able to face any of my friends again, but I thought that would be a small price to pay. I looked around and asked myself if maybe one other person felt like I did, but I think I was the only one who wanted to hide. We stood in a row to be photographed and filmed. Everybody smiled and was very relaxed. I think even I might have smiled. But I wasn't very relaxed. You see, no one at home knew. I had to go back to my flat and phone Paul here and borrow his car and drive down to Tullamore. I got there just before the six o'clock news. I knocked on the door and my mother answered; my father was in the hall. I had worked out what to say, but when I saw my mother it was no use, I couldn't say it. I just blurted out, "You're not to watch the six o'clock news," and I walked into the sitting-room and stood like an eejit in front of the television.'

'And what happened then?' Helen asked.

Larry sighed and stopped.

'Telling it is worse than when it happened.'

'Go on,' Paul said.

'Anyway, I was standing there and my mother kept asking me what the problem was, but I couldn't tell her. My father sat on the sofa looking at me like I was mad. I realised that maybe I could tell my mother, but I certainly couldn't tell him. So I said I needed to be on my own with my mother. My father said that he would go out but I told him not to. I was sure that he'd meet someone who would have seen me on the television. Or he'd go down to the pub and he'd see me himself.'

'Your son's a big girl,' Paul said.

'Shut up, Paul,' Larry said.

'So what happened?' Helen asked.

'He went into the kitchen, but I still couldn't say anything and suddenly my mother looked at me and said: "Are you after joining the IRA?" I couldn't believe it.

Can you imagine me in the IRA? I don't think there was anyone in Tullamore ever in the IRA. They're all too bloody boring. No, I said, no. And then I told her.'

'And what did she say?' Helen asked.

'She said that I would always be her son no matter what I did, but I was to get back into the car this minute and go back to Dublin and she would deal with my father and she would phone me later on. She couldn't wait to get me out of the house. She was all pale and worried-looking. I think she would have been happier if I had been in the IRA.'

'Oh come on,' Helen said, 'that's not true.'

'OK, that's not fair about the IRA,' Larry said. 'I think she was just shocked and surprised. You know, in my family my brothers and sisters – even the married ones – still haven't told my parents that they are heterosexual. We don't talk about sex. She was nice about it afterwards, and she still is OK about it, but my father just grunts at me in the same way as he did before. At least if I was in the IRA we would have something to talk about. It'd be more normal.'

'And are you and Paul partners?' Helen asked.

'Him? You must be joking,' Larry said.

'You'd want to be mad,' Paul said.

'What? To be with you, or to be with him?' Helen asked.

'With him,' Paul said. 'Or maybe with either of us.'

'So do you have a partner, Larry?' Helen asked.

'Tell them, Larry,' Paul said.

'I do, Helen,' Larry said, 'but I couldn't tell you about it.'

'Go on, Larry,' Paul said.

'I'm sure Mrs Devereux has heard enough,' Larry said.

'Oh, don't worry about me,' the old woman said. 'There's nothing would shock me. When you've gone through life like I have, there's very little you don't know.'

'Funny, it's easier to talk like this in the dark,' Larry said. 'It's like going to Confession, except there's no lighthouse in a confession box.'

'Come on, we're all waiting,' Paul said.

'We'll hear all about Paul later on,' Larry said.

'Tell the story,' Paul said.

'Stop me now if I go on too long,' Larry said. 'There's this big family a few doors down from us at home. There are five girls and four boys. My folks are friends with the parents. The parents are very religious – the father is in the Vincent de Paul and the mother is always saying Novenas. They're nice normal people. Their youngest son lives in Dublin. And I'm with him at the moment. That's been going on a few months. The only thing is that I've also been with the other three, I mean the other three sons. Two of them are married, but that doesn't seem to stop them. It's funny, they're all different. The youngest fellow is great.'

When he had finished speaking there was silence. Helen could see traces of light through the window, but the room was now entirely dark.

'They're a terrific family. It must be something in the genes,' Paul said after a few moments.

'It's in their genes all right,' Larry said. 'And in their Terylene trousers.'

'I've heard everything now,' the old woman said. Her

voice was hard and it was louder than it needed to be, as though she were addressing some higher power. 'Four of them! They must be a right crowd.'

'My mother has enough to think about at the moment, I imagine,' Helen said.

'I told you that you wouldn't want to hear it, Mrs Devereux,' Larry said.

'Oh guard your heart, that's my advice to you, guard your heart and be careful of yourself.'

Just then the light was switched on and Helen's mother stood at the door. 'What are you all doing here in the dark?' she asked.

Helen blinked and covered her eyes against the harshness of the electric light. She wished her mother would turn it off again.

'Declan is after being sick, but it's not too bad,' her mother said. 'I've cleaned it up, it's all right, but I think he might go asleep now. I hope he will. I don't know what you were all doing in the dark.'

'We were talking, Lily, we were talking, and we didn't notice the night coming down,' the grandmother said.

'What were you saying when I came in the door?' Helen's mother asked.

'I was saying to the boys that this is a very hard time and it is nice to have their company,' the grandmother said. Helen watched her as she turned her face towards Larry as if daring him to contradict her. 'That's what I was telling them, Lily,' she said.

The old woman stood up then and looked out at the night. She pulled her chair back and began to draw the curtains slowly until Larry came over to help her. As he approached her, she raised her hand as though to hit him. He moved away from her, laughing.

★

They made up the beds for Larry and Paul in the small room upstairs while Lily took her leave of them, saying that she had not been able to sleep the previous night, making her mother promise that she would turn on the mobile phone. She said she would be back in the morning. Helen walked out to the car with her.

'I couldn't sleep the first night I came here either,' she said.

'If there is a problem, you will give me a ring, won't you?' her mother said.

'I found it very strange being back here after all this time,' Helen said.

Her mother started the ignition and began to reverse the car in the yard. Helen stood out of her way.

Later, when she returned from Blackwater, where she had phoned Hugh, she found Declan by the Aga in his pyjamas and slippers. Paul and Larry and her grandmother were sitting at the kitchen table looking at a full-page advertisement in the *Wexford People* for Lily's computer company.

'She's a big noise, your mother,' Paul said.

'Lily was always very independent-minded,' Helen's grandmother said. 'Even when she was a baby, if you picked her up to cuddle her or put her on your knee, she'd want to be let down to crawl around on her own, or walk when she was old enough. You could never tell her what to do. You couldn't even tell her to get up in the morning. She'd be up before you. She was always a great worker and she had great brains, she won a university scholarship. The nuns loved her. I took in bathers first so I could pay for her to go to FCJ in Bunclody, and, you know, she nearly became a nun.'

'I never knew that,' Helen said.

'Oh, the nuns loved her,' her grandmother went on, 'and when she was in her final year and we drove her back up after the Hallowe'en break, they called us in, and they had never looked up or down at us before, oh they were very grand, the nuns, a French order. And Mother Emmanuelle, the grandest of them all, told me that she believed Lily had a vocation. I smiled at her and said that would be the happiest thing for us. It was all smiles until I got out to the car and I said to your grandfather that I was going to pray to God to stop Lily entering the convent.'

'And did you not want her to be a nun?' Paul asked.

'Lily? Our beautiful daughter? Have all her hair cut off? And a veil and a draughty old convent and only doddery old nuns for company? I did not! And I lay awake every night thinking about how to stop her. I knew that we could say nothing to her, that talking to her would make no difference. Your grandfather, who was a very good man and is getting his reward in heaven, said that we should accept God's will, and I said that my not wanting her to be a nun could also be God's will.'

'Good man, Granny,' Declan said.

'So what did you do?' Helen asked.

Her grandmother looked at the floor and said nothing.

The others looked at her in silence, waiting for her to continue.

'I'll make tea,' she said. 'I'm talking too much.'

'No, you're not, you have to tell us,' Declan said.

'I'll make the tea,' Helen said.

'Well, I thought and I thought,' she said, licking her lips. 'And I knew that I had until the end of the Christmas holidays to stop it. And I thought about Lily. You know, when other girls were playing nurses, she had to be the best nurse, and when it came to dressmaking, she'd keep me up all night with patterns and material. She always did what everyone around her did, only more so. It was the same with her studies. She had to be the best and the most enthusiastic. She was with the nuns day and night, so, of course, she wanted to be one of them. And once all that struck me, then I knew what to do. It was just before we collected her for Christmas.'

'What did you do, Granny?' Helen asked as she filled the teapot.

'Lily needed to have her head turned, that was all. And my sister Statia was married to one of the Bolgers of Bree and she had five sons and no daughters, and they were the wildest young fellows in the county Wexford. They were nice and decent, mind, but Statia loved them all, and she was softer than I was, and she'd let them roam the countryside and have parties, when no one else was having parties, and go to dances in their father's car and not come home until dinnertime the next day. And they had cousins on the Bolger side who were nearly as bad. All they thought about were hurling matches and girls and dances. Three of the cousins were on the Wexford team.

151

'I went out to Bree. I left your grandfather in the car and I talked to Statia, and Statia understood, and even if she hadn't understood she would have done what I asked. And I asked her to take Lily for the time after Christmas and let her loose with the Bolgers. So we left her in there on St Stephen's Day. She was a bit surprised but she suspected nothing, and we didn't collect her until the day before she was due back in school. And Statia let her go to every dance and hop. She flew around the country in cars and vans, wearing clothes she borrowed from one of the Bolger cousins. She was as mad as a cat, Statia told me. She had them in stitches describing oul' farmers who came to the dances. She was the best dancer and she was a great goer. Her cousins knew everyone, and their cousins knew everyone else. Soon then Lily knew every-one too. It was the same as the nuns. She wanted to be one of them, except that now she wanted to be at the dance in Ballindaggin or the dance in Adamstown. When we didn't hear from her, we knew it was working.'

'Granny, were you not afraid that she'd get into trouble?' Declan asked.

'They were different times, Declan. Her cousins were looking out for her. And she wasn't the sort of girl you could take advantage of.'

'I'm sure she wasn't,' Helen said as she began to pour the tea.

'So she went back to the FCJ, and spent her time sneaking out letters to fellows with the day-girls and keeping the other girls up late on the dormitory. She must have studied as well, because she got her scholarship, but her head was turned and we were called in before we took her home for Easter, and we were told that she was becoming a bad example to the other girls, and she had changed completely. Oh, I said to Mother Emmanuelle, I said, we haven't noticed any change. It must be something in the convent, I said. Oh, she gave me a look, and I looked back at her. And she knew she'd met her match. And that's how we stopped Lily becoming a nun.'

'And wasn't that lucky for all of us?' Helen asked.

'It must have seemed like that at the time, anyway,' Declan said.

SIX

In the morning Helen found her mother in Declan's room, cradling his head in her hand.

'You must have come back very early,' she said, and immediately realised that she sounded as though she were accusing her mother. 'You look tired,' she said then, trying to soften her tone.

'Declan wasn't well again this morning,' her mother said coldly.

Declan stared at her. The bruising on his nose had become darker, almost purple, and seemed to have spread; yet there was a strange contentment in the way he lay without moving. He did not appear to be in any pain.

'Are the boys up yet?' she asked.

'They're being fed by your granny,' her mother said. 'She's in her element – she thinks she's running a guest-house again. It's rashers and sausages and how would you like your eggs?'

'If we had rashers,' Declan said hoarsely, 'we could have rashers and eggs, only we've no eggs.'

'You've been saying that since you were about five,' Helen said, laughing, 'and I've never thought it was funny.'

'Go in and have your breakfast before they eat it all,' her mother said.

When Helen went into the kitchen, Larry was talking and her grandmother was giving him her full attention. Paul acknowledged her arrival, but the other two ignored her.

'No, Mrs Devereux,' Larry was saying, 'no, knocking down a wall costs nothing, and widening a door costs nothing. You could do the whole thing for a thousand pounds, but if I were you I'd put in the anti-damp system too and an oak floor, or at least a pine floor . . .'

'Is that fellow still talking?' Helen asked.

'Your breakfast is in the Aga, Helen,' her grandmother said.

'Granny, I hope you're not listening to him,' Helen said.

'But where would I put the kitchen?' her grandmother asked Larry.

'No,' Larry said, 'leave the kitchen where it is, but put in a ramp and a rail.'

'We're talking about if I fell, Helen,' her grandmother said. 'Or if I was in a wheelchair. And, anyway, I can't be going up and down the stairs much longer.'

'No,' Larry continued as though no one else had spoken, 'put the bedroom and the bathroom where Helen and Declan are sleeping, with a big, wide door between them, but make them both much bigger by using some of the dining-room. Sure I bet you never use that.'

'Have you brought your measuring tape, Larry?' Helen asked as she sat down.

Larry ignored her. 'I checked those walls,' he went on.

'It would take half a day to knock them down. It would be like a new house. You wouldn't know yourself.'

By the time Helen had returned from the village, having bought groceries and the newspaper, and phoned Hugh, Larry was making drawings to scale in a large sketch pad on the kitchen table. He had the measuring tape beside him.

'There's no talking to him,' Paul said. 'He's a maniac.'

'Where would the bed be, though?' her grandmother asked, turning away from her washing-up. 'I don't want it against the window.'

'Is it a double bed or a single bed?' Larry asked.

'That's a very personal question,' Helen said.

'What sort of bed do you think I should get?' her grandmother asked, turning again, her hands covered in suds.

'Oh, that's up to you now,' Larry said.

★

As soon as the sun came out from the clouds, Helen took a chair to the front of the house and sat there reading the *Irish Times*. She would wait, she thought, until her mother left Declan's room, and try to see him on his own. If Cathal were sick like this, or Manus, she thought she would want to do as her mother was doing, but she was unsure if it was what they would want.

Paul came and sat on the ground beside her, his back against the house.

'Do you think Declan is all right?' she asked.

'How do you mean?'

'I think my mother has been with him since the dawn.'

157

'No, she hasn't. She arrived just before you got up,' he said. 'But she seems to be guarding the room, keeping his evil friends away from him.'

'And his evil sister,' Helen said.

'And her evil granny,' Paul added, laughing.

'No, I wouldn't call her evil. "Bad" is the word I'd use.'

'You're in good form this morning,' Paul said.

'Years ago,' Helen said, 'when we were children and my parents were away somewhere and my grandfather was out, my grandmother caught her hand in the window and she couldn't lift the sash. I don't know what age I was, six or seven I suppose. Anyway, she says, and she loved telling the story, that I used the occasion to go through every drawer in the house, rummaging freely, while Declan sat close to her, crying and trying to comfort her. I, of course, don't remember doing that at all. And I'm sure I didn't take advantage of the situation like that. But that's what she's doing now, what she accused me of doing when I was six or seven: she's rummaging in the drawers with your friend Larry.'

'Oh come on, give her a break,' Paul said. 'She lives on her own. It isn't often that she meets a real live architect. And Larry can never go into anyone's house without suggesting that they plant a bathroom somewhere entirely unsuitable.'

'What are you saying about me?' Larry came out and stood in the sun.

'I was telling Helen that your middle name is Frank Lloyd Wright,' Paul said.

'Your granny says that we're all to go for a swim,'

Larry said. 'She gave me these.' He held up two pairs of black nylon swimming togs.

'God, I wouldn't wear one of those,' Paul said.

'I brought my own,' Helen said.

'Where did she get them?' Paul asked.

' "Left behind by bathers", she said.'

'She calls outsiders "bathers",' Helen said.

'God, they are skimpy,' Larry said, holding up the togs. 'They must have had fierce small mickeys in the nineteen-forties.'

'They're from the sixties,' Paul said, 'when blokes didn't mind having their mickeys squashed.'

'Do you think we should ask Declan if he wants to come with us?' Larry asked.

'Go in and find out,' Helen said.

They waited in silence until he came back.

'He's asleep now,' Larry said. 'I didn't even ask. I said I'd get your mother a cup of tea.'

'We'll wait,' Helen said. 'Get towels.'

Helen took her swimsuit from a bag in the boot of Declan's car, and all three of them walked down towards the cliff. If these men were not gay, she thought, she would have found an excuse not to go down to the strand with them. There would be too much tension and uncertainty. She would not have known how to behave unless Hugh were in the company as well, and then she would keep close to him. It was only when they were on the strand and Paul took off his shirt, and she saw the pale, smooth skin on his long back, that she realised how strange and new this was for her. If he saw her undressing, she thought, it would mean nothing to him. Maybe he

159

would be curious, but he would not feel what she felt when she saw him now standing up in the black nylon togs.

'Last in is a sissy,' Larry shouted and began to wade fearlessly into the water until he suddenly stopped and jumped in the air as though he had been hit by an electric current. 'It's freezing, oh Jesus, it's freezing!' he roared.

Paul walked casually into the water, but he too stopped and wrapped his arms around his torso as though protecting himself from the cold. Helen realised that she would have to resist the temptation to splash him as she passed. He was too serious and distant for teasing. She thought of whispering the word 'sissy' into his ear, but she thought he would be offended.

'Come on, Paul,' she said, 'you're a big boy.'

'Don't even speak to me,' he said, shivering. 'You never told me it was this cold.'

By now, Larry was swimming out to sea, and as soon as it was deep enough, and with as much effort and determination as she could muster, Helen dived in as well. When she surfaced, knowing that Paul was watching her, she nonchalantly tossed the seawater out of her hair.

Afterwards, they dried themselves and lay on their towels in the sun.

'Your granny says', Larry began, 'that if she broke her leg or got sick, they'd sort of capture her and keep her, and she'd never get home. She was in hospital once and the old woman in the bed opposite thought everyone was a priest, even the nurses, and was all father this and father that, and your granny says she couldn't bear it. They started to treat her like she was demented as well.'

'She is demented,' Helen said.

'God, it'd be awful, though, when you think about it,' Larry said.

'Shut up, Larry,' Paul said.

'No, seriously,' Larry said.

'I don't care about Granny,' Helen said. 'I mean, I do care about her, but not now. Now, I'd like to get Declan out of that room.'

'I think maybe he wants to be there with your mother like that,' Paul said.

'Are you sure?' Helen asked.

'I think he was so afraid that your mother would refuse to see him or something,' Paul said. 'I think he desperately wanted her to know and help him and yet he couldn't tell her, and now he's told her and he has her there and she's trying to help him.'

'It might be better in small doses,' Helen said drily.

'It might also be exactly what he wants,' Paul said. 'He talked about it so much.'

'Imagine being locked up in a room like that with your mother,' Larry said. 'I'd sooner be taken hostage by the Hizbollah.'

'Shut up, Larry, you told us your mother was nice,' Paul said.

'I suppose if I was sick, it would be different,' Larry said.

'Stop telling Larry to shut up,' Helen said.

Paul stood up and walked towards the shoreline and then began to wade fearlessly into the water.

'Maybe he'll cool off in there,' Larry said.

'What's wrong with him?' Helen asked.

'He has his own problems,' Larry said.

'Is he sick?' she asked hesitantly.

'No, not that. Boyfriend problems. Can you imagine trying to be his boyfriend?'

'I'm sure he's very nice.'

'Oh, a bundle of laughs, our Paul. He reads books about relationships.'

'And that's the limit, I suppose?'

'Well, it would be for me, big-time,' he said.

'Yes, it would be for me too,' Helen sighed.

★

Later, Larry went back to the house and Helen and Paul walked south along the strand towards Ballyconnigar and Ballyvaloo. The day was hazy, but the sun was strong and warm.

'Do you live alone?' she asked him.

He looked at her sharply. They both knew that the question had been rehearsed.

'No, I live with my boyfriend in Brussels,' he said. He sounded bored.

'Sorry, I should mind my own business,' she said.

'No, it's OK,' he said.

They walked in silence until they came to the Keatings' house, where she began to explain the erosion. He seemed interested in it, asked questions about who had lived in the house and how long it had taken this part of it to fall over the cliff.

They crossed the stream at Ballyconnigar and continued walking. Without thinking, she asked another question. 'Is your boyfriend Irish?'

'No, he's French, but I met him in Ireland.'

'How did you meet him?'

She did not know why she was so curious, and she

promised herself that, if he put her off this time, she would ask him nothing more.

'We were on an exchange scheme when we were both fifteen.'

'And did you . . .?' She hesitated, and he looked at her as though he did not understand what she was asking. 'Did you . . .?'

'I think I know what you mean,' he said. 'No, no, not until four years later.'

'But did you know?'

'I knew I was, but I didn't know he was, and vice versa.'

'And what happened?'

They sat down against one of the small sand dunes. He put his arms around his knees and stared out to sea. 'A lot of French students came to the town,' he said, 'and they all joined the tennis club so we were all down there day and night. There were hops and tournaments and all sorts of things. The way all of us – I mean the Irish boys – the way we dealt with each other puzzled the French people, but I didn't realise that until much later. We were all surprised at how they shook hands with each other and kissed each other, and they were amazed at how we slagged each other off all the time. Looking back on it, that was, I suppose, how we communicated. If anyone got a haircut, or was caught holding hands with a girl, or had any weakness, it could be anything, they'd all jeer you and slag you and it could go on for days.'

'That's what you and Declan do to Larry,' she said.

'He deserves it,' Paul said.

'Sorry, I interrupted you.'

'You'd have to know my father,' he went on. 'He's an

engineer, and he's really interested in problems in maths, and he's also big into logic. All my brothers are engineers. From the time we could talk he had us solving problems. And when we were older, if we had to decide anything, like how to spend your Confirmation money, or whether to watch television or study, he'd make you write out the problem and then the pros and cons, and then the decision. We all had slips of paper for this, and he'd love if you showed him how you worked something out. So the winter before François came to stay with us I wrote on a slip of paper: "I am gay. I feel about blokes in my class the way they feel about girls." And then I hid the piece of paper. I read an article in the *Irish Times* about a couple where the husband was gay, but they didn't talk about it until they had two children. They were going to try and stay together, the article said, but she knew that he didn't really fancy her.

'I used to take out the slip of paper and write down options: I could ignore it. I could try and forget about it. I wrote down the most outlandish things I won't tell you about. One night I wrote down the option that I should look out for someone my own age who was gay too. I remember I underlined it twice because it was less drastic than some of the other options.

'And very soon someone came along, or I thought he came along. I used to play rugby then, until I got sense, but our club was tiny and we had no showers or anything like that. We used to put our clothes back on after the game and then go home and shower and change. The first time I played in an away-game there was a communal shower and we all noticed that one of the guys on our team – he's a big barrister now – got an erection in the

164

shower. I stupidly decided that he had to be gay. He was a really good-looking guy, so I watched him, and then one night I managed to walk home with him after a debate, and I don't know what I said to him, but whatever it was he understood my meaning. He said he would be interested, but just not tonight, and we left it like that, and I went home happy. I had met somebody. I wouldn't need to consult the slip of paper again.

'The problem was that I never got to be on my own with him properly again, even during the day, and I tried everything: waiting until he was leaving, trying to find him during the breaks in school. I even called around to his house once, and every time I was about to bring up the subject, he would do something like leave the room or zap the television. It was all hopeless. But I didn't realise he had told everybody. I didn't realise that until François was staying and we were sharing a room. François' English wasn't great then. Anyway, one night, we were all in the tennis club, it was too dark to play but too early for the dancing to start. So we were all just sitting around. And there was the usual jeering or banter going on. Somebody said that François was looking for a transfer to another house and everybody sort of cheered, including the girls who were there. Is it the food, someone mockingly asked. No, someone else said. Is it Paul's oul' ma? No, someone said again. It all sounded like they had planned it. What is it then, someone shouted. It's because Paul's a queer, one of them said, and they all laughed and cheered until one of them said to François – who hadn't a clue what was going on – "Isn't that right, François?" and François, who is very polite, said "Yes" in a French accent and they all fell around laughing.

'My father's system of logic didn't mean much that night. I went home and I was already in bed when François came in. "Those boys are not your friends," he said. He tried to explain that he didn't understand what the question was, but I knew that anyway, and I told him so. He turned the light off and got into his bed. I started to cry and he came over and sat on my bed and tried to comfort me and then he lay down beside me and he said that he was my friend and we wouldn't go to the club any more. Anyway, slowly, as he lay against me, I realised that he had an erection. He put his hand inside my pyjama-top and touched my shoulder. But I'd had enough of boys with erections, so that even when he kissed me I lay there frozen. Nothing happened and he didn't do anything more. After a while he went back to his own bed.'

'And what happened then?' Helen asked.

'We became very close, especially when I went for a month to his house in France. His parents were young and he was an only child and they treated us like adults. They had a lot of time for us and they were so polite. François thought my father didn't like him because he used to banter with him all the time. But François' father always said what he meant and normally that was some-thing quite gentle and straightforward. I loved how straightforward they all were. And François was like that too, he was loyal and serious and polite. Sometimes he was also very funny, he wasn't a drip. I loved how clear he was, and how careful about everything he did and said. And I knew he liked me as well and that was amazing. His parents rented a house by the sea in Normandy and we swam and played tennis. We never touched each other, but we did things in France that we didn't do in Ireland, like we stripped off in front of each other, rather more perhaps than was necessary.'

'It sounds like true love,' Helen said.

'It was a sort of pure happiness, yeah it was,' Paul said. He stared out to sea and closed his eyes.

Helen wanted to ask him what happened next, but felt that a single question, phrased badly, could stop him now, and she desperately wanted him to go on. When he did not speak, she decided not to prompt him. Then he began again:

'François came back to Ireland when I was going into my third year in Trinity. He had changed a lot, he was taller and stockier. His face was thinner. He had new gestures and was funnier. We had corresponded over the years, but less as time went on. I had a bedsit in Dun Laoghaire but he had rooms in Trinity for the month of September, and the first night we met we found ourselves in the city with the last bus gone. I took up his offer to use the other bed in his room. It was like the old days except we were both nearly twenty. I knew that I was gay, but I had done nothing about it, except wank myself to death, if you'll excuse the language. He'd been with a guy, but only once. Anyway, that night in Trinity, we were half drunk and we made a big play of stripping off and wandering around the room. Someone had to make the first move, but it wasn't going to be me. After we'd been in bed for a while there was a silence, and then he asked me in French if he could come to my bed. I still remember the words and we often laugh at them. But I was too nervous. It was too much, I wanted him too badly, and it was all too real. I said no, but he could

167

tomorrow. I made sure he understood that I meant yes, that I wasn't just putting him off. He stretched his arm out towards me in the dark and we held hands for a while between the two beds. And then the next night we went to bed together for the first time.'

'And have you been together ever since?'

'Well, for the next two years we saw one another as often as we could, and then when I graduated I went to Paris for a year, and then we both came back here for a year. So we've been together for the past eight or nine years but the last two years have been very difficult.'

They stood up and brushed the sand off themselves and began to walk back towards Cush.

'How have they been difficult?'

'When we got together,' Paul went on, 'François' parents were just unbelievable. They bought a big double bed for us and put it in François' room. I don't think he had a single moment's problem with them about being gay. We saw them often. We usually stayed with them on a Saturday night, or saw them on Sunday. They were our best friends. And they were both killed in a car crash, killed instantly, almost two years ago, they were still in their forties. They were driving out from a side road, the car behind them crashed into them and pushed them out into the path of a lorry. And then our world fell apart. There were no close relatives as both of them were only children; there were no cousins or aunts. François was alone except for me, but after a while I was no help to him because he couldn't handle the idea that I might abandon him.

'I said I wouldn't. I tried to reassure him and I thought that soon he would be all right. He had taken time off from work, and I thought that when he went back he'd be better, but he wasn't better, and he couldn't manage – he's a civil servant – so he had to take extended leave. He believed I was going to desert him and after a while no reassurance was any use. The phone would ring at work, and the person on the other end would hang up, but I'd know that it was him checking on me. He was falling apart; he went to a counsellor and a therapist but it made no difference.

'Then I had to go to a conference in Paris. I told him way in advance that I was going, it was a job I couldn't get out of. It was a three-day conference on fisheries. I was in the translators' box on the last day and I suddenly saw François walking into the hall. He looked lost and strange, he was like someone who had gone out of his mind. All I felt was anger. I ran down and grabbed him and brought him up with me and kept him there. I was really pissed off with him, and I realised that I couldn't handle much more. Back in the hotel, I'm afraid I let a few roars at him, which I don't think I'd ever done at anyone before, and I told him he would have to pull himself together. I remember that we went to bed without speaking. We got the train back to Brussels without speaking and I realised we'd lost it.

'I thought that maybe we'd split up for a trial period and I went around with this in my head for a few days, but it was a stupid plan. I was just letting him down, I wasn't helping him, and I knew that if we split up now we'd never get back together again. So I remember one night when things were at their very worst asking him if he loved me and he said that he did. I said that I loved him as well, and I knew he was afraid of being alone, and

I told him I would do anything to prove to him that I would stay with him. I told him I would show I meant it. And I did mean it.' Paul stopped and wiped his eyes with his hands. He stood and looked at Helen.

'What did you do?' she asked.

They sat down on the hard sand under the cliff at Cush and watched the waves breaking softly and the haze on the horizon and the mild sky.

'I did two things. I brought him home and reintroduced him to all my family, including my brothers, as my partner and my lover. Only my sister knew I was gay before that, and it was all difficult and emotional. It was OK in the end, mainly because of my father, oddly enough. That was the first thing I did.'

'And what was the second?' Helen asked.

'Maybe I'm boring you with this. I'm worse than Larry.'

'No, tell me,' she said.

'So, we went back to Brussels, and every time François talked about me leaving, I just said the same thing: "I'll do anything to show you that it's not true." He still hadn't gone back to work and he was depressed, and I'd come home from the Commission and he would have been in bed all day, and he was on all sorts of pills, but I kept saying to myself that I had to try and help him. We had a photograph of his parents enlarged and framed. We selected a gravestone. We went through all their things. I just said to him all the time like a mantra: "I'll do anything to show you that it's not true. I'm not going to leave."

'Both of us were part of a group of Catholic gay men in Brussels who met on a Wednesday night. Declan used to fall about laughing at the idea, and even more when I told him some of the things that were said. He used to call it Cruising for Christ. He just couldn't believe that we went there. But anyway, we did, and we made good friends there, and I asked a few of them – I had to do this very discreetly because there were some activists in the group who were angry with the Church – I asked a few of them if there was a priest in Brussels or anywhere who would bless us. One of them was an ex-priest himself, and he told me he knew someone, and would call on him and find out and come back and tell us. He came back and said that the priest he knew was worried about being set up for a publicity stunt, so I should go and see him and tell him that this wasn't about politics or publicity.

'The priest in question was a grumpy little old man, badly shaved, with dandruff everywhere and huge bushy eyebrows. He lived in a big shabby house in a part of Brussels I'd never been in before. He was hostile, but I knew that I hadn't been sent to him for nothing. He asked me things like when was the last time I had been to Confession. I said it was years. And Communion? I said it was a long time. He let a big shout at me that I just wanted to use the Church. I had no intention of arguing with him. He said he would phone me and he hustled me out.

'A few nights later he phoned and said that he wanted to meet us in our apartment. He came and sat there and looked at the two of us. He never smiled once or was in any way friendly. He asked us questions in a really abrupt tone. And then he stood up and said he would do it on three conditions – one, that we made good confessions before the ceremony; two, that we went to Mass and Communion every Sunday for a year; and three, that we told no one. We said to him that the third was impossible, we would have to tell two people, but we would guarantee that they would tell no one – and, in fact, within a few days, we had told Declan and my sister. He mumbled something and left, and a few days later he phoned with a date and a time.

'He came to see us once more and informed us that he had something very important to say. He spelt it out carefully: he was prepared to marry us rather than conduct a blessing. He said, "I am willing to perform the sacrament of matrimony, if that is what you want." And we said that was what we wanted but we didn't think it could be done. "It can be done," he said, "but it is a grave step, and you must let me know if you have any doubts." We assured him that we wanted this. One day he rang and asked us if we were going on a honeymoon and we said that we had thought of it. "Leave a few hours free after the ceremony," he said. We booked a flight to Barcelona for later that day, which was a Saturday, and booked a posh hotel for a week. We bought suits and had haircuts. The only things missing were the photographer, the organist and the wedding guests. That morning we packed our bags and we got a taxi out to the priest's house. François couldn't stop giggling when we were waiting at the door. It was the first time he had giggled like that since his parents died and I couldn't take my eyes off him.

'The priest heard our confessions separately, and then he brought us together and asked us again if we were sure. We told him we were sure. He brought us into a small church by a side door which he then locked. The church was done in gold and when he turned on all the lights it was all rich and glittering. He changed into his vestments and said Mass and gave us Communion and then he married us. He used the word "spouse" instead of husband and wife. He had it all prepared. He was very solemn and serious. And we felt the light of the Holy Spirit on us, even though Declan thought this was the maddest thing he'd ever heard and I suppose you do too.'

'I don't think that at all,' Helen said.

'We felt that we had been singled out to receive a very special grace. All three of us knelt and prayed for a long time.'

'Why did the priest do it? What was his history?'

'We never asked and we never found out. He had a housekeeper who was nearly more dishevelled than him and just as unfriendly, but that didn't bother us after the ceremony because we were so happy. Anyway, the padre asked us to eat with him, and it was straight out of *Babette's Feast*. Have you seen that?'

'No,' she said.

'It's a film where the most sumptuous meal is made for the most unlikely people. This housekeeper brought plate after plate of pâté and lobster and prawns and stuffed everything, and then meringues and amazing cheese and a wine that the padre had removed the label from – we knew it must have cost a fortune – and champagne. Our priest barely touched it, he sat back with his hands over his little paunch like an old Christian Brother, and almost smiled. We ate what we could. He loved us cooing every time more food came, although the housekeeper who had cooked it didn't look at us once. At the end he raised his glass and said something extraordinary. He said: "Welcome to the Catholic Church." And we proposed a toast to him and his housekeeper, but he said the person to thank was not them, the person to thank was Jesus Christ. But we didn't think we could propose a toast to Jesus Christ, we felt we had pushed our luck far enough, so we nodded in agreement, and we went to the airport soon after that. When we got into bed in the hotel that night, I said, "This is our first night as man and wife," and François asked who was the man and who was the wife. "Turn off the light," I said, "and I'll show you." We laughed until we shook, and that was the beginning of a new life for us. Although François still has his bad moments, it was a turning point and we're very close now. He hates me being away like this, but he loves Declan and he understands.'

They scrambled up the cliff at Mike Redmond's and sat on the edge with the sea wide and calm and blue beneath them.

'Did you see much of Declan during all that time?' Helen asked.

'He didn't come to Brussels over the past two years, because he knew we had problems and because he wasn't well, but before that he was a regular visitor. He would come for long weekends and he'd make us hang out in bars and clubs with him, and he'd usually abandon us at a certain time and then come back home in the early hours like a half-drowned dog. My best memory of him was in the morning; he would crawl in the bottom of our bed. He was like a small boy, and he'd talk and doze and play with our feet. François always joked about adopting him; he even bought a child's pyjamas for him as a joke and folded them on his bed. François loved his visits. Usually, by Saturday afternoon, the phone would ring and some-one from Friday night, or Thursday night if Declan had come earlier, would be eager to talk to him and Declan wouldn't be interested. He checked out all our friends from the Catholic gay organisation and a few of them really fell for him – everybody fell for him – and he would bounce up and down with them for maybe two weekends, and then he'd arrive again and we'd know by something he did or said that he hadn't been returning So-and-so's calls, so we learned never to tell anyone he was coming. And then the whole routine would start again; he'd laugh about it himself. François used to say that once he went to school and met all the other toddlers he'd be all right, and Declan loved being fed and looked after and listened to and protected from his former lovers by us. He was fascinated by how we never had it off with anybody else. He was always listing out the names of actors and asking us if we'd sleep with them. He'd go "OK, Paul Newman in *Hud*," and we'd shake our heads; "Marlon Brando in *Streetcar*," and we'd still shake our heads; "Sidney Poitier in *Guess Who's Coming to Dinner?*" and we'd still shake our heads. And then he'd get fed up – he got fed up very easily – and he'd call out other names like Albert Reynolds or Le Pen or Helmut Kohl.'

★

When Paul and Helen got back to the house, they saw that Larry's car had gone and her mother's car was not there either. When they opened the kitchen door the two cats scrambled back to their vantage point. There was no one in the house.

'Do you think Declan is sick?' she asked. 'Do you think they had to take him to hospital?'

'I'll be able to tell you instantly,' he said.

175

He went to Declan's bedroom and looked into the locker beside the bed.

'No, all his drugs are here. He wouldn't have gone anywhere without them.'

'Maybe they've gone shopping,' Helen said.

She heated the soup that her grandmother had left in a saucepan beside the range and made toast and tea. She put two bowls on the table and went back to the range.

'You know that priest in Brussels?' She turned to Paul, who was sitting at the table.

'Yes?'

'Does the Pope know much about him?'

He narrowed his eyes and pointed at her. 'That is exactly the sort of thing Declan says, and he uses exactly the same tone of voice, as though butter wouldn't melt in his mouth.'

'I was just wondering,' she said.

'And I have no intention of allowing another member of your family to start. I'm sorry I told you the whole story now. It's amazing that people like you are let bring up children.' He smiled ruefully.

'Ah no, Paul, I'm sorry. I'm really sorry.'

'That's why I left this country, remarks like that. French people, even Belgian people, never talk like that.'

'You really are a sensitive boy,' she said.

'You're starting again.'

'But all the same, can you imagine if the Pope got to hear about it?'

'I'm not listening.' He put his fingers in his ears.

★

176

Later, they took deckchairs to a spot at the front of the house which still caught the sun. The day was calm, with milky clouds in the sky and a heat which had not been there in the previous few days.

'This is a beautiful place,' he said.

'I suppose it is,' she said, 'for an outsider it is maybe. I have only bad memories of it.'

'Did you ever get on with your mother and your grandmother?'

'When I was a little girl and had no choice.'

'When did you all fall out first?'

'It was years ago.'

'Over what?'

'Sometimes I'm not sure I know.'

'But when did the fighting start?'

'This doesn't look much like a guest-house,' Helen said, 'but in the old days my grandparents would move into what is now that shed, where there were two rooms. And there are, as you know, three and a half bedrooms upstairs, and two downstairs. A whole family would take over a room; the place was bedlam and they had to be fed morning, noon and night. The summer before I finished school I worked here for a month. My grandmother paid me, my mother and Declan came on Sundays and it was all fine. So I agreed to come and work again the following summer before I went to college. This time, however, my grandfather was dead and my grandmother was different. As soon as I arrived she stopped doing anything herself except bossing me around and not letting me out of her sight. I went into Blackwater one night without setting the table for the morning, and there she was waiting up for me, going on and on about how I had treated her. I know my grandfather had died not long before, but there was no need for it. I couldn't wait for the summer to be over, and by the time it was over I was exhausted.

'I loved UCD from the first moment I arrived there. I met Hugh in my first term and we started going out together, and that was great, even though there were problems because Catholic girls from Enniscorthy did not sleep with men from Donegal without a lot of persuasion. Hugh was going to America for the summer after first year with a whole crowd from Donegal, and they had guaranteed work there. He asked me to come with them and I said I would. By this time I was on the pill, you'll be glad to hear. During the Easter holidays, when I told my mother about America, she instantly became hysterical, and asked me what my grandmother was going to do. "She has a few months to find someone," I said. "And who would she find?" she asked. "Anyone she'd find would be an awful fool for putting up with her," I said. And so you can imagine the screaming and shouting and the letters that followed me to Dublin in case I had not properly understood. She didn't threaten to cut me off, or anything like that, but it was all full of stuff about my father and my grandfather and the two of them – my mother and my grandmother – left alone now and needing the support of those around them, and instead finding themselves insulted and let down by one of the people they loved most. It was all sick. And I gave in. I told Hugh I couldn't go, and when I arrived here the old witch wouldn't speak to me. And the place coming down with guests. If I asked her a simple question, she'd ignore me. And for the first month the only food she bought was ham, boiled in the middle of the day with potatoes and cabbage, in a sweltering July, and cold with a half a tomato and a few leaves of lettuce at six o'clock. The guests – some of them were the lowest forms of life – used to groan when I appeared with the food.

'Granny and I began to leave lists on the kitchen table, as a way of letting each other know that we had run out of eggs or toilet paper. One day, when there was about a week to go, she left a bar of chocolate on my pillow. That was the signal that the cold war was coming to an end. By the time I was going back she was addressing some civil words to me. And the worst part was that I went back the following year as well.

'A few days after I arrived back in UCD at the end of the first summer, I was walking down the stairs of the canteen, and I saw Hugh sitting there with a group. He glanced away and pretended he didn't see me. I thought at least he would wave and wander over to meet me and we'd have coffee together, even though I'd only had a single postcard from him all summer. All his crowd had been to America, they had money now and confidence, you'd notice them on the campus. This little mouse, on the other hand, ran scared of her grandmother, had no new clothes, was back in Loreto Hall, run by nuns, had lost her boyfriend and wouldn't meet him again for three or four years, but got used to nodding to him discreetly on the way into the library. He was always on his way somewhere. I became very interested in my studies.'

'And did you say', Paul asked, 'that you came back here the following year?'

'I knew it would be the last time, because the year after that I was sitting my finals in the autumn, but it didn't make it any easier or any better. That year, of course, she was talking to me, and if she annoyed me in any way I spoke to her in that same clear, reasonable way I use with teachers now, and she found that almost impossible to deal with.'

'Yes, it must have been very frightening,' Paul said. They both laughed.

'I missed my chance. I would love to have had those two summers in America and I learned nothing here except this awful bitterness against the two of them, my granny and my mother. And that meant that I was ready for them the next time.'

'What was the next time?' Paul asked.

'I did my Dip. hours in Synge Street, and the Brothers offered me a job and I accepted it. I had also done a course in English as a Foreign Language, and I found work for the summer teaching Spanish students. I told my mother and my grandmother this news way in advance – not the full-time job story, but the summer teaching story. This meant I was in Dublin, I had money, I worked in the mornings, I had a dingy room that I loved at the top of a building in Baggot Street, with a view right down to the Pigeonhouse. I have good memories of that summer, the freedom of it. The area has changed a lot, but up to a certain time in the evening you could go into the Pembroke or Doheny & Nesbitt's or Toner's and nobody would bother you. But I knew my mother and my grandmother thought I was coming home to teach, and I wasn't, but I hadn't told them I wasn't.

'Earlier in the year, my mother had told me that she would ask about vacancies in the schools in Wexford or anywhere around, including Enniscorthy. I remember that

I was really careful to say nothing. I didn't want to have the argument then. I never told them about the job in Synge Street. Then in July I had a letter from her to say that there was good news, it was all arranged and Mother Teresa would be delighted to have me from September. I would need to go for a formal interview, but it wouldn't be a problem.'

'Can you give jobs out like that?' Paul asked.

'You can do what you like when you run a religious school. So I wrote back and told her I had a job, thank you. And then the next day the two of them arrived up to Dublin; they were waiting in the car outside my door in Baggot Street, white-faced both of them, when I arrived home after work. There I was, sauntering along Baggot Street on a beautiful summer's day, only to find these two madwomen sitting in the car taking up valuable parking space. They wouldn't come in; they marched me to the Shelbourne Hotel, and I noticed on the way there that they had both dressed up for the occasion. They sat me down and, as they would put it, tried to talk some sense into me. Two summers of drudgery had me ready for them. It was all Mother Teresa this and Mother Teresa that. "I have a job," I said. "I don't need a job." "You've been in Dublin long enough now," my grandmother said. "You have your qualifications and you'll come home now like your father and your mother did. God knows your mother wants to put her feet up for a while." I realised that the plan was that I would skivvy for my mother the way I had done for my granny, perhaps even commute between them. They had brought notepaper and envelopes with them, and they wanted me to write a letter to Synge Street saying that I would not be accepting their job and to Mother Teresa saying that I would be available for interview at her convenience.

'I told them I was writing nothing. They were fussing with the tea things as though they were Lady Muck and ordering more sandwiches. "You'd be much better among your own people," my granny said. "Everyone is to stop bossing me around," I told them. "No one's bossing you around," my mother said. "We're both very busy and we've both come up all the way to try and talk some sense to you." You should have heard them both, and all they wanted, of course, was to be driven here and driven there, and have messages collected and dinners cooked. And where was Declan during all of this? He was on his first summer holidays after his first year doing Pharmacy in college and what was he doing? Was he washing out the floor of his grandmother's so-called guest-house? No, he was working as a ticket seller in a cinema in Leicester Square in London, and he was, as he will tell you himself, having the time of his life.'

'I know all about it,' Paul said.

'The two of them said that they weren't going to let me throw away a good chance like this. I listened for a while more and then I took my handbag and my cardigan and I went to the ladies' and then I walked out of the hotel into the street. I bought an English newspaper and I went over to Sinnott's in South King Street and I sat in the snug drinking a Club orange and reading my paper. And I suppose at some stage they went home. And that was the end of that.'

'And when did you see them next?' Paul asked.

'I haven't really seen them since,' Helen said.

'But you must have.'

'I saw them the following Christmas because Declan called to my flat and implored me to come down with him, which I did. The reception was very frosty. I nearly spat when they tried to stop him doing half the washing-up with me. And I came down again the Christmas after that. And I got used to not seeing them, and I found that not seeing them made me much happier, and I became interested in my own happiness.

'I didn't tell them I was getting married and I didn't tell them when the boys were born. Hugh's family love weddings, and they couldn't believe there wasn't going to be a big wedding, but we got married quietly in a registry office in Dublin and then there was a big party in Donegal.'

'Why didn't you want them at your wedding?' Paul asked.

'I would have hated their two faces looking at me. That's all. I told Declan and he told them. And I told Declan when I was pregnant and I suppose he told them that too. But my mother has never met Hugh or the boys.'

'And how long have you been married?'

'Seven years.'

'I knew it was a long time. It's a long time not to see people you're close to. But did something not happen last summer?' Paul asked.

'Declan organised a big reconciliation last summer,' Helen said. 'I came down here for a night with Hugh and the boys, and my mother was to drive out from Wexford, but she never turned up. My granny was full of apologies for her. And then I think they all gave her such a hard time that she rang me and we met in town one

Saturday in Brown Thomas, if you don't mind, and she bought me the most expensive coat in the shop. And she bought presents for the boys as well and they wrote her thank-you letters. And the plan was that we were all going to drive down here again later this summer for a repeat of last summer, except this time she would turn up.'

'Do you mean that this has been going on for ten years and all because of this row in the Shelbourne?' Paul asked.

'Yes, that's correct,' Helen said stiffly.

'Has it ever occurred to you that they wanted you home because they loved you?'

'No, it has not. That is not why they wanted me home.'

'Has it ever occurred to you that your mother would have been worried about you going to America with people she didn't know?'

'Whose side are you on?' Helen asked.

'I don't understand the reason you didn't want them at your wedding and the reason you didn't see them for so long. What you've told me isn't reason enough.'

'I was angry with them for the reasons I told you.'

They heard a car in the lane. When Helen looked at her watch she saw that it was almost five o'clock. Larry and her grandmother smiled and waved as they drove into the yard in front of the house, but Paul continued talking.

'They just tried to get you a job,' he said. 'If you'd said that you didn't see them much for a year, I'd have understood, or two years. But a whole ten years and you didn't let your children meet your mother and your grandmother! Wow, there must be something between the three of you, something . . .'

Paul stopped as Larry stood in front of them. The old lady was taking a bag from the car.

'I don't know what he's saying,' Larry said, 'but he has that funny, pompous, know-all look on his face. I saw it as soon as I drove around, and if I were you, Helen, I'd get away while I could. I'll distract him and you just run. People have been known to go crazy just listening to him. Look at the self-righteous set of his chin. God! Aren't you lucky we came along!'

'One of the reasons I left Ireland', Paul said and stood up, 'was to get away from this sniping and sneering and cheap stupidity.'

He went over to the car and helped Mrs Devereux into the house with her shopping.

'Sorry,' Larry said. 'I didn't know why it needed to be said. It just needed to be said.'

'Where were you?' Helen asked.

'We went for a trip to Wexford, looked at bathrooms and ended up like all good married couples in the supermarket. Incidentally, what was he saying to you?'

'He was talking about reasons.'

'Yeah, he's good on reasons. Has your mother gone to Wexford?'

'She's gone with Declan somewhere. We thought you might have gone together in convoy.'

'No, they were here when we left.'

★

Helen drank a strong cup of coffee in the kitchen as the others wandered about. She noticed Paul looking at her, and she wanted, now more than any other time in the previous few days, to be away from his interrogation, and to be away altogether from this house. She was uneasy with what had happened between them; Paul had told her the truth about himself and she had been evasive. There was something now that she needed to put words on, something she needed to hear herself saying. She made herself another cup of coffee and when Paul left the room she followed him. She could feel her heart thumping. She stopped him at the bottom of the stairs. 'I need to talk to you,' she said. She motioned him to follow her into the back bedroom. When they were in the room she closed the door. She sat on the bed and he stood close to the window.

'You asked me about my mother and my grandmother and I told you things, but there are other things I left out that are harder to understand, and maybe I should try. I feel bad because you were so honest and open with me.'

'I knew there was something else,' Paul said. 'I hope I didn't offend you by saying so.'

'No, you didn't offend me.' She drank her coffee and began to talk.

'About seven or eight years ago I worked as a career guidance and home liaison officer in a new comprehensive school on the west side of Dublin. There was a girl in the school, a student, who used to cut herself. She was about fifteen. She'd cut parts of her body that no one could see. A friend of hers came and told me, and then I met her and asked her, and eventually, after a lot of tears and denials, she told me it was true. I had to get involved in her case, even though I had no experience. So I spoke to her parents, but it was no use. There was a strange atmosphere in the house when I went to visit. It was all new to me, I was a nice middle-class girl, and there was silence and fear mixed with poverty and a sort of contempt for people like me. And the girl herself was a mystery. She was so bright in class, the teachers said, and so poised and intelligent in the sessions which I had with her.

'The only thing she would not do was talk about what she was doing to herself. I found her a psychiatrist who was in the public health system because I felt that other help was needed if she was to be all right. I thought maybe if we talked to her and made her realise that she must stop before it all went too far, she might be better. I know that sounds stupid. I was learning then and I listened a lot to the psychiatrist, who was a man in his fifties with a beard who was always in his stockinged feet. He told me that it would take time to help the girl, that we were dealing with something fundamental, something that could not be easily dislodged.

'I took the girl to and from the sessions, and I spoke to her about what was happening, and I spoke to the psychiatrist. And it all made me think about myself, why I felt no need to make up with my mother or my grandmother, that I had put away parts of myself that were damaged and left them rotting. When my father died, half my world collapsed, but I did not know this had happened. It was as though half my face had been blown away and I kept talking and smiling, thinking that it had not happened, or that it would grow back. When my father died I was left alone by my mother and grandmother. I know that they had their own problems and maybe they could not have helped, maybe even the damage was already done, but I got no comfort or consolation from them. And these two women are the parts of myself that I have buried, that is who they are for me, both of them, and that is why I still want them away from me.'

Helen's voice was hard and low. Her hand was shaking.

'My mother taught me never to trust anyone's love because she was always on the verge of withdrawing her own. I associated love with loss, that's what I did. And the only way that I could live with Hugh and bring up my children was to keep my mother and my grandmother away from me.

'I knew that it was wrong, I knew that I could not go on for ever like this, but I did not have the courage to confront them or even see them. And now that we're all here, you watch them: they are pulling me back in. So what's going on between me and them is not about how I spent my summer holidays when I was a student or where I got a job.

'I am telling you this only because you asked me. But I am not looking for sympathy or help, because Declan needs that from all of us. Someone else would probably have softened, but I haven't softened. We have to put up with these people, my mother and my grandmother, and be polite to them because Declan is here. So we should go into the kitchen and see if he has come back.'

Helen was pale when she finished talking. Paul put his arms around her and held her until she was calm again.

'I'm caught between wanting to make up with them and wanting to get away from them,' Helen said. 'But actually what I would really like to do, if you insist on hearing . . .' She smiled.

'I insist,' he said, ruefully.

'I would really love to run my mother over in the car, that's what I would really like to do.' She laughed sourly and opened the door.

★

At about eight o'clock Declan and her mother came back. From the dining-room window, Helen watched her helping him from the car. She and Paul went to the front door.

'He wants to go to the bathroom,' her mother said.

'Was there a problem?' Paul asked.

'Not until we were driving home, and then he was sick in the car.'

'I'll clean it,' Paul said.

'Sorry about that, Paul,' Declan said. He began to make his way upstairs to the bathroom.

'It was a very sad day, Helen,' her mother said. 'We were talking about the house and the garden, and it was always something I planned for him, that he would come down at weekends and take an interest in it. He has only ever been down once. But he saw it all today and he was so good. I brought him into the offices; he hadn't seen them since they were refurbished. I had to leave instructions for next week.'

Declan shouted down the stairs for fresh underwear and clothes, which his mother went to get. Helen remained surprised, almost shocked, at the tone her mother had taken with her just now, which was instantly confiding and intimate. It was like tasting something not consumed since childhood, or smelling something not encountered for twenty years. It brought anxiety with it as much as reassurance.

189

In the kitchen her grandmother was sitting by the window looking out, with the two cats on her lap. On seeing Helen, they immediately jumped and sat on the top of the dresser, although Larry had been in the room all the while.

'Some people like cats, and cats like some people, but they're not always the same people,' her grandmother said.

'Did you buy anything in Wexford then?' Helen asked.

'Oh, we've fresh everything, fresh bread, fresh eggs, fresh fish and fresh meat. All from the supermarket. "You'd swear", I said to Larry on the way home, "that we lived on a farm by the sea."'

Paul came and stood at the door. 'Declan says he wants to go for a short walk at Ballyconnigar. He says he wants to get being sick in the car out of his system. His mother is going to come.'

Larry and Helen agreed that they would also join the walk.

'Tell them I'll stay here,' Mrs Devereux said, 'and ask them if they want salmon or lamb chops for dinner. Explain how fresh everything is.'

Declan said he did not think he would eat much, but he'd try the salmon. The old lady came and watched as Helen, her mother and Declan got into Declan's car and Larry and Paul got into Larry's car. She waved at them as they turned in the yard.

'Helen,' her mother said from the back of the car, 'I wish you'd talk to her about looking after herself. Even getting in a proper telephone, any small thing would be a great improvement.'

'My husband says there's no getting around the women in our family,' Helen said.

'But he doesn't know us,' her mother said.

'I've told him about you,' Helen said.

Suddenly she looked up and saw her mother's face in the rear-view mirror; her eyes seemed magnified and unguarded and vulnerable, nervously watching her. She was tempted for one second to slow down and turn to see if the mirror were making her mother's eyes like that, or if they would appear like that too if she saw them directly. When Helen looked again, her mother's eyes were cast down.

They stopped in Keatings' car park in Ballyconnigar, Larry and Paul parking in the space behind them. They got out of the cars and walked across the small wooden bridge and moved south in the half-fading light. Tuskar lighthouse had started and they stood and watched as a beam circled towards them.

'There used to be two lighthouses here,' her mother said. 'I don't know what they needed the other for, but I suppose the Irish Sea was busy and bits of it were dangerous. It was just out there now – no, a bit further north, towards Cush and your granny's house. Do you remember it, Helen?'

'I do, Mammy, but only when we were children.'

'It was taken out of commission by Irish Lights. I don't know exactly when,' her mother said.

'What was it called?' Paul asked.

'It was called the Blackwater Lightship. It was weaker than Tuskar. Tuskar was built on a rock to last, I suppose. Still, I loved there being two. I suppose the technology

191

got better, and maybe there's not as much shipping as there was. The Blackwater Lightship. I thought it would always be there.'

Slowly, they walked towards Ballyvaloo. Helen eased close to her mother. The three others moved ahead, Larry and Paul with Declan between them, quietly protecting him. Helen noticed that the beam of the lighthouse did not flash when she calculated it should. Each time she expected it to come too quickly.

'When I was young, lying in bed in your granny's house,' her mother said, 'I used to believe that Tuskar was a man and the Blackwater Lightship was a woman and they were both sending signals to each other and to other lighthouses, like mating calls. He was forceful and strong and she was weaker but more constant, and sometimes she began to shine her light before darkness had really fallen. And I thought they were calling to each other; it was very satisfying, him being strong and her being faithful. Can you imagine, Helen, a little girl lying in bed thinking that? And all that turned out not to be true. You know, I thought your father would live for ever. So I learned things very bitterly.' When Helen looked down, she saw that her mother was clenching her fists. 'If I could meet him here for one minute now, your father, you know, even if he were to be allowed to pass us on the strand here, here now, when it's nearly night. And not speak, just take us in with his eyes. If he was only to know, or see, or acknowledge with a flicker of his eyes what is happening to us. This is just morbid talk, don't mind me, but it's what I think about when I look at Tuskar lighthouse.

'We should go back now,' her mother went on, 'we're

all hungry, I'm sure, and we've had a long day, Declan and myself, and I'm sure you've had a long day too.'

The five of them turned and walked back towards the small river which changed its course through the sand each year. There was no one else on the strand now; it was too late for walkers or bathers, and theirs were the only cars in the car park. Helen was surprised when Declan travelled with his friends and left her alone with her mother. He must have been talking to their mother about her, she thought, must have been trying to bring them together. They were together now, Helen thought, and it was awkward. She started the car and then waited for Larry's car to start up. She moved slowly behind it, the lights full on, and they drove back towards Cush as the night settled down.

★

As soon as she got back, Helen grew restless and wondered if she could find an excuse to drive back to Dublin now. This new softness in her mother was impossible to resist. She felt that her mother was waiting to approach her again with a soothing voice and a tone of easy intimacy. She could not bear it. She took the keys of Declan's car, slipped out of the house and drove into Blackwater.

She dialled Hugh's number from the callbox in the village. When his mother answered the phone, Helen's asking for Hugh was so urgent that she called him immediately and did not make conversation.

'Are things all right?' Hugh asked.

'No, they're not. I'm desperate to get out of here.'

'How's Declan?' he asked.

'There's no change.'

'The boys are fast asleep,' Hugh said.

'It was mad me not going with you. I'll never do that again. I don't think I can leave them like that again.'

'Helen, it's just a few days.'

'How can you tell whether they're all right or not?'

'Of course I can tell,' Hugh said. 'They're fine. They're on their holidays. They know they'll see you soon.'

'When my father was sick, they all thought it was OK to leave us down here too.'

'There's one big difference,' Hugh said. 'I'm their father, I'm with them. You're talking about them as though I don't exist. I'm looking out for them all day.'

Helen listened and said nothing.

'What you have to do,' Hugh continued, 'is imagine how it would have been all those years ago if your father had been with you. And you mustn't sound worried when you talk to the boys, or they'll get worried too. At the moment they haven't a bother on them. And if there were the slightest problem, I'd tell you.'

'Maybe it's myself I'm worried about. Maybe I'm just afraid to tell you that.'

'I'm here all the time and I'll come down if you want me to, even just for a day.'

'The worst part of it is that my mother is going all soft on me.'

'That sounds like good news.'

'Stop making everything seem good.'

'What are you going to do? Are you going to stay?'

'I'll stay for another day,' she said. 'And I'll call you again in the morning. It's good to talk to you.'

SEVEN

That night before he went to sleep Declan asked them to put another bed in his room; Larry and Paul found a camp bed upstairs which they dismantled and took downstairs and put together again beside Declan's bed. Helen came in and sat on a chair and watched them as they made it up.

'Do you want me to sleep here?' she asked Declan.

'Maybe. I don't know. Sometimes I wake and it's not easy.'

'You can call me. I'm just in the next room.'

'They'd all wake, or you'd think there was something wrong.'

'No I wouldn't. Call me if you need company. Cathal and Manus wake me all the time.'

'Do they never wake their daddy?'

'Sometimes,' she said and smiled, 'but their daddy is a great sleeper.'

'Anyway, I'm going to take a Xanax tonight, so I'll probably be all right. If I'm not, Paul or Larry can sleep here.'

'Is Mammy smothering you with attention?' Helen asked.

'She's finding it all very tough. She's jealous that I

didn't want to come to her house. She brought me there today to show me where she would have me sleeping and how much space there was for my friends. No mention of you. But it won't be long before she has a room for you, too. I have a new word to describe her which I picked up from Paul.'

'What's the word?' Helen asked.

'The word is "needy",' Declan said. 'She's needy and she never was that before. I mean she's become needy over the past year or so.'

'Earlier, when we walked on the strand,' Helen said, 'she was different, she was mellow and sort of sad, and I feel she's going to embrace me and all I can do is cringe, but otherwise she's been a complete bitch to Paul and Larry.'

'Yeah, they can't get over it. But Granny is making up for it, isn't she?'

'Granny', Helen said, 'is all charm.'

★

Larry woke Helen in the night to say that Declan needed company. For the length of a breath she could have been twenty years younger, moving hastily from her room to his. It was just a flash, but it was real and almost perfect; she was surprised at how little the memory disturbed her, how natural the connection seemed.

She put on a pullover and went and sat by Declan's bed.

'Now I feel I've woken the whole house,' he said. 'The Xanax has worn off. There's no point in trying another.'

Larry had been sleeping on the camp bed. Now he

and Declan lay on their beds, each with his hands behind his head, while Helen sat on the edge of Declan's bed. They listened to the distant roar of the sea and the moths' brittle wings against the window-pane, but they said nothing. Helen was tired and she wondered what they would say if she said that she wanted to go back to sleep.

'I'd love to have a real house to go back to – you know, a house of my own,' Declan said. 'Somewhere bright and clean.'

'Even an apartment?' Helen asked.

'Even an apartment,' he said.

'Why don't we find you one next week?' she asked.

'No, I mean that was my own, that I had painted and furnished myself.'

'But we'll do that,' Helen said. 'We'll paint it and furnish it, and it will be all bright and clean.'

'Maybe,' Declan said. 'What do you think, Larry?'

'I'm all for it,' Larry said.

Helen made tea in the kitchen and was joined by Lily, who wanted to know if everything was all right. She gave her mother a mug of tea and told her that Declan was almost asleep and it would be a mistake for her to disturb him. When Helen had drunk her tea, she felt even more sleepy.

'I'm going to bed for a while,' she said. 'Wake me if you want me. I'll drive to Dublin and rent you an apartment and furnish it and decorate it, if you want, Declan. You should think about it.'

★

She did not wake until nine in the morning. She wished there was a back door to the house so that she could

197

sneak out to the car and drive to Blackwater, make her phone call and buy the paper without having to consult anyone. Instead, she would have to go into the kitchen and brave them all. It struck her for a moment how simple Hugh and Cathal and Manus were compared to these people, how settled their relationships, how easy and modest their requirements. In the kitchen now, she was sure, as she got out of bed and went on tiptoe to the bathroom, warring factions were already at work, strange demands and alliances, energies that no one could understand. Soon she would leave, she thought, if only for a day or two, and once she began to imagine a possible escape she felt satisfied, more secure in her mind.

It was Saturday now. Declan was already up, sitting in the chair beside the Aga, taking his drugs. Larry was doing the dishes, the rest of them were sitting at the kitchen table.

'I'm going into the village to get the paper,' Helen said.

'We already have the paper, thank you,' her grandmother said.

'I have to phone Hugh.'

'You phoned Hugh last night,' her mother said.

'I'm going into the village,' Helen said firmly.

'Helen always does what she sets out to do,' her grandmother said.

'I'll come with you,' Larry said, his hands covered in suds.

'No, I'm going now and on my own and I won't be long,' Helen said. She closed the kitchen door behind her.

She knew that Declan had given up his flat in Dublin, but it had not occurred to her until now that this left him at everyone's mercy. Surely they could rent him a comfortable apartment somewhere in Dublin with a garden and large windows. She knew that it would be better if her mother thought of this and did all the organisation. When she went back, she would try to plant the idea in her mother's mind.

Hugh was still in bed when she rang, but the boys were up; she asked Hugh's mother if she could talk to them.

Cathal came first to the phone.

'How are you?' she asked.

'Fine,' he said quietly.

'You were in bed early last night,' she said.

'I think so.'

'Are you having a good time?'

'Yes.' He sounded subdued.

'Is your bed comfortable?' she asked.

'Yes.'

'I'll be up soon, so you'll be able to show me all the sights.'

'Do you want to talk to Manus? He's trying to grab the phone,' Cathal said.

'OK, and tell your father I rang.'

Manus came on the phone. 'We're going fishing,' he said.

'For what?' she asked.

'For all morning,' he replied.

'Is your daddy asleep?' she asked.

'He's not coming. Uncle Joe is coming.'

'Have you got a fishing rod?'

'We're allowed to use the ones here. But we have to go now.'

'You sound very busy,' she said.

'Will you ring again later?' he asked. He was trying to sound like an adult.

'Yes, I will.' She laughed. 'I'll ring again later.'

Manus put down the phone.

Helen bought the paper and sat in the car on the bridge reading the headlines, turning the pages. She looked through the section *Apartments to Let*, and realised that her mother would relish this work, dealing with landlords and leases.

Lily was in the lane when she returned. On seeing Helen she waved, as if to flag her down. Helen let the car roll down the hill towards her.

'Declan's gone blind in one eye,' her mother said.

Helen parked the car and went with her mother into the house. Declan was sitting exactly where he had been in the kitchen.

'What happened?' Helen asked.

'I felt over the past while that I was losing the sight in it, and now it's gone. It was always going to go, but the other one's fine, the other one's taken care of. I've explained it all.'

'Helen, tell him we should call the doctor,' her mother said.

'Declan, we should call the doctor,' Helen said.

'There's nothing the doctor can do,' Declan said. 'Ask Paul, he's the expert.'

'Paul isn't a doctor,' his mother said.

'He's read a big book and he knows all about the new therapies. Ask him,' Declan said.

Paul was sitting at the kitchen table.

'I have a few books out in the car. I'll show them to you if you want, but everything Declan is saying is true.'

'He's as calm,' his grandmother said. 'Look at him. I'd be tearing my hair out.'

'I've done all that,' Declan said. 'And I'm not calm. I only look calm.'

'There's a good eye man in Waterford,' his grandmother said.

'It's not the end of the world,' Declan said. 'I just have one eye, but I can see fine. Does the left one look a bit funny?'

'No, it looks perfectly normal,' Helen said.

'Yeah, well I'm going back to bed to sleep on it. If I lose my nose or my mouth or one of my toes, I'll let you all know.'

'Have you taken all your pills?' his mother asked.

He stopped and looked at her.

'You sound exactly like my mother,' he said.

*

'Is this serious?' Lily asked Paul when Declan had left the room.

'No, he's right about it, it's been coming for the last while. It's the end of something, rather than the beginning. They'll check the other eye more closely now, but they won't be able to do that until next week.'

'Should we not just let the doctor know?' Lily asked.

'On a Saturday morning? No, we should leave her alone.'

'Oh, I got a terrible fright when he said it,' his grandmother said. 'It's the one thing I dread. Your eyes are your most precious possessions. And Declan has the most beautiful eyes. His father, God rest him, had beautiful eyes as well. Lily used to go on and on to me about his eyes.'

'Declan's going to be buried with him now,' Lily said.

'I think Declan wants to be cremated,' Larry said.

'Oh, no one down here has ever been cremated,' Mrs Devereux said.

'Well, he says he wants to be cremated,' Larry said.

'No, he'll be buried like all the rest of them,' Mrs Devereux said. 'I wonder what put it into his head about cremation.'

No one spoke until there was the sound of a door banging upstairs.

'Oh God, listen to that! Oh God, listen!' Mrs Devereux said, standing up.

'What's wrong, Mammy? What's wrong?' Lily asked.

'You remember it well, Lily. My mother and my sister Statia were great believers in it. And that banging door just reminded me of it now. Two knocks would come to the door before someone in the family died. I heard it clearly the night before Statia died. And I woke your father and said we may get up now and drive into Bree because that's the sign for Statia. I got it for my mother, God rest her, we all got it.'

'Did you get it for my father?' Helen asked.

'No; I was just thinking, I didn't. Ah, it's part of the old ways, you'd hear no one talking about that any more, none of the neighbours. And there were other families like ours who had it too, a special warning that someone was dying. It was a gift, I suppose, but there's no one believes in it any more. It's died out.'

'But you did believe it?' Paul asked.

'I did believe it,' Mrs Devereux said. 'I do believe it. I know that I heard it when my mother was dying and I heard it when Statia was dying, but I haven't heard it since, I don't think. I don't know what it is about now, but whatever it is, something like that wouldn't have the same meaning. I don't know what it is.'

'And did you think the door banging upstairs was a sound like that?' Helen asked.

'It just reminded me of it, that's all,' Mrs Devereux said and walked over to the window and looked through the curtains.

Helen noticed her mother saying nothing, seeming disturbed. She wanted to ask her if she too had heard this sound in the past, but decided not to.

'One of the things about having children,' her mother said as though she had not been listening to them, as though involved instead in another conversation, 'is that you fear for them so much. I always felt with Declan that he wasn't able for things. He'd wake easily and cry easily and he was afraid of school and he got sick easily. And when I saw him going anywhere on his own, I always felt that he needed more strength than he had, or someone to watch out for him. The feeling never left me. Helen was always leading the other kids around. You never had to worry about her. But Declan, I've never stopped worrying about him.'

'He'll sleep for a while, Lily,' Mrs Devereux said. 'I don't think he slept very well last night.'

'Where does he stay in Dublin?' Helen asked.

'He stays with Larry, or with a friend of ours, Georgina, who has a big house,' Paul said.

'That's something we could do, isn't it, Mammy?' Helen said. 'We could find him his own place.'

Her mother nodded distractedly; clearly she wanted to talk more about Declan as a child or wanted to avoid talking about the warning knocks to the door when someone was dying. Helen knew that she had raised the subject at the wrong time, and now it would be hard to raise it again.

★

Declan slept for some of the morning and then woke complaining of a stomach pain. It had begun to drizzle outside as Helen and Larry changed the sheets and pillowcases for him; he sat and shivered in the chair in his room.

'Declan, if you want us to get you an apartment or a small house in Dublin, just say it, say it in front of Mammy, and we'll do it, we'll get it this week.'

'Thanks, Hellie,' Declan said. 'I'll think about it.'

He sank back into the bed and moaned. The bruise around his nose seemed to grow darker every day. 'Leave me,' he said. 'I'll try and sleep again.'

'No,' Helen said; 'you should try and stay awake so you can sleep tonight. Let us stay with you for a bit.'

'OK, bossy-boots,' he said, laughing, 'but I might sleep.'

Larry brought him the *Irish Times* and Declan leafed through it and then left it down. Larry sat at the bottom of the bed and told Declan and Helen all his plans for making the house more comfortable for their grandmother.

As the afternoon went on, Declan began to go to the toilet at fifteen-minute intervals and came back looking drained. He still had the pain in his stomach, he said. Helen and Larry sat with him while Paul hovered in the room outside. The older women stayed in the kitchen.

'It's a funny thing about the eye,' Declan said. 'It's a relief to have it all over. I used to see all sorts of floaters in front of it, but now I see nothing. That part is finished, anyway.'

The others nodded. It was hard to think what to say in response. After a while, Helen went into the kitchen and left Paul to take her place.

Her mother was in mid-sentence when Helen opened the door. She stopped, and put her cup down.

'Say it to her,' her grandmother said. 'Say it out.'

'Say what?' Helen asked.

'No, I was just saying, Helen,' her mother said, 'I would have loved a daughter who cared a lot about clothes and furnishings and colour schemes and all that. You know, when you came into my house the other day, I would have loved if you had made suggestions about colours or where to put things. I'd love if you had come into my bedroom and looked at my wardrobe and picked out some dress or suit that I never wear, or some jacket, and admired it.'

'It's a new daughter you need then,' Helen said. 'With all your money, why don't you buy one?'

'No, Helen, you're being too hard,' her grandmother said. 'She was just saying that you don't have a great interest in clothes.'

'I'd love if you were the sort of daughter who'd come down and see me and take an interest in my house and my garden and my clothes,' her mother said.

'Your house is very nice,' Helen said coldly.

'Declan loved my garden and was full of ideas yesterday as to how to improve it,' Lily said.

'It's a pity I'm not Declan,' Helen said.

'How is he?' her grandmother asked.

'He's starting to get bad diarrhoea,' Helen said.

'God, the poor man,' her grandmother said. 'You know we should kneel down now and say a decade of the Rosary for him.'

'You can leave me out of that, Granny, if you don't mind,' Helen said.

'I'll say the Rosary with you later, Mammy,' Lily said.

'Oh, I'll pray on my own. I don't know what's got into the two of you.'

'Mammy,' Helen said, 'I'd love if one of my sons was a really good musician – his father would love it too, but they're not, neither of them, and we just have to live with them as they are. I suppose I wish one of them had been a girl, I'd like to have had a daughter, but I don't think about it. I wish you'd been satisfied with me at some stage, even though I'm not what you wanted. I wish you'd stop wishing I was someone else.'

'Helen, I've always accepted you,' her mother said.

'That's a lovely word for it, thanks,' Helen said.

'Helen and Lily, stop the two of you and make up,' Mrs Devereux said.

★

Later in the afternoon when Paul came into the kitchen, he looked worried.

'It's very difficult to get rid of diarrhoea once it starts,' he said. 'He's taken a few things to stop it, but they don't seem to be having an effect.'

'What should we do?' Helen asked.

'Hope it goes, but if it continues into tomorrow he'll have to go back to St James's.'

'Is it something he ate?' Mrs Devereux asked.

'No; he's had problems with his stomach for the last year,' Paul said. He went out and the three women sat at the kitchen table.

'He knows it all, that young man,' Lily said.

'I think he's been through a lot more with Declan than we have,' Helen said.

'I don't think there's ever any substitute for your own family,' Lily said.

Helen wondered if everything her mother said was designed to irritate and provoke her.

'Declan has been very lucky with his friends,' Helen said.

'And not so lucky with others,' Lily said.

'What do you mean?' Helen asked.

'Well, there must be people who led him astray. I wonder where they are now.'

'I don't think he needed much leading,' Helen said.

'When Declan left my house, he was a young man anyone would be proud of,' Lily said.

'He was also gay,' Helen said.

'The two of you will have to be separated,' Mrs Devereux said.

'But isn't it funny that his two friends are healthy and he's sick? It's easy for them being around him now,' Lily said.

'I don't know what you mean,' Helen said.

'Your grandmother told me that one of them gave a very vulgar account of himself. He's lucky I was in the other room. I would have run him out of here. And you all laughed and egged him on!' Lily said.

'Including Granny,' Helen said.

'Oh Helen, when I thought about it afterwards, I imagined your grandfather and things like that being said in this room,' her grandmother said.

Helen addressed her mother directly: 'It was funny, and you weren't here for it and you missed it and there's no point in making moralistic comments about it.'

'Listen to the teacher with her class,' Lily said.

'You'll just have to learn to tolerate people,' Helen said. 'And it seems really odd to me that you can talk about what sort of daughter you'd like to have had in front of me.'

'Would you rather that I did it behind your back?' her mother asked.

'Yes I would, actually,' Helen said.

'I just wish you'd take an interest in me and my life,' Lily said.

Helen noticed her mother's face changing, as it had done in the car the previous evening. Suddenly, she seemed vulnerable, desolate, as though she were waiting for the one remark to which she would have no reply. Her eyes were filling with tears.

'Mammy, I will do that,' Helen said. 'When all this is over, I will do that, but you'll have to stop wishing I was somebody else.'

'And I'd love to meet your children and Hugh,' her mother said.

'The younger one is a little terror,' her grandmother said.

'I'm sure they'd love you, Mammy,' Helen said.

'Oh would they, Helen? I don't think they would.' Lily began to cry. Mrs Devereux came and put her arm around her shoulder.

'I'm sure they would, Mammy,' Helen said again.

Lily wiped her eyes and took out a mirror and began to reapply her eye make-up. Helen could see that she was getting ready to say something else. 'The fact that you didn't ask us to your wedding', Lily began again, 'is not nothing, not just something we missed for a few hours one day. We never saw you smiling and happy, having something you wanted, being with someone who loved you and who you loved. We never even saw photographs of it, if there were any photographs. And we never saw you with your babies. We missed all of that.'

The crying and the sympathy, Helen saw, had given her mother strength and courage. She spoke as though she believed that no one would contradict her, or reply to her. Helen sat back and smiled before she spoke.

'I didn't want you at my wedding. It was important for me that you would not sponsor me, or take credit for me, when it had nothing to do with you. You had all my life to see me smiling and happy, and since you took no notice of me in private, I wasn't going to have you make a big play of me in public. But I do agree with you that it's not nothing.'

'You've said enough to each other now,' Mrs Devereux said. 'Helen, I've never known a child who was as loved as you were by both your father and your mother, who was brought everywhere and given everything. They would come down here on a Sunday and their biggest boast would be that you had walked two steps, or said a word, or grown your teeth. I've never known a child who got as much attention as you.'

'Sorry, Granny. I know Declan's sick and it sounds petulant and spoiled to be complaining.'

'What are you complaining about?' her mother asked.

'I'm complaining that you don't love me the way I am, you want me to change. I'm complaining, actually, that you don't like me.'

'Helen, do you think if you had a problem that I would not drop everything to help you, to come to your assistance?'

'But that's not what I want from you. You've just invented a person in extreme need. I'm not that person, stop inventing me and projecting things on to me.'

'You're a very cold person, Helen,' her mother said.

'You can say anything about me and it will sound true,' Helen said.

'You know, after your father died, I could never get you close to me. I came home, and I noticed it first at the funeral that you wouldn't meet my eyes. When we settled back in together, the three of us, you were distant, you gave me no affection, you never told me anything and you brought no friends home, there were no girls whispering or watching television together. It was you studying, or going to bed on time, or moving around the house like a ghost passing judgement on us all.' Her mother's eyes were sharp; her voice was full of contempt.

'I never understood,' Helen said, 'how you could leave us down here for so long without visiting us when my father was sick.'

'Is there a need to rake over everything?' her grand-mother asked.

'You don't know what happened to your father,' Lily said, 'how afraid he was, and how lonely and upset he was in the hospital even though I was there every day. I had no choice. Is that what's been eating away at you all these years?'

'Declan and I felt abandoned then, even though Granny and Grandad were nice to us, we felt abandoned, yes, if that's what you want to know. Yes, and I suppose it's true that it has been eating away at me all these years, as you put it. I'm the one who took it to heart.' Helen was almost crying now.

'And carried it with you,' her mother added.

'I've never trusted you again, that's all. And it's not true to say that I was distant and you couldn't get through to me. You were never on my side.'

'I did what I could for you,' her mother said, 'and you never gave me an inch. Even I remember when your exam results came in, you just looked at them, you wouldn't even smile. But that's all long past now. I'd love to see you in your own house, to see if you're any different there.'

'I remember one of those summers,' Helen said, 'after I finished my degree and I was alone in that flat in Baggot Street. I had bought a book on cookery, and there was a brilliant vegetable shop around the corner just beside the Pembroke, everything fresh, and herbs and spices and even vegetables I'd never seen before. I used to go in there and over to Stephen's Green, and I'd wake in the morning with the whole day to myself, to walk around in the sun, cook something, read the paper, read a book. I loved the area, the freedom, the quietness, and I thought to myself, If nothing ever happens to me like marriage or friendships, I'll have achieved this. I'll have got away. And I still feel that, and there's no point in saying I don't. I feel I got away.'

'From what?' her mother asked.

'From you.'

'What did I do to you?' her mother asked.

'I don't know, but as you yourself put it about the wedding, it was not nothing.'

'So why do you want your children to see me?'

'Because we can't go on like this.'

Helen went to the window.

Earlier her grandmother had made sandwiches, which were now piled up on a plate. She went towards Declan's room to announce that sandwiches and soup were ready.

Declan wanted two people to have their soup and sandwiches in his room. He did not want to be left alone. Helen and Larry joined him.

'I've just been fighting with Mammy,' Helen said.

'One of the things I've noticed about the women in your family,' Larry said, 'is that they talk like they run things.'

'They do run things,' Declan said. 'But you've never seen them with men. I mean real men, not wimps like us. When real men are around, they shut up and make tea.'

'That is pure nonsense,' Helen said, laughing. 'Mammy has never once shut up in her whole life and when Granny makes tea it's a form of power play.'

As Declan went to the toilet, he told them to say nothing until he came back. He did not want to miss anything. Larry and Helen ate in silence.

When Declan came back, Larry resumed. 'I mean that even if there were men around, I bet that wouldn't change them very much. They'd still go on the same way.'

'Fighting with each other,' Declan said. 'What were you fighting about?'

'We were fighting about why she wasn't invited to my wedding.'

'Oh yeah, I've heard that one before all right,' Declan said.

'Your granny says that the two of you are exactly alike,' Larry said.

'That's all rubbish,' Helen said. 'I'm not like her at all.'

★

In the hour Helen and Larry sat in the room with Declan, he went to the toilet five or six times and came back each time looking exhausted and dispirited, curling up in the bed and closing his eyes. The morning's drizzle had cleared up now, although the ground was still wet. When she touched Declan, Helen knew that he had a temperature. The room, she thought, was too hot, the atmosphere too stuffy. She opened the window.

In the kitchen she told Paul that Declan was getting sicker.

'At some stage,' Paul said, 'he'll have to go back to the hospital, but nothing happens in hospitals at weekends, so there's no real point in him going back until Monday.'

Helen looked at her mother, who looked away. She realised that her mother was not speaking to her.

Helen told them that she was going to walk alone to Ballyconnigar along the strand and then take the road to Blackwater, where she wanted Paul to collect her in an hour and a half. She went to her room to change her shoes and put on a pullover.

'Maybe you'll think about some of the things I said to you,' her mother said when she came back into the kitchen.

Helen left without replying.

As she made her way down the rain-soaked edge of the cliff, she realised that at some point in the afternoon the opportunity had come and passed for her to put her arms around her mother, cry alongside her, forgive her everything, and promise to start a new relationship. She shuddered. Most people, she thought, would have been tempted, and would regret not having gone some way towards an enormous reconciliation. She shuddered again at the thought as she stepped on to the damp sand.

In all the talk about the past, there was one scene especially which haunted her, which remained strangely beyond her understanding. She could not tell her mother how that day when she came from Dublin with her husband's body, and Helen met her in the foreground of the cathedral for the first time in months, her mother had seemed regal, remote, the last person a little girl would want to hug or seek comfort from. She watched her mother that evening as much as she watched the congregation or the coffin. She seemed totally transformed. Helen knew as she knelt there why Declan had been kept away; her mother could not have maintained this stance, this proud, public bearing, with a small boy clinging to her. An older girl could be kept at bay much more easily. Her granny could look after her, or her father's sisters.

Helen remembered that the house that night was filled

with people, with cups of tea and sandwiches being passed around, and more people arriving. She stayed close to her grandmother, and made sure that she and no one else was sleeping in her own bedroom. What she hated more than anything else was the familiarity people had with her; strangers knew her name, and, because her father had just died, impressed the idea on her that they were full of sympathy for her. They pointed at her and introduced her to people, and she wished, as soon as they arrived, that they would all go. Her mother held court.

Those days after her father's death were dream-days, as though captured on badly processed film. And all the time, as her father's body spent its first long days in the grave away from everyone who had loved him, her mother was at the centre of the strangeness, utterly placid, beautifully dressed, receiving people, talking calmly. Her daughter watched her from the bottom of the stairs, or caught a glimpse of her each time a door opened, thinking sullenly: When all these people go, you will just have me, but you don't know that yet. And after a week or two, but especially when school term began, that was how it worked out. On nights when they did not go to Cush, and Declan went to bed, Helen sat by the fire relaxing, watching something on television in the half-hour before going upstairs. Her mother sat opposite her with no idea how to talk to her, how to treat her, none of the cosy companionship Helen had built up with her grandmother. Helen did nothing to help her; she turned the television off and stared into the fire and stretched. Without even trying, she was creating a barrier which would be hard now to break. Her mother smiled at her, asked if she was tired, and Helen nodded and packed her books for the

215

next day, and yawned and went to her room, to her own realm, where she lay in bed and thought about the uneasy presence down below. Even then, she was dreaming about getting away.

She walked close to where the waves broke and withdrew and broke again. There was no one else on the strand. She wondered where the small stones came from that studded the shore between here and Ballyconnigar. Did they come from the land or the sea? Did they remain deeply embedded in the mud and marl that made up the face of the cliff? And then when the slice of cliff or big boulder of cliff fell, did the sea wash them clean and deposit them here?

She listened as a wave knocked them against each other like chattering teeth, and then retreated. In the time when they had come here after her father died, when all the funeral crowds and sandwich eaters had gone, and there was just Lily and Helen and Declan and their grandparents, Lily would sit at her mother's kitchen table and innocently talk without stopping: all her woes, all her hopes would spill out. Helen could not listen to her; she had vivid memories of coming down here to this strand with the landscape slowly being eaten away and willing the sea to come more quickly towards them, taking the house and the fields, removing all trace of where her grandparents had lived. She imagined the sea, angry and inexorable, moving slowly towards the town, everything dissolving, slowly disappearing, the dead being washed out of their graves, houses crumbling and falling, cars being dragged out into the unruly ocean until there was nothing any more but this vast chaos.

She pictured her mother now, sitting at the kitchen

216

table having more tea made for her. At some stage when she was a little girl, Helen thought, Lily had worked out a way of doing whatever pleased her, of liking and disliking people and things at will, and of always being supported. For years no one had argued with her, or asked her to stop, and for three days now she had been openly rude to Paul and Larry, clearly hostile to them. The first thing she would do when she got back, Helen thought, would be to shake her mother, force her to be polite to Paul and Larry, treat them like friends of Declan's who had been there for him when no one else was. But thinking about changing Lily was stupid, Helen knew; no amount of shouting or shaming would make any differ-ence. Her mother was best left alone, tolerated and kept at bay, because nothing now would change her or improve her. It was too late.

Helen inspected the ruins of the Keatings' house. She stopped once more to look at the shreds of wallpaper and the floorboards and the half-rooms open to the wind and the sea. She wished that she could pray now for some-thing – for Declan to be better, or for Declan not to be worse. But she realised as she walked through the car park and then up through the fields that she could not pray. She could only wish; and she fervently wished that what was coming could be delayed or stopped as she made her way along the road into the village.

It struck her as she walked along – still brooding over her mother – that the view of Lily she had been offered during the previous four or five days confirmed all her prejudices. It was that hopeless mixture of looking for sympathy and demanding attention; it was the ability to turn hot and cold, swamp you with affection and then

217

turn her back because she was busy. As Helen passed the limekiln she could picture her mother's head over the crowd at the funeral, and she pictured her again now as she sat at the table in Cush, and Helen saw in both versions of her mother's face a desolation and a helplessness, and, more than anything, a fear that would never leave her now.

Helen realised that she would never in her life experience that fear and desolation and helplessless she had seen in her mother's face. Some time in the year around her father's death, she had trained herself to be equal to things, whatever they would be. And this was what she was now resisting, something she had killed in herself, which in her mother was coming to the fore again, unadulterated and unashamed. All those early raw emotions which Helen had watched her mother direct at everyone but her, emotions which were flaunted in public and hardly used in private, these were now back at the kitchen table in Cush. And she was being asked to become friends with their owner.

Hugh would smile and say that she was taking things too hard. It would all mend, that was his view. He wanted her to see her mother and grandmother, but he would not accept that this would mean yielding something in her own nature. 'Talk to her, that's all you can do,' he said.

They had been married for more than a year when Hugh's father died. Helen had loved her father-in-law in the short time she had known him, and deeply regretted – she was pregnant with Cathal then – that her children would not know him. He had been a big, smiling, friendly man and he lay in an open coffin in the hallway of the house. The expression on his face was mild and satisfied. Helen's mother-in-law sat close to the coffin, turning sometimes to look at him, or touch his face, as though to admire it or make sure that no great change was coming over it. And Hugh's brothers and sisters wandered in and out of the hallway, stopping for a while to touch the coffin or touch their father's hand. All of them cried at various times, and all of them took turns to sit by the coffin while their father's body lay there, lit only by candles, his skin waxen in the flickering light, his presence increasingly shadowy and distant.

No one in Hugh's family watched things as Helen did. She looked out for a niece or nephew or cousin or aunt or brother or sister who watched everything, who took everything in as though it were not happening to them. But there was no one like that except Helen herself at this funeral; they were all involved in being themselves, and this surprised her and impressed her. She wished she had been like that at her father's funeral instead of watching everybody, instead of observing her mother as though she were someone she had never seen before. And she wondered, as she passed the ball-alley on her way into Blackwater, how different she would be now if she had spent those days after her father died openly grieving for him. Would she be happier now?

In the village she found Paul outside Etchingham's pub. He was agitated.

'I thought I should phone the hospital,' he said, 'but there was no one there I could talk to, so I phoned Louise at home, but she's out. They're expecting her back any minute but not for long, so I've got to keep trying. Your grandmother is going to have to get her mobile phone working, if only just for one or two nights.'

'Is Declan really sick?' Helen asked.

'If he's like this so early in the evening, there are real possibilities for serious diarrhoea and high temperatures and headaches in the middle of the night.'

'Does he have a headache?'

'He's beginning one.'

'And what's his temperature?'

'At the moment it's a hundred and two, which is very high for so early in the evening, and he could be dehydrated too.'

'And what could they do?'

'If the headache got worse, there's a slow-release morphine they could use, and there's an injection they could give him, but you'd need a doctor to write the prescription or give the injection.'

'You sound like a doctor,' Helen said.

'I've been through this with Declan a good few times, and I know Louise,' Paul said.

After a while he got through to Louise. Helen watched him talking to her, knitting his brow and listening and then talking again. He hung up. 'She'll be back at ten o'clock,' he said, 'so if things are worse we're to phone again. We're to keep him cool. She's worried about the diarrhoea and she knows how bad the headaches have been in the past. So we'll call her at ten if we need to.'

They drove back to Cush in silence. As soon as they came into the house, they could hear voices in Declan's room. Paul walked past Helen, sensing that something was wrong.

'It's all right. It's nothing,' Declan was saying as his mother and grandmother stood over the bed.

'He's had a bit of an accident,' Larry said, having signalled Paul to leave the room with him. 'I think there's diarrhoea all over the bed and vomit as well.'

Paul went back into the bedroom. 'It would be better if everyone left the room,' he said. He turned to Mrs Devereux. 'Could you get fresh sheets?' he asked her. He turned to Lily then and asked her to switch on the shower and make sure that it was hot enough. He asked Larry to get a basin of water and some soap. His tone was brusque, almost bossy. 'Could we clear the room? It needs to be much less stuffy in here.'

When Lily did not move, he gestured to her to leave. 'It really would be better if we had some privacy in here,' he said.

'Could I talk to you outside?' she asked.

Helen followed them both to the kitchen.

'Could we talk afterwards?' Paul asked.

'Don't you dare speak to me in that tone!' Lily shouted.

'We'll talk afterwards,' Paul said calmly. 'I have a job to do.'

He went back to Declan's room, where Larry was waiting for him with a basin of water. Mrs Devereux had already brought the fresh sheets. Larry went upstairs to run the shower. Helen stood in the kitchen looking out of the window.

'I don't know who he thinks he is,' her mother said.

Helen sighed.

Her grandmother came into the room and sat down. 'We put all the sheets into a bucket outside. Paul said he'll wash them once they've soaked for a while. Isn't he very good?'

Helen felt that her grandmother was deliberately provoking her mother.

'We could easily put them in the boot of my car and I'll stick them in the washing machine when I go home,' Lily said.

'Well, it's a pity you're saying that now rather than doing it at the time,' Mrs Devereux said.

Helen watched her mother bristle quietly at the table as Paul came into the room.

'His headache is getting worse,' Paul said. 'Also, he needs to drink a lot if he doesn't want to become dehydrated. I should have got him 7-Up when I was in the village.'

'How dare you speak to me the way you spoke to me in there!' Lily stood up and faced him. 'I don't know what you think your place is here.'

'Look,' Paul said, 'I knew as soon as I came in that Declan felt humiliated and I decided that he needed privacy and I didn't notice him saying that he wanted you all back in when you left.'

'As far as we are concerned you have no business here,' Lily said.

Helen sought to interrupt her, but Lily continued. 'Maybe it's time you and your friend thought of taking yourselves out of here.'

'Like now, immediately?' Paul asked patiently. 'Just because you want us to?'

'As soon as you can, yes,' Lily said.

'And just because you want us to?' Paul asked again.

'Well, I do live here,' Lily said.

'No you don't,' Helen interrupted.

'It is my mother's house,' Lily said.

'Declan asked Larry and myself to come down here,' Paul said. 'We have, Larry more than me, the two of us have been looking after him during very difficult times when I didn't notice his family around.'

'We weren't around because we were told nothing,' Lily said.

'I wonder why you were told nothing. Maybe you could ponder that, instead of getting in the way and making pointless arguments,' Paul said.

Helen felt that he had gone too far, but he remained placid and in control, weighing each word he said.

'I wasn't in the way,' Lily said.

'Well, it looked like that to me,' Paul replied.

'I'm his mother!' Lily shouted.

Paul shrugged. 'He's an adult and he has got a bad headache and he needs a drink and there's no room for this sort of hysteria.'

'So are you going to leave?' Lily asked.

'Listen, Mrs Breen,' Paul said, 'I'm here as long as Declan is here and you can take that as written in stone, and I'm here because he asked me to be here, and when he asked me to be here he used words and phrases and sentences about you which were not edifying and which I will not repeat. He is also concerned about you and loves you and wants your approval. He is also very sick. So stop feeling sorry for yourself, Mrs Breen. Declan stays here, I stay here, Larry stays here. One of us goes, we all go, and if you don't believe me, ask Declan.'

'What do you mean, "not edifying"?' Lily asked.

'He's nearly thirty years old and he's afraid to tell you

things, for God's sake,' Paul said. 'I haven't time for this. Larry, could the mobile phone be got working, could the battery be recharged?'

Lily began to cry and went upstairs. Helen left the room and went and sat on Declan's bed.

'What happened?' Declan asked.

'Mammy had a row with Paul,' Helen said.

'She shouldn't have done that. He always wins rows, he always knows what you're going to say next,' Declan said. He put his hands over his eyes and winced. 'The pain comes in waves,' he said and got out of bed again to go to the toilet. 'I'm feeling really sick again.'

★

Helen met her grandmother at the foot of the stairs.

'That was a bit rough,' Helen said.

'Oh, she's all right,' her grandmother said. 'She'll cry it out of herself. She can put people out of her nice house in Wexford if she likes, but she can't put people out of here. They'll go in their own good time.'

They went back to the kitchen, where Larry was trying to recharge the mobile phone.

'Sorry, everybody, if I sounded offensive,' Paul said.

'You'd feel sorry for poor Lily,' Mrs Devereux said, 'putting her big foot in it without a leg to stand on, as the fellow in Ballyvalden used to say.'

'Does anyone have a screwdriver or a pen-knife?' Larry asked. 'I need to check this plug.'

'I have a knife here.' Mrs Devereux reached into her apron pocket.

'Granny, that's a flick-knife!' Helen said.

Mrs Devereux pressed the switch and the blade flicked open. It looked dangerous. She handed it to Larry.

'Granny, why do you have a flick-knife?' Helen asked her.

'Helen, I don't know if you saw all the programmes about old people being attacked, old people living alone. Oh, it was all they talked about around here; the Kehoes nearly built a moat around their house and the guards in Blackwater were nearly driven out of their minds by the strange sightings. People kept asking me how I was managing. I had no peace and, as you can imagine, Lily was out here day and night with brochures about alarm systems. It was madness. But I'd seen this thing' – she pointed to the flick-knife – 'on the television and it seemed even better than a gun. So I went into Wexford and I asked Mr Parle in Parle's Hardware and he said he didn't stock them, they were too dangerous, and no one in Wexford would stock them. So I explained what I wanted it for. I think he thought I wanted it as a present for a grandson or a nephew. But when I told him he brightened up no end and said he would order one for me, and we talked about shapes and sizes. He said I was quite right to take the law into my own hands. He seemed to know all about flick-knives. And a few weeks later I went into Parle's and there it was, new and shiny.'

'But, Granny,' Helen asked, 'can you use it?'

'Use it, Helen? You just press the switch.'

'And what would you do if an intruder came into the house?' Helen asked.

'I'd stab them, Helen. I'd disfigure them,' her grandmother said.

'God, you sound as though you mean business,' Larry said.

'You're a lesson to us all, Mrs Devereux,' Paul said. 'I'm glad I didn't try and break in here.'

'Does Declan know about the flick-knife?' Larry asked.

'No,' Mrs Devereux said.

'I must go and tell him. This battery should be recharged in about half an hour,' Larry said.

Larry bumped into Lily at the door. She addressed Paul across the room.

'Declan says you're his best friend and I mustn't be rude to you, so I agreed to do what he says.'

'Actually, I'm his best friend,' Larry said.

'Actually, you're just a young pup,' Mrs Devereux said, smiling at him.

'It's OK, I understand. I'm sorry too,' Paul said to Lily.

'Declan's getting sick into the basin all the time,' Lily said. 'He says the headache is getting worse, and he's back in the bathroom again now.'

'What time is it?' Paul asked.

'It's nine o'clock,' Helen said.

'We'll try Louise on the mobile at ten,' Paul said.

★

While they had dinner each of them took it in turn to stay with Declan. He spent most of the time going to and from the bathroom.

At a quarter to ten Paul established that the mobile phone was working. He asked Mrs Devereux for the name and number of her doctor in Blackwater so that Louise could phone him if she needed to.

'I'll have to draw the line now,' Mrs Devereux said. 'I've been going to old Doctor French for years and I go to his son as well now that he's home, and they know more about me than I do myself, and they're as nosy, God bless the two of them, as the two Kehoes. And I don't want them to know anything more about me.'

'That's fine,' Paul said, 'except you don't have a phone book or a Yellow Pages so we can find some other doctor.'

He rang Directory Enquiries and found the number of the Garda station in Kilmuckridge, the village north of Blackwater; the guard gave him the number of two general practitioners, including the doctor on duty that night.

'You are the essence of efficiency,' Helen said to him.

He rang Louise, and left a message for her to call the mobile number when she returned. As Mrs Devereux poured tea for everyone, Helen noticed that her mother was trying to smile at Paul.

With the first sharp ring of the mobile phone, the two cats sprang from their perch, bringing with them plates and bowls from the upper shelves of the dresser which crashed to the floor and broke into small pieces; the cats leaped across the room and escaped in a flash through the kitchen door as Mrs Devereux screamed at them. 'The whole house will be destroyed,' she said.

Lily tried to calm her down while Paul took the phone into the hallway. Helen began to pick up pieces of crockery and delph.

'The cats have such a quiet life normally,' Mrs Devereux said when Lily had forced her to sit down. 'It must have been the last straw. It was the same when I bought the electric mixer. Six feet into the air they went, the two of them, but they broke nothing that time. They wouldn't come back into the house for two days.'

When they had picked up and swept away most of the shards which lay all over the kitchen floor, Paul came in to say that a Doctor Kirwan from Kilmuckridge was going to visit, that Louise had spoken to him, he would know exactly what to do, and someone would have to go to Wexford, to the chemist shop which was on all-night duty, to get the slow-release morphine for Declan.

When Larry came back from Declan's bedroom Paul told him what had happened.

'I got one of those plates as part of a dinner service as a wedding present, nearly sixty years ago,' Mrs Devereux said.

'They're a bad business, cats,' Larry said. 'We'll drown them if we find them.'

'A little pup, that's the best description of you all day,' Mrs Devereux said.

'Sure you couldn't have two cats up on a dresser like that,' Larry said. 'They'd be bound to knock everything over at some stage.'

'I'd say they take a very dim view of you lot,' Mrs Devereux said. 'And if that terrible handphone goes off again, I don't know what will happen.'

'Two scalded cats, Garret and Charlie,' Larry said. 'I'm raging I missed it.'

★

When the doctor came, Declan was in the bathroom. He walked downstairs slowly, wearing boxer shorts and a T-shirt. He seemed to Helen almost impossibly thin. The

228

doctor went into the bedroom with him; the rest of them stayed in the dining-room and kitchen. Helen saw that her mother had changed her clothes. When her grand-mother did not come to the front door to greet the doctor, but waited nervously in the kitchen, Helen realised that she did not want the doctor to see her or recognise her.

Having finished with Declan, the doctor stood at the dining-room table and wrote a prescription. Helen noticed that his hair, which hung in loose strands around his head, had been badly cut. It was as though someone had put a bowl around his head and then applied a pair of scissors. She spotted Paul watching it as well.

'I've given him an injection which will control his bowels for a while. He needs to drink a lot of liquid. This prescription is for the morphine. I'll phone the chemist when I get back, and he'll have it ready for you. He's on the quays in Wexford town, close to the Bank of Ireland.

'This is a very remote place,' he said as Lily paid him.

'It's very good of you to come,' she said.

As soon as the doctor started up the car, Larry and Paul went into Declan's room to talk about his hair.

'You'd think with the amount of money he makes he'd get a proper haircut,' Larry said. 'If I went around like that, people would laugh at me, but just because he's a doctor he gets away with it.'

Mrs Devereux came into the bedroom.

'I knew his father, old Breezy Kirwan,' she said. 'He's very nice. His mother is very nice too, she was a Gethings from Oulart. I didn't know he was home.'

'Is his father's hair like that too?' Larry asked. He gave Mrs Devereux a description of the doctor's hair.

'Oh stop now about his hair. I'm sure he's saving up to get married, giving good example, which is more than I can say for some.'

★

Declan was quiet now. Larry and Paul drove into Wexford to get the pills for him. Mrs Devereux stood in front of the house, calling the cats in whispers. And Lily and Helen sat in the bedroom, Lily holding a packet of frozen peas on Declan's forehead. 'This will keep the pain down for a while,' she said. She fixed his pillow and pushed his hair back.

Helen was uncomfortable in the room; her mother was still not talking to her. She began to speak to Declan as though Helen were not there.

'Helen says that I abandoned you and her when your father was sick.' Lily's voice was gentle and soft as she spoke, as if they were children still and she was telling them a comforting story before they went to sleep. 'I wrote all the time,' she went on, 'and your granny assured me that if I visited it would just unsettle you, that you were happy here, and it would be better if there were no interruptions to your routine, that she would have to get you settled all over again if I came. So that's why I never visited. You can ask her and she'll tell you. I wanted to come down and your father wanted me to come down, even if just for a day, but your granny said it would be too much for you, me arriving and then going away again. It would be too emotional.'

Lily was almost crying now, but Helen saw that Declan was watching her and his eyes were hard. She wondered if he believed his mother. Helen did not.

'Why did you leave me in Byrnes' house for the funeral and never see me?' Declan asked.

'That was everyone's advice at the time; they all said that you were too young to take in your father's death, and you'd be too young to see the coffin and the grave. And Declan, I would have broken into pieces if I'd seen you in those days, I would have broken into pieces.' She was crying now as Declan softened and held her hand. 'I couldn't have done anything else, Declan and Helen,' Lily said. Her crying had become louder.

Helen did not notice her grandmother coming into the room. By the time she saw her she was already holding Lily, rocking her back and forth.

'It's a vale of tears, Lily,' she whispered to her. 'It's a vale of tears, and there's nothing we can do.'

★

The pills had no immediate effect. Between one and two in the morning Declan's pain became almost unbearable. Helen and Lily and Paul and Larry took turns sitting with him in the dark, but they could not touch him or speak to him.

After three o'clock his pain began to ease. He took a sleeping pill and a Xanax and said he would sleep until the morning now if he was lucky.

When Helen went to bed, she thought about Hugh and the boys and the words of reassurance which had come from Donegal. Cathal and Manus were all right; they did not notice her absence, they were having a good time. How would she know, she wondered as she lay there, if one or both of them was miserable and missed her, but learned to mask it and disguise it, and did not complain? Manus would know how to complain, but Cathal would not. He would say nothing, as he had said nothing on the phone that morning. She thought about Hugh and how easygoing and dependable he was, and how much she loved him and the boys loved him. For a moment, as she lay there in the night, she felt the glow of his love, and felt reassured that nothing that had happened to her was being passed on to her children. She resolved to think harder and pay more attention so that Cathal and Manus could feel secure in the world and feel none of the currents which went through her grandmother's house now every moment of the day. As she turned and tried to sleep, however, she knew that anyone who was close to her must have learned long ago to live with and manage this web of unresolved connections. She clenched her fists and swore that she would do her best to protect them.

EIGHT

It was after nine when Helen woke to the sound of shouting and laughing. She listened and heard the revving of a car and then some more voices. She heard her mother coming down the stairs and shouting something. She wondered if the cats had returned, or if morning light had unveiled them on the roof of one of the outhouses. A car revved again, as though someone were having trouble starting the engine.

She looked into Declan's room when she got up, but his bed was empty. From the dining-room window she could see what was happening in front of the house. Her grandmother was trying to drive Larry's car; Larry was giving her lessons in the front seat. Her grandmother would start the car, rev the engine, get into gear and move forward in a sudden jerk, and then the engine would cut out.

Declan and Paul were sitting in the morning sunlight watching this, laughing and applauding. Lily was at the front door, where Helen joined her.

'She'll crash the car and then she'll blame someone else,' Lily said.

'She can't go far,' Helen said.

This time Mrs Devereux had edged the car slowly

towards the gate before it cut out. She opened the window and shouted, 'Lily, Paul, Helen, put your cars out in the lane. I don't have room enough here.'

'We're afraid to move. You'll kill us all,' Lily said.

'Helen, hurry up now!' her grandmother said.

Mrs Devereux listened carefully as Larry explained the gears to her once more. Helen turned Declan's car under her grandmother's impatient gaze. Lily followed her, as did Paul.

'Helen, my flat shoes!' her grandmother shouted as she made her way back to the house. 'They're in the hall.'

She found a pair of flat shoes in the hall and brought them out. Her grandmother had already taken her other shoes off, which she handed imperiously to Helen, immediately going back to Larry to discuss a point about the gearstick.

'Come on, Granny!' Declan shouted. His thin legs were folded around each other.

Mrs Devereux started the car again as they all watched. She changed the gear and then took her foot off the brake. She let the car forward until it began to shake. She shouted at Larry, 'What'll I do now?'

'Indicate, Granny, indicate,' Declan shouted.

The car stopped. She pursed her lips and looked ahead. Then she opened the door of the car and turned towards her audience. 'Go inside, all of you! I can't learn if you're all going to be watching me and jeering me. No one can learn like that.'

'She's serious about learning,' Helen said. 'I thought it was a joke.'

'Since she got the money for the sites, she's gone cracked,' Lily said. 'Cracked! And wait until the winter comes and she gets depressed and she won't speak to anybody and Father O'Brien will ring me up like he did last year to say that she's been seen walking into Blackwater with a string bag for the second time in the same day, and she won't say a word to anyone she meets.'

'Are you serious?' Helen asked.

'Cracked,' Lily said again. 'And she'd a sister Statia, you'd be too young to remember her. She sent me into her in Bree one Christmas. I had an awful time. She was cracked as well. All that family were cracked. So don't start blaming me now for leaving her on her own out here, there's nothing I can do about it.'

'I'm not blaming you,' Helen said.

'What was that yesterday then?' her mother asked.

★

Declan had gone back to bed. Paul, Lily and Helen had breakfast together while Larry and Mrs Devereux continued their driving lesson.

'I told Declan', Paul said, 'that he should go back to St James's today, but he says that if it remains fine as it is now, he'll stay. Louise is worried about his stomach: there are various things it could be and they would require treatment, but only after a good deal of testing.'

'Could they do the testing today?' Lily asked politely.

'No, but they could start very early in the morning. Louise doesn't want to mask the symptoms any more, so she won't treat him until she knows what it is.'

'You mean treat him with drugs?' Lily asked.

'Right,' Paul said.

Paul and Lily looked at one another across the table and nodded gravely. Helen made more tea for them as they continued talking. After a while, Larry and Mrs Devereux came into the kitchen.

'It's that first gear has me flummoxed,' Mrs Devereux said.

'And second and third too, I wouldn't be surprised,' Lily said.

'No, Mrs Breen, she has great potential,' Larry said. 'My father taught my mother to drive only last year.'

'You'll have to get a provisional licence,' Helen said.

'Oh, sure that's no problem, Helen,' her grandmother said. 'Didn't I tell you what Kitty Walsh from The Ballagh did last year, and she's so blind she can't see in front of her nose, and that's God's truth. Didn't she go into the eye man the day before her appointment, and she just said she was looking at spectacle frames – her sister Winnie told me this – and didn't she look closely at the letters when the door was open, you know, the letters you have to read. She wrote them down and went home and learned them off. So by the next day the eye man complimented her on her sight when she could hardly see the colour of the money she was paying him with. And she driving a Mazda mad all over the country now. Get into the ditch if you see her coming. A red Mazda.'

'Someone should report her,' Lily said.

'It was Winnie told me, and she thought it was a terrible thing. But there was never any talking to Kitty. Their mother was an awful oul' rip and she lived into her nineties. Kitty had put up with a lot, and nothing would do her but a car once the mother was dead. So watch out for her now!'

★

236

At a quarter to eleven Mrs Devereux and Helen, Lily and Paul drove into Blackwater for eleven o'clock Mass.

'Walk straight back to the car now after Mass,' Mrs Devereux said. 'No dawdling around the paper shop, and no talking to people.'

Helen had not been to Mass in Blackwater for well over ten years, since her last summer working at the guest-house. She had forgotten the scene at eleven o'clock Mass: the women in headscarves or mantillas or fancy hats on one side of the church, the men on the other side in suits – even the young boys in suits – and the sense of awe and unease in every face, the silence and the watch-fulness, and the soft, old-fashioned edge to everything. The respect and the conformity was broken only by visitors, people from Dublin or from towns who walked up the church and sat together as a family and wore summer-holiday clothes.

When the Mass started she was aware of Paul praying beside her, calling out the responses firmly and loudly. Her grandmother, her mother and Paul went to Com-munion, but she sat back and watched as each communi-cant walked down the church in bowed, concentrated prayer. Paul, she noticed, was dressed conservatively and could have fitted in as a local farmer's son, a staunch pillar of the community.

As soon as the Mass was over her grandmother nudged her. 'Come on now, quick, before the crush.'

People she half knew smiled at Helen in recognition as they joined the queue to leave the church. She wished she had worn a scarf or a mantilla like her mother and grandmother. She felt oddly conspicuous, as though by coming here bare-headed and not going to Communion she was trying to make a statement. As soon as they reached the porch of the church, her grandmother caught her by the wrist and began to talk to her animatedly so that no one else could get her attention. Lily had gone ahead; Paul was coming close behind.

'Oh there'll be people raging,' Mrs Devereux said when they got into the car, 'wondering how we slipped by them. People who wouldn't look high up or low down at me for the rest of the year would love to detain me now that I'm with Helen and Lily. And they'll think Paul is your husband, Helen. And they'll say what a clean-looking man she's married. I don't know what they'll say about you, Lily.'

'Well, that priest would put years on you. I don't know what his name is,' Lily said.

'Start up the car,' Mrs Devereux said to Paul, 'and just drive it out. Someone will just have to give way.'

'When you get your own car, Granny, you'll learn all about giving way,' Helen said.

'Oh, I'll need a lot of practice first,' Mrs Devereux said.

When they arrived home, Declan and Larry had everything packed for them to go to the strand. Mrs Devereux, however, refused, said she hadn't been down there for years and if she went down now, she would never get back up. 'And furthermore,' she said, 'you'd never know who you'd meet down there, and you could get a pain listening to people.'

Declan appeared frail and white in a pair of shorts, sandals and a T-shirt. Lily carried a basket with a flask of tea, sandwiches and biscuits. As they turned in the lane, they heard Mrs Devereux whispering the cats' names, trying to entice them back into the house, but they did not appear.

In the previous few days, a number of boulders of mud and marl, studded with stones, had fallen on to the strand from the cliff; soon, they would disintegrate as the tide came in and washed over them. After a few days there would just be stones, until they too, or some of them, in the winter and spring, would be swept out, or buried in the sand.

Lily stood behind one of the boulders and changed into an old-fashioned swimsuit she must have found somewhere in the house. There were a few families further down the strand, but no one near them. Helen spread out a rug and Declan lay down on it, but sat up again to watch as his mother marched down the short strand, blessed herself as soon as she touched the water and swam out without a moment's hesitation.

'She's a brave woman, your mother,' Larry said.

'She met her match with Paul,' Declan said. 'Paul would put the fear of God into anyone's mother.'

'Leave me alone, everybody. That Declan fucker, saving your presence, Helen, has me awake all night.' He smiled at Declan.

'We'd tickle Paul, only Helen's here,' Declan said. 'You see a whole new Paul when you tickle him.'

'I can't think of anything I'd like more than to see Paul being tickled,' Helen said. 'But maybe we should wait until my mother comes back.'

Paul, who had already changed into his bathing togs, stood up and charged down the strand and into the sea. But he stopped as soon as he was up to his thighs in the cold water and jumped to avoid each wave. Eventually, to cheers from Larry and Declan, he swam out. Helen joined him, and as soon as she was down in the water, and almost warm as long as she kept moving, she noticed Declan, still in his shorts, paddling on the shore with Larry beside him. She knew that Declan could not swim because of the line which the doctors had put in his chest.

Later, when the sun left the strand in shadow, Larry, Paul and Declan went back to the house, leaving Helen and her mother alone. It was still warm and the sky was clear, except for a few clouds in the distance over the horizon. They lay on the rug first without speaking once they had changed from their swimsuits into their day clothes. After a while, when Helen was almost dozing, Lily began to speak.

'I don't think Declan is going to last much longer. It's funny how we've all absorbed the shock, and we're used to it now. It's a part of life. Sometimes, he looks like your father; there's something he does with his face, some way he turns.'

'Was my father thin before he died?' Helen asked.

'Not noticeably, no. Not like Declan is. But he was like Declan in that he was sitting up in bed and laughing, well, not laughing so much, but talking. And, of course, he didn't know he was so sick.'

'But you knew?'

'No, the thing was I didn't know either. They all thought they had told me, but they hadn't, none of them, and when after the operation the surgeon asked to see me, I went to his office, but he was never in, I never could find him. So I left it. And your father was different in hospital. He was like all the men around here, he didn't talk much, he left all the talking to others, but he loved company and he listened and he was never without company. So he found the hospital lonely, but it was a new world for him, and he'd notice everything and remember everybody, and when I'd come in he'd talk about everything that had happened during the night. And, of course, I was staying with my cousin Pat Bolger, and there were all sorts of comings and goings in the house, so I'd have my own news, and we'd read the paper and we'd talk. There was a man opposite said he never saw two people talking as much. And we planned everything out, what we were going to do.

'We were going to have another child if we could,' her mother went on, 'maybe even two more, like a second family, to thank God for him getting better. We talked about having another boy and another girl, or maybe the opposite way around. We planned everything in detail, and I learned a lot about him even though I'd been married to him for years. We had our own little world there. He was in a corner bed by a window, and nurses came and went, and doctors came and went, and I never asked them a question. Maybe I knew he was sick, and avoided it, but really I didn't know, and one day I was walking up and down the corridor waiting for the nurses to finish with him when one of the nuns came up to me and asked me if I would come down to the chapel and pray with her. She lit candles and we knelt down.

' "We'll ask Our Lady", she said, "that he has a happy and a peaceful death." Well, I prayed with her, and she held my hand, but I thought she had mixed me up with somebody else. She was a slow, placid old woman, and I'd noticed her from as soon as we arrived, and she'd noticed me, and I knew she wasn't making a mistake, but still I asked her. She brought me down to meet the consultant, who was very arrogant and brusque and had no time for me. Then I had to go back to your father, and pretend nothing had happened. They had given him an injection, and he weakened after that and was dead within two days, and after he died, if that nun hadn't been there I don't know what I would have done.

'I couldn't part from him. You know, I wanted them to draw the curtains and leave me on my own with him, but they kept coming in to say I would have to go. I knew I'd never see him again. And the nun brought me back down to the chapel and I prayed for him, but the praying made no difference, I did not know that there could be blackness like I felt that day.'

'Did you let Granny know he was very sick a good length before that?'

'Well, she knew he was sick.'

'I mean that he was dying.'

'Sure I didn't know myself. I suppose I would have let her know the day I knew, or the day after. I left it all to Pat Bolger. But your father was dead within a day or two. He was so young, he was ready for another life, he was looking forward to coming home. He was the light of my life and he loved you and Declan so much. He didn't want to let you out of his sight. And now he was cold, like he was nothing.

'And I made a promise that day in the chapel, after they'd taken his body out of the ward, that I'd do my best with you and Declan, that I'd try to be as good as the two of us would have been. I made a promise to do my best, but I don't suppose, looking at it now, that I did very well.'

Her mother's hands were trembling as she looked out to sea. Her last remark was made so flatly, the tone so factual and melancholy, that Helen did not feel she should say anything in reply. They sat in silence listening to the waves sweeping in towards the shore. Eventually, Helen spoke.

'I was just thinking,' she said, 'that I have a son who reminds me of my father sometimes, just like you said about Declan, when he turns his head.'

'Which son is that?' her mother asked.

'He's Cathal, the older one, he's quiet, he's like the men down here, he loves not having to talk. And then the other is the opposite.'

'Declan was the opposite to you when you were small. Your father loved having the two of you in the bed on a Saturday morning or a Sunday morning. I never wanted it, but if there was a sound out of you he'd bring you into our bed, and if you came, Declan was sure to follow. And you'd be quiet, you'd suck your thumb, but Declan would crawl all over us, he'd pull his daddy's ears, or he'd want to tickle his feet, and you'd hate all the noise, and Declan would get worse until we got up.'

'I always wanted to be an only child, especially when I was around that age,' Helen said.

'All I ever wanted was a sister,' her mother said. 'Your granny tried to adopt. She was all ready and then a woman in a tweed suit — I don't know who she was, some sort of inspector — came down and asked her where the adopted child would live when our house fell into the sea, and was there an insurance policy? And, of course, there wasn't. And my mother was raging. "You couldn't bring a child up here," the woman said to her. And we were turned down for adoption. She was in a terrible state, your granny; that was the winter she didn't speak to us at all, me or your grandfather.'

'A sister would have changed everything, wouldn't it?' Helen asked.

'It would, yes, it would,' her mother said thoughtfully, regretfully. She said nothing for a while, and then began to shake her head and frown.

'What is it?' Helen asked.

'There's something I will never forget about the funeral,' her mother said. 'It's hard to talk about it. Coming home like that from Dublin and your father so young, and everybody looking and watching, there was a sort of shame about it. It sounds mad, doesn't it? I know it does, but that's what it felt like, so exposed, or maybe that isn't the word. But it felt like shame, those days after he died when we came home.'

'But you didn't look like that,' Helen said.

'I don't know how I looked. I spent those days trying to put back time. And maybe trying to stop time too, because I knew when it was all over and the people went away I would be alone, I'd be sleeping alone, I'd be alone at night, and the job of dealing with you and Declan I'd have to do alone. And I couldn't manage, you know I couldn't manage. I don't know why I'm thinking of all this now. I suppose it's because of Declan.'

The strand grew colder as the afternoon wore on. Helen and her mother folded the rug, and took their swimsuits and towels from where they had half dried on the boulder, and they walked until they came to the gap at Mike Redmond's house, where they scrambled up the cliff.

As they made their way back to the house along the lanes, Helen stopped for a moment.

'There's something I've never realised before, that's just struck me now,' she said. 'I've always believed that you took him away and you never brought him back. I know it's irrational, but that's what it was, that's what I felt. I thought that you had locked him away somewhere, that you knew where he was, that it was all your fault. Somewhere in the back of my mind, I believed all this.'

Lily shivered as she stood there.

'I locked no one away, I'm afraid, Helen,' she said wearily. 'He died in my arms. I watched him go. I know I came home to you all without him. There was nothing I could do.'

'I know, Mammy, I know,' Helen said, and linked arms with her mother and they continued walking.

★

At the top of the lane they saw Madge and Essie Kehoe approaching.

'Say nothing now,' Lily said.

'Well,' Madge Kehoe said as she came close, 'we've just been down to Dora's house and we were wondering where you were.'

'Dora will kill someone,' Essie interrupted. 'You'll have to stop her. She nearly drove into the ditch.'

'Oh, but she used to be a great driver,' Lily said. 'She'll learn again in no time.'

Helen knew that what her mother had just said was untrue; she felt that the Kehoes also knew that.

'Did you hear about Kitty Walsh from The Ballagh

245

and her poor mother hardly cold?' Madge asked. She spoke quickly, breathlessly.

'There should be a law, you know,' Essie said. They were both excited at what they had just witnessed.

'There is a law,' Madge said, 'but it's the guards, they won't stop her.'

'Sure she's too blind to see them. She wouldn't stop for them,' Essie said. 'And now Dora is driving.'

'Oh, it'll be a while now before she hits the road,' Lily said. Helen noticed that her mother was sounding aloof, almost posh.

The Kehoe sisters' eyes darted from Helen to her mother. 'And is your husband still in Donegal?' Essie asked.

Helen nodded.

'And isn't Declan looking very thin?' Madge said. 'He'll never get a wife if he doesn't fatten up a bit.'

'Oh I'd say there are girls only waiting for him to make up his mind,' Essie said and smiled sourly.

Neither Lily nor Helen spoke; the sisters slowly seemed to realise that they had said too much too quickly. For a second or two they said nothing more until it was clear that Lily and Helen were going to move away. Eventually, Madge broke the silence.

'God knows who we'll have driving next. Old Art Murphy, or Kate Pender.'

'I'd say it'll be a while now before they get their provisional licences,' Lily said, laughing.

'And the judge is a queer dangerous driver,' Madge said.

'We'll all have to watch out so,' Helen said, and made as though to move.

'And who is the other fellow in the car teaching Dora?' Essie asked.

'He's a friend of Declan's,' Helen said.

'Is that so now?' Essie asked. 'And is he teaching in your school?'

Helen did not answer.

'God, you've a right crowd,' Essie continued.

The Kehoe sisters searched their faces to see if there might be some more information for them to gather.

'We'd better be going,' Lily said.

'Call in before you go back,' Madge said.

'We'll have the kettle on for you,' Essie added.

'They're mad, they were always mad,' Lily said as soon as the Kehoes were out of earshot. 'You should be down on your knees thanking God, Helen, that you didn't have to go to school with people like that. I pinched that Essie so hard one day that her oul' father came down home to complain about me. God, when I was growing up here I couldn't wait to get away! Even seeing the two of them puts years on me.'

★

The driving lesson had just ended when Lily and Helen arrived at the house. Mrs Devereux and Larry were standing beside the car; Declan and Paul were sitting on chairs outside the front door. Declan's face, Helen noticed, was almost green; she had not seen him looking so sick and so strained before. But he was smiling now and laughing. She realised as she watched him that he was making an effort to keep going.

'Show them now,' Larry said to Mrs Devereux.

247

'We met the Kehoes,' Lily told them.

'They were full of admiration for you,' Helen said to her grandmother.

'Show them,' Larry repeated.

Mrs Devereux got into Larry's car, closing the driver's door and seeming to concentrate hard. She started the car and let the engine rev for a minute. She acted as though no one were watching her as she put the car into gear and let off the handbrake and then slowly and smoothly edged forward towards the gate. As she prepared to turn into the lane, the car began to shudder and the engine cut out. She started it again, the engine revving and revving until thick, black smoke poured out of the exhaust. She turned the corner and made her way up the lane. All of them went out to the gate to watch her. She stopped the car with a jolt and applied the handbrake and waited until Larry reached her. She moved over into the passenger's seat and let Larry reverse the car and drive it back down. When the car stopped in front of the house, Mrs Devereux got out and dusted herself down. Larry, Paul, Declan and Helen applauded. Lily stood still, stony-faced.

'She's high now,' Lily whispered to Helen, 'but wait until the winter and she'll be screaming at me from the coinbox in Blackwater, or she'll be walking the roads like Moll Trot.'

★

In the late afternoon Declan's mood darkened. When they had tea in the kitchen, Declan sat apart from them in the armchair by the Aga. All of them were aware, Helen realised, that he was lower now than he had been at any time in the week. He did not speak, but stared straight ahead; no one at the table spoke either, and finally when Larry said something, it was clear that he was merely trying to break the silence by making jokes about Mrs Devereux's driving and the disappearance of the cats. No one laughed or responded, and Larry gave up and became oddly morose in a way which disturbed Helen more than anything.

When they had drunk their tea, Mrs Devereux fussed nervously about second cups. All of them had, at some stage, left the room to use the bathroom and come back. Paul now tried to ease the tension by asking Declan if he wanted to go to bed.

'No, I don't want to go to bed, Paul, I don't want to go to bed. Leave me alone. Do you have a problem with me being here?'

Helen watched Paul's face redden; it was the first time she had seen him at a loss. He said nothing. Mrs Devereux clattered the teacups and saucers in the sink.

'Leave them. I'll do them later,' Helen said.

Her grandmother went to the window and looked out. 'We'll have the dinner later on,' she said. 'I don't have the energy now.'

'I'll make the dinner,' Helen said.

Declan still did not speak, and paid no attention to any of them. He was pale now; the bruise-mark on his nose had spread into his cheek and turned ugly and dark. Helen noticed for the first time how thin his hair had become. He crossed his legs and then crossed his ankle around his leg again, emphasising his thinness. In the dim light of the kitchen, as Helen watched him, he seemed strangely beautiful, despite the spareness of his face and

249

frame, like a figure in a painting, with shadows under his eyes and dark shadowy tufts where he had not shaved. She observed his long, bony fingers.

He caught her looking at him and she looked away. By this time, all of the others except her grandmother had left the kitchen. Mrs Devereux went to the window over and over, as if expecting some sudden arrival, and then went back to the sink, where she had started to peel potatoes. Helen went to help her, noticing as she crossed the room that Declan had turned the sickly, almost green colour he had been outside the house earlier.

Helen and her grandmother worked at preparing the vegetables while Lily came in and out of the room and Declan sat silently staring ahead. Whatever was happening to him filled the atmosphere so that they became conscious of every sound they made – the scraping of vegetables, the clattering of saucepans, the turning on and off of taps – as a disturbance, an irritation, a direct breaking of Declan's fierce and anguished concentration.

Helen could not wait to get out of the room. She wanted to close the kitchen door behind her as she left, with only her grandmother and Declan in the room, but she felt it would be like closing the lid of a pressure cooker. She left the door ajar.

Larry and Paul were in the dining-room.

'Larry is going back tonight,' Paul said. 'He should really go back to work. I'm going to hang on. I think Declan should go back up tomorrow.'

'I'll wait around until after dinner,' Larry said.

As the meat sizzled in the oven and the vegetables boiled and the smell filled the kitchen, Declan sat impassive and immobile, staring at a fixed point ahead of him as though ready to explode in pain or anger. Paul and Larry remained out of the room while Helen and her mother set the table in the kitchen, carefully including a place for Declan, knowing, however, that he would not sit with them. They moved gingerly, silently, aware that every sound seemed to grate on his nerves. Mrs Devereux filled a saucer of milk and went outside and put it near the shed for the cats.

Eventually, they sat down to eat. They left a chair for Declan but he did not join them, nor did they ask him to. They busied themselves passing food, alert all the time to Declan's brooding presence.

'Would you not eat something, Declan?' Lily asked.

'No, leave me alone,' he said without looking up.

'Leave him alone,' his grandmother said. 'He's my pet.'

Helen saw how uneasy Paul and Larry had become. Declan's sunken mood had rendered them useless; if the family were not there, she felt, his friends would have been able to do something, but the signals in the room, the connections, were too tangled and complex now, and no one could think of anything to say, and a strange embarrassed sadness descended on the company.

When Larry got ready to go, Declan did not move. Larry left his bag in the hallway and came into the kitchen and tossed Declan's hair. Declan held Larry's hand for a moment and squeezed it, but he did not turn to look at him, and did not say anything.

In the dining-room, Larry stood and discussed the plans for renovation with Mrs Devereux. 'I have all the measurements now, and I know what you want, and I'll draw up the plans, and we'll find a good local builder, a real reliable fellow, and I'll do the talking. And all these plans will come free of charge. Rob the rich and feed the poor, that's what I say. No offence meant now.'

Helen noticed her mother standing in the shadows listening suspiciously to this.

'Oh, I'm very grateful to you,' Mrs Devereux said. 'I don't know where I would be without you.'

'And you should get the work done before the winter,' Larry said.

'Oh, indeed, indeed,' Mrs Devereux replied.

'So I'll post the plans to you during the week for your approval, and I'll come down again when we get the builder.'

'Oh now, that's very kind.'

'So you'd need to be sure now this is what you want,' Larry continued.

'Come on, Lar,' Paul said. 'It'll be midnight and you'll still be talking.'

As Larry got into his car, the two cats appeared briefly on the roof of the shed, miaowing sharply and watching the departing guest. Mrs Devereux ran in and filled another saucer of milk for them. Accompanied by Helen and Paul, she moved up and down the space in front of the house, and then, alone, she walked up and down the lane, calling to them, but when it was clear that they had gone back into hiding, she returned to the house.

★

It was almost dark and the beam from Tuskar had begun to wash across the front of the house when Declan's stomach cramps started. Helen noticed the spasms coming lightly at first, with Declan gasping and holding his breath, and then as time went on she witnessed Declan's panic each time the spasm approached.

All of them tried to talk to him. Lily knelt down in front of him and held his hands, but he would not look directly at her or speak to her. Paul sat quietly at the kitchen table, watching him. Mrs Devereux did the dishes and swept the floor and went out again in search of the cats. Helen stood at the window.

'Could you turn off the light?' Declan asked.

There was still a faint glow in the sky so that after a while when they got used to the semi-darkness, they were able to make out shapes in the kitchen. At regular intervals now Declan began to groan. He asked for the basin under the sink to be put near him, and soon, with each spasm, he vomited and retched into it. When he had vomited the first time he put his head back and cried out. When Helen came near him, he motioned her away. He was breathing heavily all the time, waiting for the next heave to begin, holding his stomach and then moaning when it came, and putting his head back when it was over.

Helen signalled to Paul to come outside; Lily and Mrs Devereux were already in the dining-room. They left the kitchen door ajar, aware that Declan had observed them crossing the kitchen.

'If everyone stays outside here,' Paul said, 'I'll talk to him. It's probably too late to ring Louise, and we could ring the local doctor again, but he really wouldn't know what to do. I think I know what it is; it's one of the common opportunistic infections, and it can be treated. So if it lasts much longer, and doesn't look like going away, then Declan will have to go to Dublin, whether by car or by ambulance.'

Helen felt that Paul was enjoying his authority and the sound of his own voice. Her mother and grandmother listened to him respectfully, grateful that he knew what to do. He moved quietly back towards the kitchen and closed the door. The women waited in the dining-room.

'I don't know what the two of you are doing,' Mrs Devereux said, 'but I am saying a prayer.'

'Do you know if it is the first time he has suffered like this?' Lily asked.

'I don't think it is,' Helen said.

'Say a prayer now that his suffering will be eased,' Mrs Devereux said. She knelt down and bowed her head, but Helen and her mother remained seated.

They waited for something to happen in the kitchen, hearing at intervals the sound of retching and spluttering and hearing, too, low cries of pain. Helen could not imagine what Paul was saying to Declan. In all the years she had known her brother, she had never seen him rude or sulky or difficult. As she sat there and waited, she regretted her feeling when Paul spoke earlier that he was pompous and self-regarding. She realised that if Paul were not there they would be helpless, unable to deal with Declan or know how to manage.

After half an hour Paul came out of the kitchen with Declan leaning on him. 'He needs to go to the bathroom,' Paul said, 'and he wants to go to bed.'

Paul helped Declan up the stairs. Lily and Helen went into Declan's bedroom and smoothed his bed, putting his pillows in place, switching his light off but leaving the light on in the dining-room. They sat in the dining-room waiting for Declan to finish in the bathroom. When Paul called down for fresh pyjamas, they went into Declan's

254

room again and rummaged in his bag. Helen brought the pyjamas upstairs and handed them to Paul through a chink in the bathroom door. She could hear the shower going.

'We won't be long,' Paul whispered to her and closed the door again.

When Declan came down the stairs he was still leaning on Paul, gasping at each step he took as though moving caused him pain.

'You're all right now, Declan, you're all right now,' his grandmother said as Paul brought him into the bedroom.

'He's too hot,' Paul said. 'And he just needs a sheet. And he needs water, maybe with ice in it if you have ice, and he needs the basin and a towel.'

As Declan lay down on the bed, the light from Tuskar spilled across the wall of the room.

'Do you want us to draw the curtains, Declan?' Helen asked.

'No,' he whispered, 'but don't go away, stay around, will you?'

'Of course,' she said. 'I'm just going to get you some water. Are you all right?'

'No,' he said and looked at her evenly. 'I wish it was over.'

'You'll be all right,' she said, and immediately felt sorry she had said anything. She gripped his hand, still wondering how she could have said such a stupid thing. He was watching her, and she tried to smile, but she could not think what to do. She waited with him, and held his hand until her mother came into the room.

★

In the hour after midnight, Declan's stomach cramps began again. He had been sweating heavily; Helen and her mother were sitting by his bed, her mother holding a towel to wipe his brow. He had been still for a while, with his eyes open, and light coming from a covered lamp in the corner. Suddenly, he started to heave; he sat up and held his stomach, pressing hard as though to prevent the cramp coming, and then moaning under his breath in small fits and starts until it died down.

Helen called Paul, who was in the kitchen, and moved so that Paul could take her place beside the bed. Declan had his eyes closed now. Paul told Helen to get an ice pack or a packet of frozen peas to cool him down. She found her grandmother in the kitchen, sitting alone at the table, studying the veins in the back of her hands.

'I think we're in for a night of it,' her grandmother said.

'He's very sick,' Helen said.

'I'm praying for him. Do you think we could tell him that?'

'I'll tell him,' Helen said.

Helen, Lily and Paul sat in the room with Declan and waited with him each time for the pain to come, and tried to comfort him as he held his stomach and let out deep cries. But after an hour or two the cramps subsided, and Declan lay back in the bed with his eyes closed. He was sweating profusely, but shivering at the same time, and they could not tell whether he was too hot or too cold.

When he quietened, Helen convinced her grand-mother to go to bed. And after a while, she decided to go herself. Paul and her mother said they would wait until Declan fell asleep. Paul whispered to her in the kitchen that he did not think the cramps had ended, merely stopped for a while. He was almost sure, he said, that they would return during the night, or the following day. He said he had told Declan earlier that he should return to Dublin. Declan had said that he didn't want to go.

★

As soon as she fell asleep, Helen heard him crying out. She got up and dressed. It was almost three o'clock in the morning. Her mother and Paul were sitting by the bed in the darkened room. The pain this time did not seem to come in waves as it had done before. Declan now held his stomach all the time. When he opened his eyes, it was clear that he was frightened. He tried to talk, and mur-mured something, but they could not make out what he was saying. They asked him if he wanted water, but he shook his head. Helen realised that there was nothing they could do, except stay with him; whatever was happening in his stomach was getting worse. Several times over the next half-hour they brought him to the toilet. Paul went in with him, while Lily and Helen changed the sheets and opened the window of his room and encour-aged Mrs Devereux to go back to bed when she appeared in her dressing-gown.

Declan lay on the bed, covered only in a sheet. As soon as he drank some water, he vomited into the basin, his whole thin frame shuddering with the nausea. He tried to turn on his side, but he could not manage it and lay on his back again. Sometimes the pain intensified, and he cried to himself, beyond their comforting.

Paul signalled to Helen to come to the kitchen again. 'He's not going to sleep,' he said, 'and he's not going to get better down here. There's no point in going near the hospital until about eight or eight-thirty. So we should think of leaving here at six or six-thirty. I'll have to take my car, and if you could take his. I don't know what your mother wants to do, but she can drive separately with Declan, if she wants, or she can come with one of us. I'll go first and alert the hospital and do all that, or I'll take Declan with me, if that's what you want.'

'Has he agreed to go?'

'He knows he has to go.'

'Has he ever been as bad as this before?'

'Yes.'

When Helen went back to the bedroom, Declan was having cramps again, this time more severe. While waiting for the next attack, he mumbled and muttered words which she could not make out. But as Lily wiped his face and forehead and held his hand, and talked to him softly, he began to call out under his breath and, when the next attack came, Helen for the first time understood what he was saying.

He was saying: 'Mammy, Mammy, help me, Mammy.'

Helen wanted to leave the room; she felt she was in the way. Declan's tone when he spoke was abject, child-like, desperate as he called out again: 'Mammy, Mammy, help me.' Lily whispered to him words which Helen could not hear.

Helen tiptoed out of the room, and when she told Paul in the kitchen what was happening in the bedroom, tears came into her eyes.

'He's been wanting to say that for a long time,' Paul said, 'or something like it. It'll be a big relief for him.'

★

Slowly, hesitantly, the dawn came up in the eastern sky, the sky over the sea. From the window, Helen saw chinks of vague light between the black clouds. It was four-thirty; she did not know that the dawn began so early. She watched from the kitchen window waiting for more light to appear, but what she had witnessed was merely a glimmer, a hint at the beginning of day, and there was no change in the sky for some time. She felt alone now, isolated from everybody, and so tired that she could not summon up, even in her imagination, how she felt about Hugh and Cathal and Manus. Just then, there at the window, she felt nothing except a hardness in her heart against the world.

When it brightened, she put on a pullover and walked down towards the sea. The air was cold and there was a sharp, thin breeze coming from the east. She stood at the edge of the cliff and watched the sea, waves gathering way out and moving deliberately to form and break in a dull curl on the strand, and pull back out.

The sea was a deep metallic blue; there were black rainclouds on the horizon, but the sun was coming through now and it was almost bright. There was no one to be seen; it would be a while before the people in the smallholdings around here woke and got up and started the day. She imagined them locked in the privacy of sleep, or turning slowly, wakened for a second by the dawn light, and then falling back into their sleep.

For some time, then, no one would appear in this landscape; the sea would roar softly and withdraw without witnesses or spectators. It did not need her watching, and in these hours, she thought, or during the long reaches of the night, the sea was more itself, monumental and untouchable. It was clear to her now, as though all week had been leading up to the realisation, that there was no need for people, that it did not matter whether there were people or not. The world would go on. The virus that was destroying Declan, that had him calling out helplessly now in the dawn, or the memories and echoes that came to her in her grandmother's house, or the love for her family she could not summon up, these were nothing, and now, as she stood at the edge of the cliff, they seemed like nothing.

Imaginings and resonances and pain and small longings and prejudices. They meant nothing against the resolute hardness of the sea. They meant less than the marl and the mud and the dry clay of the cliff that were eaten away by the weather, washed away by the sea. It was not just that they would fade: they hardly existed, they did not matter, they would have no impact on this cold dawn, this deserted remote seascape where the water shone in the early light and shocked her with its sullen beauty. It might have been better, she felt, if there never had been people, if this turning of the world, and the glistening sea, and the morning breeze happened without witnesses, without anyone feeling, or remembering, or dying, or trying to love. She stood at the edge of the cliff until the sun came out from behind the black rainclouds.

★

In the kitchen, her grandmother was at the Aga, still wearing her dressing-gown. 'There's tea on,' she said, 'but maybe you want to make a fresh pot.'

Helen sat at the table. The house was cold and the smell of damp brought her back years. She covered her face with her hands. When Paul came into the kitchen, he told her that she should sleep, that they would go to Dublin in about an hour, and she would need a small amount of sleep if she was going to drive.

'Is Declan asleep?' she asked.

'No, but he's calmer, and he's not in pain, but I don't know how long that will last.'

On the way to her room, she noticed that the door to Declan's room was closed and there was no sound coming from it. She lay down on her own bed, leaving the door of her room open, covering herself with an eiderdown. She curled up, burying her face in the pillow. She dozed lightly and woke with a start and dozed again. She lay there in the grey light feeling that she never wanted to move again; she tried to concentrate on Declan's pain and the need to get him to Dublin, and when she fell asleep she dreamed that she was driving in her sleep, and kept trying to wake, knowing that she would crash if she did not open her eyes. She held the wheel, but saw nothing that was coming and understood that if she did not wake up in the next second she would wreck the car and injure herself. She braced herself for the accident but then found it was Paul standing over her, telling her that Declan's cramps had started again, and there was no point in waiting, that Paul was going to drive ahead, and Helen and her mother were going to follow with Declan in Declan's car and they could take turns driving.

Helen felt sweaty, in need of a shower and a change of clothes, but she knew that she had nothing clean left, not even clean underwear. She packed her things with her eyes half shut, wondering if she should go into the kitchen and invite her grandmother to Dublin – she could travel with Paul, and stay with Helen – but she knew that she would not ask her, that they would leave her grandmother here alone, fretting about her cats, her attitude as steely and direct as ever, but with a loneliness which had only been intensified and deepened by her visitors.

Declan was still in bed. Helen went into his room, where Paul was sitting, and heard him whispering weakly with pain.

'He's going to try and get up soon,' Paul said.

'Do you think you're OK for the journey, Declan?' Helen asked.

He nodded. 'I'll get up soon,' he said.

★

When she went into the kitchen Helen saw that her grandmother was wearing a bright dress with blue dots, and a navy-blue angora cardigan. She had put on a light lipstick and some make-up. It was as if she were coming to Dublin with them and wanted to look her best, but it was, in fact, Helen knew, that she did not want to appear as though she were being left behind.

When they helped Declan out to the car, Lily insisted on sitting in the back seat with him. Paul and Helen tried to make him comfortable, with two pillows Mrs Devereux had offered them, but he could not settle, lying slumped with his eyes closed. They suggested to Lily that she move into the front seat, but she would not budge from where she was, saying that she wanted to be close to him.

Mrs Devereux came out and stood beside the cars.

'Drive carefully now, and stop if you feel sleepy,' she said.

'Keep that phone turned on,' Lily said.

'Oh God, that phone!'

'Keep it turned on,' Lily repeated.

Declan pulled down the back window of the car.

'Thanks for everything, Granny,' he said weakly.

'Mind yourself now, Declan, mind yourself.'

His grandmother had tears in her eyes.

It was six-thirty when they set off, Paul driving ahead. As soon as they were beyond Blackwater, Lily put the pillows on her lap, and Declan rested his head on the pillows. He was in pain still. In the rear-view mirror Helen could see Lily stroking his face.

'I've a terrible pain,' he said to her, half crying.

'You'll be all right now,' Lily said. 'Paul says they'll have a bed for you and they'll know what to do and we'll all stay close to you.'

As they drove north, through Gorey and Arklow, Helen felt oddly alert, realising that if she stopped or thought too much about sleep she would need a rest, and she knew, as Declan's pain worsened and he tried to vomit in the back of the car, that she could not stop, she must go on until they reached the hospital.

'You'll be all right, Declan,' her mother said. 'You'll be all right.'

As they reached the twisting road between Rathnew and Ashford, Declan's pain became intolerable.

'Where exactly is it?' Lily asked.

'Here, here,' he said.

'Is it his stomach?' Helen asked.

'Yes, it's still his stomach, but it won't be long now. We're nearly there.'

Declan tried to vomit again, but it was all dry. As she drove, trying to concentrate all the time on the stretch of road ahead and nothing else, she realised that he had soiled himself. Carefully, hoping that she wouldn't be noticed, she opened the driver's window.

What she heard then in the back of the car surprised her. It was her mother's singing voice, which she had not heard since she was a child; thin and shaky on high notes, it started softly as though Lily were nervously checking to see if she could still sing. Then it became louder and stronger. It was a song she used to sing at night when Helen and Declan were very young, when they still slept in the same room:

> October winds lament around the Castle of Dromore
> But peace is in the lofty hall, a pháiste bheag a stór,
> Though autumn winds may droop and die, a bud of
>   spring are you.

And then, making her voice husky and low, she sang the chorus.

When she had finished the chorus for the first time, she stopped. 'Help me, Helen,' she said, and began the next verse. Helen knew the words, she had sung the song in a choir in school. She joined in with her mother and together they finished the song.

As they joined the Monday-morning traffic into the city from Bray, they sang any song they could think of –

Brahms' Lullaby, 'Oft in the Stilly Night', 'The Croppy Boy' – as Declan lay still. Helen dreaded the traffic lights as they approached Stillorgan; if she stopped for too long, she was afraid that she would fall asleep, or not be able to go on.

'Think of something else, Helen,' her mother said.

'I wish I knew the words of more songs,' she said. 'You think of something and I'll join in.'

When they arrived at the hospital, Helen could not remember how to reach the building where Declan had been when she visited him first. St James's was a sprawling complex; she turned at a roundabout towards a set of buildings, but these all turned out to be modern, unlike the wing where Declan had been. She wanted to ask Declan to sit up and help her, but from the silence in the back of the car she knew that he was asleep. She found a modern car park and waited for the barrier to lift. She drove in and found a space. 'I'll find out where we should go,' she whispered to her mother. Declan's head lay peacefully on the pillow. Her mother could not move. She closed the car door carefully and made her way to the main reception area of the hospital.

She realised when she began to talk to the receptionist that she had no idea what to say. There was, the receptionist told her, no AIDS ward in the hospital, although there was a clinic, but that didn't open on Mondays. The consultant Dr Louise Farrell had beds all over the hospital. If her brother was very sick, the receptionist said, he should go to Casualty. Helen tried to describe the building she had been in before, but the receptionist was now suspicious of her, and was ready to be unhelpful. Helen, in her tiredness, felt a sudden burst of temper, and made herself turn away.

She walked out of the reception area and decided to turn right. There were signs for everything, but she recognised nothing. She knew that in the hallway of the old building Paul would be waiting for her, and he would be impatient at her inability to find it. She hoped her mother would have the sense to stay in the car.

In another building she found a porter sitting by a desk. He was reading the paper, and although he had seen her approaching him, he looked down as she came near. She turned away and left. She tried to think back: how did she come into the hospital grounds that day with Paul? She believed she was moving in the right direction, but she could not be sure. It struck her that she should have asked the receptionist to put her through directly on the internal telephone system to Louise or one of her staff; as soon as she could find another porter she would ask to speak to Louise, she thought. As she entered another building and realised it was a kitchen complex she was so frustrated she was close to tears.

By the time she found Paul in the lobby of the building where Declan had been before, she could barely speak. He made her walk with him to a hallway where he had a wheelchair ready. 'Has something else happened?' he asked her.

'No, just the car is miles away.'

'We'll get a porter to wheel him over,' he said. 'It couldn't be that far. Is it the pay car park?'

She nodded.

'That's OK. We can handle that.'

Declan woke as soon as they came back to the car. He

said nothing, appearing stunned by his new surroundings. He got out of the back seat without any difficulty and sat into the wheelchair. The porter put a blanket around him, and Paul carried his bag as they wheeled him through the hospital grounds. Lily and Helen walked behind.

When they reached the ward, Paul handed the bag to the porter.

'They won't need us now,' Paul said. 'He'll be given tests and he might even be sedated. There's no point in us waiting around here.'

Helen now realised that she had her mother on her hands, with only one car between them. 'I need to make a phone call,' she said.

Paul directed her to a callbox in the lobby, while her mother went to the toilet. She dialled the number and Hugh picked up the phone. She told him where they were and what had happened.

'You sound terrible,' he said.

'We had a bad night.'

'Do you want me to come down?' he asked.

She said nothing.

'Helen, you can't be on your own like this. You've got to let me help you.'

'What about the boys?'

'They're fine, they're happy. Let me come down.'

'No, we can't both leave them.'

'Helen, why won't you let me help you? It would take me four and a half hours to drive down, that's all.'

'Hugh, I had the worst thoughts during the night.'

'Why don't I drive down now,' Hugh asked, 'see you, spend the night in Dublin, and take you back up tomorrow? You can see the boys, and then you take the car back so you won't even be a night away?'

Once more, she did not reply.

'Helen,' he said.

'Hugh, can you come down now?'

'I'll leave in a few minutes and I should be there by two or three. Will I come to the hospital or the house?' He sounded relieved and eager.

'The house.'

Helen stood in the lobby with Paul, waiting for her mother.

'I'm going to go home and sleep,' he said. 'I'll come back in the afternoon. Tell your mother I'll see her then.'

'We're very grateful to you,' Helen said. Paul embraced her before he left.

★

Her mother walked slowly towards her, as though she had injured herself.

'We should go back to my house and have a rest,' Helen said.

'I've no clean clothes.'

'I have clean clothes at home,' Helen said. 'Or we can go to the shopping centre. Hugh is coming down from Donegal.'

'Hugh? Oh Helen, I don't think this is the right time to meet him.'

'You've no choice now,' Helen said and linked her mother through the hospital grounds.

When Helen got into the car, she felt an overwhelming tiredness. As she reversed out of the parking space, she had to force herself to turn and look behind. She wondered where Declan was now, if he was lying in bed, or being tested for something by doctors. She and her mother should have left a note for him before they walked out of the hospital, she thought, to say that they would be back later to see him. She put the car into gear and drove it slowly to the barrier. 'You need fifty pence. Do you have a fifty-pence piece?' she asked her mother.

Her mother searched through her bag and found a purse with loose change. She handed Helen a fifty-pence piece and Helen opened the window and put it in the slot. The barrier lifted.

'We should have gone to the other car park,' Helen said. 'You don't have to pay there.'

It was a mild, hazy morning, with a promise of sunshine. Helen realised that she would have to phone the school and speak to her secretary and cancel the interviews for Wednesday. All she wanted now was sleep, even an hour or two of sleep before Hugh arrived.

'It's funny,' her mother said, 'how time flies. Here you are driving me through Dublin, and I remember when you were a little girl and we were taking you to Dublin, you and Declan on the train all in your good clothes.'

Helen drove along Thomas Street and Patrick Street and turned into Clanbrassil Street.

'We used to think the train was going to fall into the sea, it went so close to the edge,' Helen said.

'They were the happiest times,' her mother said. 'Declan and you were so different, but on these trips you were the same. Neither of you would be able to sleep the night before, and you'd both be up in the morning long before us, and you'd both be exhausted on the way home.'

'The strangest thing for me', Helen said, 'was how Daddy used to cross the street in Dublin. At home we were trained to look left, look right and look left again. And if we caught sight of a car coming or heard one in the distance, we were told to wait. But in Dublin, he'd walk out, he'd work out the distance and begin crossing when cars were coming, and then he'd dodge them. Declan and myself couldn't believe it.'

'I remember that there was one thing you loved and one thing Declan loved. Do you remember what they were?' her mother asked.

Helen drove towards Templeogue. 'No, I can't,' she said, 'unless it was Moore Street, or the zoo.'

'No. You both loved Moore Street and you both loved the zoo. It was something else. Declan loved the self-service restaurant in Woolworth's in Henry Street. His eyes lit up when he got in there. You know, he hated ordinary restaurants, the few times we took him; he had no patience, he couldn't understand why it took so long for the food to come. And now in Woolworth's he could get a tray and pick whatever he liked and have it immediately. You were different, you liked restaurants, and had plenty of patience, you liked the ordering and the waiting and the looking around. So Woolworth's was Declan's special treat, and then after it, or before it, you got yours.'

The car was stopped at traffic lights near Templeogue now.

'The escalators,' her mother went on: 'you loved the escalators in Clery's and Arnott's. Declan was afraid of them. He couldn't be persuaded to get on to one. But you could have gone up and down them all day. Do you remember?'

'I do, yes, but I think I liked the self-service as well,' Helen said.

'Yes, but not as much as Declan,' her mother said. 'I have photographs of the two of you at the zoo and in the airport. I must give you some of them so you can show them to your boys. You both look so happy in them. I'll wait for a while now, because seeing Declan in them would make us all too sad.'

Her mother stopped for a moment and sighed. 'I'd love if some of the happiness could be there in his spirit when he goes, as well as all the suffering.'

They were almost home now. Helen knew that as much as she wanted sleep, she needed silence: no more raw memories, no more of the soft-voiced tenderness that her mother was using in the car. She was dreading her mother coming into her house.

'I hope we were some comfort to Declan, Helen,' her mother said when she had reached the house and stopped the car. 'Do you think we were?'

'Maybe he's easier in his mind,' Helen said. 'I hope he is. I don't know.'

Her mother looked at her searchingly, clearly in need of further reassurance. Helen tried to think of something to say which would cause her mother to relax and cease to be such an uneasy presence.

'We're here, we're here now,' Helen said. 'We'd better go in.'

Her mother did not move, but looked at her again, as though pleading for an answer.

'I think we did our best,' Helen said and got out of the car. She waited for her mother at the gate. She linked her slowly along the path to the front door.

'Yes, that's right,' her mother said wearily, 'and what more could we have done?'

The house seemed cold and strange and, as she walked down the hallway, Helen felt she had entered an unfamiliar place. She would have done anything not to have to make tea for her mother. She forced herself to think that this was her house, where she lived, and it could not be taken away from her now. But she could not step out from her mother's dark shadow. When she turned in the kitchen to face her, she was shocked to find how helpless and broken her mother seemed. In those first moments, as they walked down the hallway to the kitchen, she had imagined someone forceful and pushy coming behind her, determined to stop her having her life. Instead, her mother looked bewildered and shocked.

'Well, this is lovely, Helen, it's lovely, it's very bright,' her mother said. Her voice was quiet and sad.

Helen made tea while her mother sat at the table. When she realised that she had no milk, she offered to go to the shop, but Lily said she would drink it black.

'Declan told me about this house, so I knew what it was like,' her mother said, 'but it's nice to be here.'

'I should go upstairs and make up a bed for you,' Helen said.

'Don't go yet,' her mother said. 'Stay here. You don't have to talk. Sometimes when I'm with my mother, I wish I didn't have to talk.'

'Granny is a great talker,' Helen said.

'Your granny wears me out,' her mother said, 'and now that you and I are talking again I don't want to do that to you.'

'I'll stay up for another few minutes.'

'I come up to Dublin on Saturdays sometimes,' her mother said. 'I'd love to come out here to your house for my tea. I mean I wouldn't stay the night. I hate staying the night in my mother's. And it's your house, and you don't want your mother nosing around too much.'

She sipped her tea and sighed and looked out at the garden. She stared into the distance as she spoke. 'I could see the boys. And then I'd drive home. It'll be all quicker with the new bypass. And that's what's keeping me going, Helen, that's what I dream about now, that you and I could sit here talking about nothing, and watch the boys playing and Hugh coming in and out of the room. And I could stand up and go, and it would be all easy and casual. That's what I dream about now.'

'That's a lovely thought,' Helen said. 'And I promise I'll have milk when you come.'

'Let's go to bed now,' her mother said. 'I've said what I wanted to say.'

She stood up and brought her cup and saucer to the sink.

'We'd better be in good form when Hugh comes,' she said. 'And we'll go and see Declan later, but we'll sleep for a while first, we'll sleep for a while.'